ZANE

A NOVEL

SCANDALICIOUS

SCANDALICIOUS

Dear Reader:

What can I say about Allison Hobbs other than she is phenomenal? There are very few writers that I can say that I actually admire. Allison is on the top of that list. She has churned out her sixteenth novel with all of her signature elements.

A cupcake bakery, Scandalicious, is the main focus where all ingredients lead to temptation. There's Solay, the owner, who seeks comfort in the arms of a rented escort; Melanee, the "innocent" by day and "naughty" at night employee who creates seductive names for their delectable treats; and Vidal, the flamboyant, in-your-face worker who thrives on gossip with his daily routine. Throw in Lincoln, who is facing the seven-year itch in his marriage, and his wife, Chevonne, whose affair has caused their relationship to sour, and you have a host of racy characters. Allison spins another lustful tale to add to her list of edgy novels.

For more relationship drama, check out Allison's, *Put a Ring on It*, featuring three women on a desperate quest to reach the altar.

As always, thanks for supporting myself and the Strebor Books family. We strive to bring you cutting-edge literature that cannot be found anyplace else. For more information on our titles, please visit Zanestore.com. My personal web site is Eroticanoir.com and my online social network is PlanetZane.org

Blessings,

Zane

Publisher
Strebor Books International
www.simonandschuster.com/streborbooks

ZANE PRESENTS

ALLISON
HOBBS

A NOVEL

SCANDALICIOUS

STREBOR BOOKS
NEW YORK LONDON TORONTO SYDNEY

SBI

Strebor Books
P.O. Box 6505
Largo, MD 20792
http://www.streborbooks.com

ISBN 978-1-59309-369-3
ISBN 978-1-4516-1809-9 (e-book)
LCCN 2011928049

First Strebor Books trade paperback edition October 2011

Cover design: www.mariondesigns.com
Cover photograph: © Keith Saunders/Keith Saunders Photos
Cupcake art: © Nikiparonak/Shutterstock.com

10 9 8 7 6 5 4 3 2 1

Manufactured in the United States of America

CHAPTER 1

An hour before dawn Solay was out of bed, dressed and ready to take on the new day. Situated beneath her modest apartment was her cupcake bakery, called Scandalicious. In six short months, Solay's store-front business had taken off like a rocket. Known for their eye-catching appearance and scandalously delicious flavor, Solay's cupcakes were all the rage.

Keeping costs down, Solay offered limited selections. Racy menu items like Double Chocolate Decadence (chocolate cake and frosting), Red Hot Passion (red velvet cake with cream cheese frosting), and Vanilla Kiss (vanilla bean cake topped with hot pink butter cream) added to the allure of Scandalicious.

For special orders only, Solay offered gourmet and savory cupcakes.

The Moulin Rouge-themed bakery was filled with antique furnishings and elaborate embellishments. A crystal drop chandelier cast sultry lighting upon walls that were painted a shameless, bright red. In the center of the back wall was a provocative wall sculpture—hot-pink, neon lips. A full-length floor mirror was draped with matching feather boas on either side. The latest sensual addition to the dining area was a foot-and-a-half-tall pair of legs that were adorned with seamed stockings and stilettos.

Solay walked swiftly past the black velvet couch that was situated in a cozy corner. A red brocade chaise lounge was directly behind bistro-style chairs and tables. Feeling a twinge of dissatisfaction, she stopped suddenly and looked around the small dining area. She needed a bigger space. The wrought-iron tables and chairs were crammed together; there wasn't nearly enough seating to accommodate her growing clientele.

An unfamiliar sweet and spicy scent wafted from the kitchen. Holding a clipboard, Solay strolled behind the empty display case and pushed open the door to the kitchen with her hip. Her baking assistant, Melanee, was hunched over a butcher block table, chopping ginger root—of all things! Her work station was cluttered with oranges, lemon peels, ginger root, a vast assortment of spices, and expensive-looking cellophane bags filled with gourmet caramel.

Solay scanned the odd assemblage of ingredients, and scowled at her baking assistant. "What's going on? What're you baking, Melanee?" Solay tried to keep an even tone, but the quaver in her voice indicated that she was livid.

"I've been working on some new flavor profiles," Melanee said confidently as she carefully sliced oranges.

"We discussed a new addition to the menu, so I came up with an orange ginger cupcake, with a couple of twists." Melanee gave Solay a conspiratorial wink, and then jumped up and pulled a tray of cupcakes from the oven.

Solay felt anger settling around her, infuriated by the gall of Melanee. Melanee wasn't the loud, in-your-face type. She was quietly willful. And somewhat sneaky, in Solay's opinion.

Melanee picked up another orange, cut it down the middle. "I'll use our signature butter cream frosting, but it's gonna be kick-ass when I mix in some tangy orange and lemon zest. I'm gonna drizzle it with caramel, and then I'll add extra flair and drama by topping it off with a caramelized orange slice."

Solay found it odd for Melanee to talk about flair and drama. Everything about Melanee was drab. She was straight up and down, and very thin. She seemed to have lost so much weight in the past month, she was beginning to look undernourished—scary skinny. She wore big, unflattering eyeglasses, and her wardrobe was nondescript. She came to work every day, wearing loose jeans, sneakers, and T-shirt—and of course, the Scandalicious logo apron. She never changed her hairdo, kept her dry-looking hair pulled back in a boring, short ponytail at all times. Melanee didn't know the meaning of fashion or glamour.

Normally quiet and extremely focused on baking, Melanee didn't engage in a lot of chit-chat while on the job, but when she started yakking about one of her signature recipes, she could go on and on until your eyes glazed over. Solay felt a yawn coming on as Melanee droned on about her ginger- and orange-flavored cupcake.

When Solay heard Melanee say, "I'm gonna call my creation, the Screamin' Orgasm," she became totally alert.

"Screamin' Orgasm?" Solay repeated, shocked that Melanee, the seeming prude, was talking openly about an orgasm.

"The family-friendly version will be simply called The Screamin' O," Melanee continued, covering her mouth as she giggled nervously. Then she took a deep breath and returned to her normal personality. "I thought it would be real cool if we featured each of my creations on the chalkboard. At the top of the menu it should say: 'Melanee's Delectable Special.'" Melanee eyed Solay, wearing a challengingly serious expression.

Solay's jaw became unhinged. *Breathe, Solay. Count to ten before you go off on this heifer.* Melanee was in serious violation. Who did this mousey little chick think she was, telling Solay what she was planning to put on the chalkboard? A violation of this magnitude warranted a long rant, but time was ticking, and Solay didn't have the time for the luxury of giving Melanee a piece of her mind. Too angry for words, she pointed at the clock on the wall.

"I lost track of time, but when you see how popular my gourmet cupcakes will be, you'll understand that it was well worth the time invested," Melanee said, with a smirk.

"I can't believe you're playing around with a new addition to the menu without asking for permission. Do you realize that business opens in a few hours?" Solay snarled.

Sulking, Melanee grudgingly rose from the butcher block table. "I'll start mixing up the red velvet batter while the Screamin' O's are cooling off."

"The display case is empty! It should be at least half-filled with trays of red velvet, chocolate, *and* vanilla cupcakes. What would possess you to waste precious time, experimenting with new flavor profiles?"

Melanee pinched her lips together and gave Solay a piercing look of irritation. "I'm not experimenting. I'm a trained pastry chef and—"

"You're a pastry school dropout," Solay reminded her, snarling. "You have a lot of gall referring to yourself as a pastry chef. Furthermore, I run this business…not you! How dare you take the liberty of ordering a bunch of expensive items without my asking?"

"I thought you wanted to keep up with the competition. Improving that boring menu is the first step," Melanee said boldly.

"I don't have to keep up with anyone. My cupcakes sell like crazy; obviously my menu doesn't require improvement." Solay slammed the clipboard on a table, and huffily tied on a full-length apron. Pissed off, she yanked the fridge open and began grabbing ingredients: eggs, cream, and butter. In a metal bowl, she blended several cups of flour and sugar in with the dairy products and began beating the hell out the mixture.

Melanee touched the tops of her freshly baked cupcakes, and began scooping them out of the twelve compartments. "Wanna taste one?" she offered, ignoring Solay's foul mood.

Solay turned her nose up. "Look, I don't have time to taste a damn thing. At exactly seven-thirty, customers are gonna come stampeding through the door. You're wasting time, Melanee. No, start hustling. I wanna see tons of velvet coming out of the oven."

Melanee looked at her fragrant creations and gave a loud sigh. "What do you want me to do—trash the Screamin' O's?"

"I don't care what you do with that ginger crap. Eat them for lunch…give them to the homeless." Solay looked at her clipboard. "I came downstairs to tell you that I have a huge special order. One hundred cupcakes for a bridal shower. I planned on personally working on the order for most of the morning. But now that I have to pitch in and help you, I don't know how I'm going to get it all done."

Solay was piping frosting onto a batch of chocolate cupcakes when the old-fashioned bell ding-donged above the front door.

"Morning, ladies" Vidal called with a musical lilt to his voice. Vidal worked the cash register, took phone orders, ran errands, and did a little bit of everything, except bake.

"Vidal! I need you in the kitchen," Solay yelled.

Fashion savvy, Vidal was looking particularly dapper in a cotton twill driving cap atop neck-length hair that was highlighted and coiffed by a stylist. Dark gray tailored trousers fit his lean body to a tee. His cherry gingham-checked shirt was coordinated with a dark cardigan sweater and a bold gray plaid scarf was knotted around his neck.

He owned more shoes than both Solay and Melanee. He possessed oodles of accessories to complete his look: belts, ties, cuff links, hats, scarves, pocket squares, sunglasses, brooches, and earrings. You name the trinket, and Vidal not only owned it, he wore it well. It was a mystery to Solay how the man maintained such a stylish wardrobe with the meager paycheck he earned from the bakery.

Peering through tinted shades, and clenching his chin as he appraised the women's aprons that were dusted with flour and splashed with frosting and other unidentifiable stains, Vidal quipped, "Y'all look like hell. What's been going on back here—a cupcake war?"

"There's no time for humor," Solay chastised. "We have a situation, and I need you mixing batter—"

"Nuh-uh," he protested, shaking his long hair that was flat-ironed daily for a bouncy look. He pulled off his shades, revealing a subtle stroke of dark brown guyliner on his lower lid. Annoyed, he blinked mascara-covered lashes and waved a manicured finger. "I don't know anything about stirring up batter, chile." He scowled excessively, as if he'd been asked to kill, pluck, and cut up a chicken. "I can't work back here with my Dolce and Gabbana pants on," he said, folding his arms.

"This is a crisis, and I'm not going to argue with you, Vidal," Solay informed with a penetrating stare.

Vidal folded his arms. "You should have warned me. Had I known that you expected me to get all dusty, I would have thrown on something raggedy—something cheap and Old Navy-ish."

Solay was unfazed. "Grab an apron, Vidal, and get to work on the vanilla cupcakes."

"Solay, I can't be back here in this stuffy kitchen with all these ovens going. I'm a people pleaser, that's why I work the front."

Solay held up her hand. "You're whatever I need you to be, Vidal. Now get into an apron. Follow the recipe; don't get creative." She pointed to the recipes posted on the wall. "I have an important client that I have to focus on. I'll be damned if I'm going to lose business because Melanee decided that she wanted to get fancy today."

A look passed between Vidal and Melanee.

"I'll be working in my apartment for a few hours. Call upstairs if you need me."

Vidal folded his arms and grumbled under his breath.

"Listen, I want this problem rectified. If that case isn't filled up by the time customers begin arriving, both of you can start looking for work elsewhere!" Solay grabbed her clipboard, then wheeled around. She banged open the kitchen door with her shoulder.

"Oh, my Gawd, what's Miss Thang's problem?" Vidal inquired in a voice raised in exasperation.

"Dick! She needs to get laid," Melanee said with a snort. "If Solay wants to rectify something, she should start by ending her sex drought. Some good dick would put a smile on her face, and we wouldn't have to deal with her being so mean and cranky all the time."

Solay heard Melanee's bitchy remarks, and felt offended. *I'm not mean and cranky! I'm a businesswoman. My schedule is too demanding to put up with the emotional attachments that always develop whenever I attempt to have a friend with benefits.*

CHAPTER 2

A delicious aroma filled Solay's small kitchen. In the privacy and serenity of her personal space, she sifted, poured, measured, and stirred, until she'd whipped up a hundred stunning cupcakes. The task could have been completed much quicker if she'd used the industrial equipment downstairs, but there was too much tension in that kitchen.

Mission accomplished, she admired the pretty little masterpieces that she'd created. The cupcakes were frosted with French Vanilla butter cream that was piped into the shape of a rose, sprinkled with shimmering, edible pearls, and then dressed in silver cupcake liners. The assemblage of white rose cupcakes looked like a huge and elegant bridal bouquet.

As she began the task of carefully packaging them— twenty-five cupcakes per each oblong box, she thought about Melanee's snide comment, and wondered if it were true? She shook her head. How could she be sexually frustrated with a drawer filled with a vast selection of sex toys?

But there was something to be said about the human

touch. Where could she find the kind of intimacy she desired? She had neither the time nor inclination to go club hopping or cruise local bars. Besides, experience had taught her that the men who frequented meat market environments were the bottom of the barrel, not even worth a sleazy one-night stand.

Solay wanted sex—on her terms. Having to check in with anyone with a text message or a phone call to keep them from feeling insecure was asking too much of her. Women were accused of being clingy and needy, but from Solay's experiences, men were the ones that needed to be reassured with text messages and phone calls. Men were the ones calling her and asking, "How was your day?"

"Busy as hell!" she'd reply, allowing the stress to ring loud and clear in her voice.

"I was thinking about you."

"Oh, that's nice," she'd say, with uncomfortable laughter.

"Were you thinking about me?" the one-night stand would ask, totally testing her patience.

Hell, fucking no! she'd scream in her head, and then dryly respond, "Uh-huh."

At the point when he'd start to hint that he was interested in seeing her again, Solay would have already labeled him a nuisance, and her fingers would begin rapidly tapping, as she deleted him from her contact list.

Call her selfish, but it was what it was. Solay was married to her business, and had scant time for an extramarital affair.

Everything about Scandalicious screamed sex, from the intimate French bistro décor to the provocatively sexy names of her cupcakes, and now Solay was feeling somewhat fraudulent, running a sex-themed business when she wasn't getting any action.

There had to be a way to get the sex she desired without the complications of a relationship. After a few minutes of pondering her options, she went online.

Wearing a naughty smile, she Googled the phrase, "rent a dick." Her smile broadened when numerous possibilities popped on the screen.

She clicked on "Rent-A-Man Escort Service." A variety of muscle-bound hunks represented the available offerings of that service. Solay was pretty sure that the beautiful images on the website were merely stock photos and not part of the actual selection. Undeterred, she perused the site, and learned that she had the option of hiring a man by the hour or renting his services for the night.

An hour's worth of no-strings-attached sex was all she needed to improve her attitude, and give her some of her swag back. Wheeling and dealing in the business world, required her to exude confidence and sex appeal.

Credit card in hand, she called and boldly requested a one-hour date, making it clear that she didn't need a dinner date, and she wasn't going to a business affair. All she wanted from her hired man was to be escorted straight to her bed!

As she swept through the dining area, Solay noticed that the place was jam-packed. Not one available seat. And there was a mob of people waiting at the counter. Business was good.

Vidal was entertaining the customers, joking and making quips as usual, enjoying the spotlight, and working the front as if it were his personal stage. Vidal had survived the kitchen war and had emerged without any noticeable battle scars. His clothing and his appearance were as impeccable as always.

"Here you go. A dozen Passionate Kisses," Vidal said to a female customer. "I threw in a free Screamin' Orgasm to complete your sinful night," Vidal said, giving the patron a conspiratorial wink. The customers who were in line waiting for their orders were not impatient. Thoroughly charmed by Vidal, the customers were completely entertained while waiting.

"What's the Screamin' Orgasm?" someone in the line asked.

"Check out the menu." Vidal pointed to the chalkboard menu that hung on the wall behind him.

Solay's eyes wandered upward. *Melanee's Delectable Special: Screamin' Orgasm (orange/ginger cupcake with tangy orange butter cream frosting) $5.00 each.*

Solay was appalled at Melanee's willfulness, and intended to put her on a one-day suspension. Her thoughts were interrupted when she heard the next customer's request.

"I'll have a dozen cupcakes," said a woman carrying a briefcase and dressed in a conservative business suit. "I want four red velvet, four double chocolate, and four vanilla," she said, carefully avoiding the provocative cupcake names.

"Do you want the free Screaming O?" Vidal asked, his eyes gleaming with mischief as he put the business-woman on blast.

"Sure, I'll try it," she said, lashes lowering in embarrassment, face flushing red.

Helping out in the front, Solay began packaging the woman's order.

"We'll have a half-dozen Screamin' O's," said two giggly college girls.

"Coming right up!" Vidal disappeared into the kitchen and then came right back, carrying a tray of six gorgeous creations.

Customers glimpsed the pastel orange-colored delights, and murmured, "Wow!"

The caramelized orange slice embellishments gave the cupcakes an award-winning look. "Folks, we're down to the last half-dozen of Screamin' O's."

The customers released a collective groan. The two college girls clapped their hands as if they'd won a prize and then shelled over thirty dollars, plus tax.

While helping out in the front, Solay witnessed numerous customers who had gotten the free cupcake, returning to buy more.

"Those Screamin' O's went like hot cakes," Vidal told a customer. "We'll have more tomorrow."

"No we won't," Solay disagreed. "We'll be back to our regular menu tomorrow."

"You must not like money," Vidal muttered under his breath.

Solay let the comment slide. Vidal had no idea how expensive and time-consuming it was for Melanee to create those cupcakes. She'd have to hire more help if she kept those Screaming O's on the menu.

By closing time, Solay had gotten over her anger and realized that she'd be only hurting herself if she put Melanee on suspension for even a day. Unfortunately, Melanee was right; to Solay's dismay, the Screamin' O's were a success.

"Good night, ladies, it's been fun," Vidal said, after tying his dramatic, fringed scarf around his neck. Before leaving, he bent and reached under the counter behind bags and cupcake boxes. "*Voilà!*" he said.

"Ooo, you're such a sneak," Melanee said, laughing.

"And you're the Picasso of pastry," he said, eyeing the cupcake with admiration.

Flattered, Melanee smiled. "Thank you, Vidal."

"I have to have at least one Screamin' Orgasm after all that foreplay I put in today!" Vidal twirled around and headed for the door.

After Vidal left, Solay and Melanee cleaned up the kitchen. "In the future, you need to ask permission before you tamper with the menu. Nothing should be on that chalkboard or baked in my ovens without my explicit permission."

"But we discussed it…"

"Yes, we had a conversation, but nothing was finalized. Your cupcakes were a huge success, but I don't see how I can afford to allow you to bake anything other than the items on the menu."

"I can come in an hour earlier. Or stay a few hours later…start making up the batter for the next day."

"Why would you put yourself through that? I can't raise your pay."

"I'm bored doing the same thing every day. I need to express myself creatively."

"Well, that's something you can do on your own time. Seriously, Melanee. I can't afford to buy those ingredients…even at five dollars a pop, I'll only break even."

"Okay," Melanee said with an indifferent shrug, but Solay could see something that looked like anger in her eyes.

CHAPTER 3

S he was so fuckin' beautiful. His dick was rock hard and ready to burst. Though his eyes were closed, he could see her incredible, sexy body behind his eyes. He cupped her ass cheeks, tugging her closer, until his dick was embedded to the hilt.

Gritting his teeth and squeezing his eyes shut tightly, he forced back the load that swelled his shaft.

She squirmed beneath him, urging him. Her moans were almost too much to bear; he pulled back and then deepened his stroke. Going hard. Disregarding self-control.

Getting a grip, he shook his head. He wasn't ready. Desperately, his lips found hers. He put some tongue into the kiss, taking his mind off the juicy pussy that enveloped his dick. He stopped his stroke and lay motionless. Further movement would cause a premature eruption.

His mouth moved downward. He buried his face in her breasts, brushing his cheeks against the softness of her satiny skin. Licking, tasting. Lips hungrily surrounding the aching tips.

Overcome by her womanly softness, his dick throbbed urgently, straining for release. It took every ounce of his willpower to deny himself her womanly pleasure. She felt so good, so wet and creamy, he wanted to stay inside her forever. With a soft groan, he withdrew himself. Palms pressed against the mattress, he slithered downward until he was kissing her inner lips. Making her moan. Causing her to spread her legs in helpless invitation.

His tongue slashed between her thick folds, and thrust toward the tiny entrance to her sex. Inside her walls, he daringly explored the moist and softly padded confines. Her pussy clenched and spasmed around his gliding tongue.

"This is good pussy, baby. So sweet," he uttered, as his finger began toying with her clit, creating unbearably pleasurable friction. He knew her body well. Could feel the pulse of an ongoing orgasm.

She writhed violently, her moans becoming shouts of pleasure. Her body bucked wildly. She cursed. She prayed. And then her womb spasmed in grateful relief.

And then she came.

It was his turn now. Sweat soaked her skin as he repositioned her languid body, pulling her to unsteady knees. He wanted to mount her...fuck her doggy style. One hand flat against her back, the other holding his swollen dick in his hand as he steered himself into her gently at first. *Good pussy*, he thought as he thrust with a pounding force, until he spurted his seed and collapsed. Drenched with perspiration, his chest molded to the curve of her back.

Good pussy motivated men to achieve their dreams. Good pussy was the reward for working your way through school and obtaining a college degree; it was the just desserts for making a good living and enduring the pressures that come with a successful career. Good pussy was constantly on his mind. But keeping this pussy happy was becoming next to impossible.

Chevonne shifted. "You're smothering me, honey. Get up," she said with a grunt.

Lincoln opened his eyes. He was back in his bedroom, no longer in paradise. He closed his eyes again, unprepared to return to the reality of his life.

A career in peril. A dying marriage. An unhappy wife.

CHAPTER 4

Though Scandalicious faced busy South Street, Solay's apartment could be accessed by a narrow side street. The cobblestone path was a pain in the ass when it came to parking, but for an unconventional date with a male escort, the isolation and privacy were appreciated. At the thump of the door knocker, Solay braced herself. She had no idea what kind of a freak was going to be standing on the other side of the door. She hoped her escort hadn't shown up, dressed in some silly stripper costume. *Does it matter?* As long as the man had an erection and possessed stamina, his appearance, personality, and fashion sense were totally irrelevant.

A glimpse through the peephole revealed a young, brown-skinned brother. She frowned at his thugged-out attire. Beneath a multi-colored hoodie was a T-shirt bearing the image of Notorious B.I.G. He was wearing sagging jeans, sneakers, a baseball cap, and two flashy chains hung from his neck. *Is this a joke? I paid good money to rent some dick. If I wanted a young hustla, I could have taken a spin around the hood and picked up this fool.*

That Rent-A-Man agency must have jokes, but I'm not laughing. I'm calling their asses to demand every cent of my money back.

Before grabbing the phone, Solay took another look. Through one squinted eye, she noticed that her escort was kind of cute. With more scrutiny, she decided that "fine as hell" was a more accurate assessment. And from his expression—the sensual set of his generous lips, the knowing glimmer in his dark eyes, and his confident stance, she guessed that he could tear it up in the bedroom.

Her mouth suddenly watered.

Dressed for the occasion, Solay had on a black stretch lace slip dress. At five-foot-five, Solay weighed 140 pounds. She was thick in all the right places. She ran smoothing hands over her rounded hips, and then pulled back the chain and let the male escort in.

"Solay, right? My name's Deon," he said in a silken voice. He looked Solay over, his eyes gliding over ever inch of her voluptuous frame. "You ain't even gotta answer my question. From the looks of things, I can see that it's all good with you."

His compliment felt like a gentle caress—every word, a sensual invitation. She could tell that Deon was street smart, slick, and overly confident, but she couldn't stop herself from blushing under his gaze. From her estimation, Deon was over a little over six feet tall. His baggy clothes were draped over what appeared to be around 190 pounds of lean, rock-hard masculinity. The man was oozing all kinds of sexy thuggishness, and he knew it. He'd entered her apartment with his guns blazing.

Solay was enthused. Her boring life could use a dose of edgy excitement.

In the real world, Solay's male acquaintances were more mature and refined. But in this fantasy life, where all she was expecting was some stiff dick, a thug was just as good—perhaps even better, than the kind of man with whom she usually became romantically involved.

He glanced in the direction of the kitchen. "Smells good in here, like cookies or cake."

The aroma of the dozens of cupcakes she'd baked earlier still hung in the air. And no doubt, the lingering fragrances from her bakery had wafted upstairs. But none of that information was any of this hired hand's business. "Oh, that's a cookie candle burning," she said, motioning toward the bedroom.

"Is that right?" His words emerged slowly…lyrically, and with a hint of seduction. As if prompted by the word, "bedroom," Deon came out of the hoodie and his T-shirt. He casually tossed the garments on a chair. Bare-chested and flaunting a six-pack, Deon moved in Solay's direction. What a body! She'd only seen men that looked like Deon in photographs. Deon was so cut…so ripped… he didn't look real; he looked like a piece of golden-hued sculpture. He wasn't dark and he wasn't a redbone; he was a golden-honey color—gorgeously delicious.

She couldn't take her eyes off his tattoo—a wide strip

of black ink. Some sort of Chinese writing was draped over his right shoulder and traveled down his back. So sexy!

His stride was fluid and rhythmic, as if he were slow dancing toward her.

He had swag, and the word "trouble" was written all over his gorgeous face. But Solay didn't have to heed her inner warnings. Thank God she was only renting Deon for his stud services. She pitied the woman who thought she could get anything that closely resembled a relationship with this kind of man.

"You're real pretty, Solay," Deon said with a smile of appreciation. His flirty words caught her off guard, causing heat to creep along the back of her neck. And his lips...they were some kind of sexy. Plump and succulent, provoking a hot, melting sensation between her legs. *Damn, I must be hornier than I realized.* Embarrassed by her reaction, Solay cast her eyes to the floor.

With a gentleness that he didn't appear to possess, he pulled her into his arms. He pressed the back of her head until her cheek rested against his bare chest. His fragrance was sensual, masculine. "Mmm," she murmured, momentarily letting down her guard. In those split seconds of defenselessness, she was filled with an extraordinary sense of well-being and bliss.

"Did you miss me, baby?" Deon whispered.

Huh? What kind of game was this? How could she miss someone she didn't know? She supposed that pretending that Deon was her man was part of the fantasy she'd paid for. In a way, though, she really did miss him. Well, maybe not Deon in particular, but she missed what he represented—a man who cared. She missed having someone to hold her at the end of a long, eventful day.

"Yes, I missed you," she finally said, looking up and meeting his gaze. Then she felt a sudden impulse to explain. "Calling an escort service…well, that isn't something that I normally—"

He cut her off with a kiss, nudging her mouth open with the sweetness of his lips. As he kissed her, his hands slid down to her ass, caressing and squeezing the twin mounds. The heat from his mouth and his hands made her squirm with need. Releasing a deep gasp, her arms looped around his neck; her hungered body sank into his. Smoldering heat shot through her, settling between her legs. Her clit was hard and aching; she could feel it throbbing against his stiff dick.

"Let's take this to the bedroom." It was more a command than a request.

Solay nodded. She sensed that Deon's performance was going to be well worth the money spent. It took a lot of effort not to push him onto the sofa, hop on top of him, and take the dick right there and then.

Pull yourself together. Calm down, be patient, she lectured herself as he led her toward the bedroom.

She lay on her back. Deon, a large and beautiful mass of nakedness, straddled her. It was hard to concentrate on the sensual massage while the heat from his hefty and curved dick pulsed against her flesh.

"Let's skip the massage," Solay murmured, feeling hot from the touch of his hands on her bare skin.

"Relax. Lemme help you get rid of all this tension."

"But—"

"Shh." He silenced her. And with skillful seduction, he rubbed her back.

Annoyed that she'd allowed some thugged-out dick-for-hire, to talk her into getting something she didn't want, Solay lifted her head to protest. "Seriously, I don't need a massage. I just want—"

"I got you, ma. What's the rush?" His strong hand continued squeezing, working through the kinks in her neck.

"Well, I didn't want you to think that I required…you know, uh…I don't really need prolonged foreplay."

Deon chuckled. "I'ma make you feel good. Dig me? And all you have to do is lie here and allow yourself to receive the pleasure. Can you do that?"

Hmm. He's got it twisted. I'm paying to call the shots. I determine how I want to receive pleasure. "Look, I don't have a problem—"

"Solay…." The way he spoke her name held a ring of patient tenderness. "You're so wound up and tense. Chill, aye. You don't have to lift a finger. This is your night.

The only thing you need to do is relax. Just enjoy yourself."

Solay had expected to dictate the direction of this sex session, but Deon was obviously an alpha male and he wasn't giving up control. Conceding, she lowered her head, her cheek resting against the pillow.

He plied and kneaded her tense muscles until her anxiety melted away. Then his hands slid away from her neck and shoulders, long fingers gliding down the length of her back, delivering a touch that was so light and teasing, Solay shivered.

He lifted the lace slip, displaying buttocks separated by the strip of black fabric of her thong. Her pulse kicked up a notch; her body shuddered in anticipation. Deon placed a kiss between her shoulder blades. That sweet and sudden contact sent shockwaves zinging to every nerve in her body.

His hot kiss traveled down to the small of her back. His lips were so devilishly close to her ass, it was tantalizing. Rocked by delicious tremors, she buried her face in the pillow, and released a soft moan of pleasure.

He covered her buttocks with kisses. Solay gave a choked gasp, and shifted restlessly. As if being pulled by invisible strings, her legs slowly parted.

He stroked her pussy through the slip of fabric. His finger encircled her clit until she was moist with longing. Gently, he pulled her thong over her hips and past her thighs, leaving them confined around her ankles.

With desperate little kicks, Solay swiftly ridded herself of the delicate restraint.

He dismounted her. Crouched by her side, Deon inserted a sturdy finger. His finger spiraled deep inside her soft confines. He stirred the hot liquid that pooled around his finger. Completely aroused, Solay quivered with excitement.

"I wanna taste you."

His words alone had the impact of a hard shaft of dick ramming her pussy. Reflexively, she moaned. Her fists curled around the lace trim of the pillowcase. Still on her tummy, Solay trembled. The muscles in her pussy tightened in anticipation.

"Can I lick that thing?" His voice was coarse with need.

She wanted to cry from happiness. Swallowing a sob, she nodded her head, whimpering consent. Without further prompting, Solay spread her legs for him.

His flicking tongue coaxed Solay to her knees. Crouching, she tooted her butt in the air, giving him ample access. His tongue slid between pussy lips, swirling and licking extravagantly.

"Oh, damn," she cried. Her pussy sputtered in appreciation.

"Yeah, baby. You know what it is. Turn that pretty ass over so I can get all up in it. I'ma suck the first nut out of you, and then...."

Oh, my God! Deon was going to suck and fuck her to sweaty exhaustion. Solay twisted around, collapsing on her back. Thighs wide apart, she offered him a broad view of neatly groomed, hot pussy.

He dipped his tongue inside an opening that was pooled with sultry moisture. His tongue swam through pulsing tidal waves of liquid desire.

Slowing his tongue laps, he began leisurely dragging his tongue up and down her narrow slit, causing Solay to vibrate and purr. Suddenly, his tongue took on a different rhythm and movement, undulating and rolling in an uncanny manner. Deon was working his tongue gymnastics with such skill and dexterity, Solay's pussy clenched up and began to spasm out of control.

Screaming for Jesus, she gave into a toe-curling, flooding climax.

As she lay panting and murmuring in relief and satisfaction, Deon covered her body with his. She was acutely aware of his erection that throbbed against her inner thigh. But she couldn't move. Not yet. She was still trying to catch her breath.

"Did you cum real good?"

"Mmm-hmm," she murmured.

"I'm not finished with you. I got something else for your sexy ass."

Shaking her head, Solay smiled. "I'm good. Completely satisfied."

"Nah, I wouldn't even feel right if you didn't bust two or three times—at a minimum," he said, laughing.

She was about to protest when she felt him cupping

her breasts, pushing them together as he took turns sucking each nipple. Sensations of pleasure took over her body, making her widen her legs, lifting herself, arching with desire as she offered herself—once again.

He separated the wet folds of her sex and rubbed the head of his dick along the slippery entry.

"Ahh," she gasped, gripping the powerful muscles of his shoulders.

"I want you to feel good." He eased the swollen head of his dick inside her, and then slid several inches of pulsing dick inside her slick softness. Possessively, her pussy puckered around his rock-hard length, trying to gobble up even more. Every tiny muscle clung to his shaft.

"You got it, baby. This is all for you," he said as he shoved in the full length of his big, hard dick. His voice was a melody, a crooning love song that heightened the delicious sensations.

Oh, my God. This man is amazing. She wondered if the escorts at Rent-A-Man went through sex training session. If so, she was sure that Deon had been a star pupil.

In and out, he stroked with an undulating rhythm that was driving Solay crazy, provoking her into wanton writhing and helpless whimpering.

"Don't stop," she said breathlessly.

"Your pussy is too good for me to stop," he told her in a husky voice. "I'm not stopping until you cum. Can't stop until my dick is soaking wet with your nut."

Solay was astonished by what he was saying…the way he was making her feel.

"You like it?"

"Love it. Never had dick like this before. Never," she said, panting and gyrating so fiercely, she wondered if she'd become sexually possessed.

It was a dick-down, delivered so thoroughly, she couldn't hold back the succession of orgasms that rocked her body. It seemed as if her very essence was swept into the sensations. She saw streaks of vibrant colors; brilliant sparks of light burst behind her eyes. "Deon…Deon…Deon," she cried over and over as a series of tiny eruptions, combined into massive, volcanic explosion.

Afterward, Solay and her paid fuck lay cuddling together; the sweetness of the intimacy surprised her.

CHAPTER 5

A goddamn tube of Krazy Glue! That's all he wanted. That's what he'd been searching for inside his wife's top drawer—her junk drawer. The drawer where she kept a mishmash of things from safety pins, batteries, needles and thread, pens, scissors, phone chargers—you name it. And the only thought on Lincoln's mind as he scattered around miscellaneous items was replacing the name plate on his six-year-old son's football trophy.

The trophy and the plate bearing his son's name were now tossed onto the bed—discarded. Unimportant. Beneath the clutter inside the drawer, Lincoln had discovered an envelope with his wife's pay stub. That envelope should have been filed away with credit card receipts and other important papers. They filed joint tax statements, so there was no mystery about his wife's income, but his gut instinct told him that this particular pay stub possessed a secret that Chevonne didn't want him to know.

Not knowing what he was looking for, Lincoln scrutinized every item on the pay stub. And then he saw it. Two personal days had been taken during that pay period.

He searched his mind. Had Chevonne mentioned a doctor's appointment for her or the kids? No, she hadn't.

It all made sense now. The new lingerie, the gym membership, late nights at work—the terrible sex. With embarrassment, he recalled how impossible a task satisfying his wife had become.

Now he knew why. Chevonne was cheating, and the knowledge of her betrayal was suffocating. Seemed like all the air had left the room. Feeling lightheaded, Lincoln sank heavily onto the bed, next to the Pee Wee League football trophy.

He couldn't fight off the mental images of his wife lying up in a motel room with her legs spread, writhing and humping. The idea of Chevonne moaning in ecstasy while another man was on top of her, sliding dick in her…the thought of it made Lincoln groan out loud. He punched his open palm, then clenched his teeth when he had a flashing image of his wife down on her knees, giving her secret lover the kind of pleasure that she seldom bothered to give him.

"We're home, Daddy! We have pizza," five-year-old Tori yelled, her happy voice carrying upstairs. His little girl's voice usually gave him immense joy, but not even her musical lilt could loosen the choking knot around Lincoln's heart.

How could Chevonne do something so destructive… so sneaky…so fuckin' emasculating? What kind of mother would knowingly commit an act that could potentially destroy her family? Lincoln was so wound up, he could hear his heart as it banged against his chest, booming in outrage and indignation.

Jealousy and rage propelled Lincoln to his feet. His manhood was under siege and he needed to do something about it. He snatched up the pay stub, preparing to confront his wife with the incriminating evidence, and get physically violent with her if that's what it took to relieve himself of the all-consuming pain. For months now, he couldn't understand why his wife was so unresponsive in bed. Her indifference toward him had begun to fill him with insecurity. He swallowed, recalling the nights when he couldn't please her. Remember that feeling of utter helplessness—and self-loathing.

After seven years of marriage, how could she do this to me—to us? Pure hatred for his wife twisted his features, had him thinking malicious thoughts.

An outburst of childish laughter startled him. The tinkling sound of his children chortling with innocence brought Lincoln back to reality.

One of his fists was balled in fury. Realizing that he was practically hyperventilating, he unfurled his hand and stared at his open palm as if it belonged to a madman. *I have to pull myself together. Can't allow myself to explode. Not in front of my kids.* Getting a grip on his emotions, Lincoln took a deep breath. He put the pay stub back inside the envelope and methodically returned it to its hiding place inside the drawer.

In their well-appointed kitchen, Chevonne had her back to him. She was wearing sneakers, blue tights, a clingy print top—her workout clothes. Her ass looked plump and toned; her waistline looked as if several inches had been whittled away in the gym. Or was it all that extracurricular sex that had his wife looking so sculpted and vivacious?

"I bought an extra-large cheese pizza for the kids, and now Amir wants macaroni," Chevonne complained as she shook the noodles into the pan of steaming water.

"Those workouts at the gym are really paying off," Lincoln commented in a cool tone, though each word was intended as an indictment.

Chevonne turned around and beamed. "You think so?"

Lincoln wanted to slap that proud smile off of her lips. If it were possible to get away with murder, if his violence would not traumatize his children, he could have easily strangled his no-good wife right there in the kitchen.

Two boxes were untouched. Lincoln opened one. He regarded the medley of vegetables with a sneer, and then closed the lid.

The other box contained Lincoln's pizza. Topped with five different kinds of meat, it was called "The Manly" pizza.

"Daddy, can I have a slice of yours?" five-year-old Tori asked.

"No, Tori. Eat your cheese pizza. Daddy's pizza has

sausage, ground beef, and all sorts of unhealthy meat on it," Chevonne cut in disapprovingly.

"A little bit of meat won't kill her," Lincoln said, his voice low and controlled as he handed Tori a slice of pizza.

Using both hands, Tori carefully accepted the heavily topped slice of pizza. "Thanks, Daddy."

"I want a slice, Daddy," Amir piped in.

"No problem. Here you go, son." Lincoln gave out another slice of his forbidden food.

Frowning, Chevonne looked over her shoulder. "We both agreed that the children should eat a healthy diet."

Lincoln smirked. "All pizza is unhealthy. If you're so worried about their health, why are you whipping up a box of mac and cheese for Amir? How healthy is that crap?"

Chevonne stopped stirring, and turned completely around. She stared at Lincoln with an expression of bewilderment. "Where is this coming from?"

"If you're so concerned about the health of our children, then cut out some of your *workouts*. Come home and fix them a healthy meal."

"You want me to stop going to the gym?" She looked incredulous.

"Apparently all that working out is interfering with your responsibilities on the home front."

"The home front! Do you hear how archaic and narrow-minded you sound?"

Indifferent to how he sounded, Lincoln shrugged.

"When's the last time you stir-fried some vegetables in that wok of yours? You remember that three-hundred-dollar frying pan with the chrome-plated handles that you simply had to have?"

Lincoln's hostile gaze wandered around the kitchen. "Look at all this," he said sneeringly, as he waved a hand around the sparkling, sun-filled luxury kitchen that was equipped with top-of-the-line appliances, white marble island and countertops, white cabinetry, a hanging stainless steel pot rack, and cherrywood flooring.

"Lincoln!" Chevonne's voice cautioned him to be mindful of the children.

But Lincoln continued his rant. "You just love throwing money away. I guess all these gadgets…this big house… all this ostentation is just for show."

"I don't know where any of this is coming from, but we need to discuss whatever is bothering you, later." She cut her eyes at the children, who were staring at their parents, wide-eyed.

Lincoln folded his arms and made a snorting sound. "I want to talk about it right now. We have all the trappings of prosperity, but my son has to eat a ninety-nine-cent box of mac and cheese for dinner," he said with disdain.

Chevonne placed a hand on her hip. She used her other hand to point and gesture agitatedly. "Amir asked for macaroni and cheese, and that's why I'm making it for him. Don't label me a bad parent, because I'm not.

It wouldn't kill you to cook dinner for the kids sometimes."

"No, it wouldn't, but who knows what it would do to them? According to you, my meal choices aren't healthy enough." Lincoln put air quotes around the word "healthy." "It seems like I can't do anything right, lately." He gave his wife a long and meaningful look.

Chevonne's eyes slid guiltily away from his gaze.

The children stopped eating, uncomfortably aware of the sudden change of climate.

CHAPTER 6

H e'd never put a hand on Chevonne or any other woman, and so he dropped the subject, waiting for the murderous rage to subside. He waited until the children were asleep. He waited until Chevonne came out of the shower. She came into their bedroom wearing a loose cotton nightshirt and smelling delicious. Her hair was pulled high into a ponytail on the top of her head. With little effort, Chevonne had sexy on lock.

He noticed that her face was slowly twisting into an expression of pain. Her antics were almost laughable now that he knew the truth. At any moment now, Chevonne would play the headache card. She had a million handy excuses: headaches, cramps, upset stomach, not in the mood. And when she did give up some pussy, she acted like it was a major sacrifice.

Initially, Lincoln had believed that Chevonne's sex drive had diminished due to motherhood, job stress, being mired in debt. Mostly, he blamed himself, thinking he was boring her with the same sexual routine. Trying to spice things up, he'd worked hard at being inventive, bringing home porn for them to watch together, giving her flowers and other sentimental gifts to show how much he loved her.

With the kids both attending private school and with all their trappings of affluence, they couldn't afford one more additional expense, but he'd even suggested they pay a nanny for a date night, once a week. He had a zillion ideas for their date night. They could hop on Amtrak and go to New York to catch a play, or dine in any elegant restaurant of his wife's choosing. He even offered to take a vegetarian cooking class with her. Lincoln had been willing to do whatever it took to reignite the intimacy and the passion that he and Chevonne once shared.

All to no avail. Using one excuse after another, Chevonne had shot down all of his ideas.

Why hadn't he realized that she was creeping? Seething anger raged through his system. It felt like he would implode—spontaneously combust if he didn't punch something. Or someone. He wanted to beat the shit out of the motherfucker who had the gall to touch his wife intimately.

"You took two personal days a couple of weeks ago. Why?" Lincoln spoke with quiet menace. His words were a statement of fact, but his tone was a clear accusation.

"No, I didn't," Chevonne stammered.

"Yeah, you did. Two days in a row."

Chevonne ran a shaky hand through her hair.

"You're fuckin' around. I know you are." Lincoln took steps toward his freshly showered wife. "Who is he?"

"I don't know what you're talking about. Lincoln, what's wrong with you?"

"What's wrong with me?" He gestured with his arms outstretched, and then gave a short, crude-sounding laugh. "My problem is that I've been listening to too many lies, trusting and believing all the bullshit that's been coming out of your mouth," he said in a lethal tone.

"I don't know what you're talking about."

"Yes, you do," he said with certainty.

"If I knew, I would…" Chevonne began looking around, as if groping for a word—searching for a lie.

Lincoln glared at her, daring her to insult him with more deception. "Why don't you just admit it?" He stalked over to her dresser, and yanked open the top drawer.

Chevonne squinted in bafflement, indicating that she had no idea why he was rifling through her junk drawer. Her eyebrows shot up in surprise when Lincoln pulled out the envelope with the pay stub she'd carefully tucked away. Then she let out a sigh of resignation.

"Now do you want to explain why you took two days off?"

"I didn't know I had to account for every moment of my time. Look, I didn't expect that taking some *me* time would cause such—"

"That's bullshit, and you know it," Lincoln exploded. "You left here on both those days, dressed in your work clothes and carrying your briefcase, pretending that you were going to your job. You came home, acting exhausted…" He paused, and dragged a hand down the side of his face. "Hell with all that. Who is he, Chevonne—and how long have you been fuckin' him?"

Her mouth moved, but no sound emerged. Trembling, she looked trapped and in a panic. For a brief moment, he felt sorry for her. Instinctively, he wanted to comfort her and assuage her fear. Then he remembered that despite his wife's expression of sheer terror, she was not the victim—he was! He was the one who had been screwed over.

"Admit it!"

Chevonne's face twitched slightly, giving the impression that she was on the brink of tears. "I'm sorry, Lincoln. I didn't mean to hurt you—"

Lincoln groaned. The anguished sound was loud and long. "Whatchu mean you didn't wanna hurt me? Ain't no fuckin' way you thought that giving up some ass was gonna make me feel good!" No longer speaking like an educated man, Lincoln reverted back to the dialect of the hood. He'd risen above his circumstances. College educated, a promising career, and he'd married well. Or so he'd thought.

He was losing control of himself. Clearly on the verge of flipping out, he snarled and bared his teeth like a wild animal.

"You had me practically begging you for sex—but you had pussy galore for that nigga you was fuckin'." His body language and mannerisms were so threatening and primitive, Chevonne flinched and uttered a sound of fear.

Invigorated by renewed rage, he crushed the pay stub in his fist and then flung it across the room. "I could choke the shit out of you right now, bitch!" He advanced toward her, biting on his lip and breathing furiously.

"Haven't I been a good husband—and father?" His voice cracked.

"Yes." She nodded briskly as if vigorous agreement would stop Lincoln from stalking toward her.

Chevonne took backward steps in the direction of the bedroom door. "Lincoln, please. You're scaring me."

"You need to be scared, bitch," he said with venom. Twice in a few short minutes, he'd called his wife a bitch. Something he'd never done before. Calling her vile names seemed to take some of the sting out of being emasculated.

"In seven years of marriage, I never cheated on you, Chevonne. Not once!" He towered over her, bending as he met her face to face.

"I know, Lincoln. I know. What can I say, except, I'm sorry."

"You can start by telling me that muthafucka's name!" Vicious anger rose in his chest, and he was having trouble breathing.

"It was just a fling. Nothing serious. He's married, too."

"Married, huh? So that makes two cheaters—two deceitful muthafuckas!"

Chevonne wiped the sweat that was spreading across her forehead. "It wasn't supposed to happen." Guilty as hell, her voice was apologetic. She'd lost all the sass and arrogance she'd exhibited in the kitchen when she thought the discord was over pizza.

"Oh, no? So why didn't you stop yourself. You didn't give a damn about me or your children. Did you think about Amir and Tori when you were laying up, spreading your legs for that nigga?"

Chevonne dropped her eyes in shame.

"I married a skank-ass bitch! Lovely and respectable on the outside, but underneath the façade, you're nothing but a filthy hoe!"

"I think you should leave, Lincoln," Chevonne murmured as she inched away from him.

"Leave!" His voice boomed with incredulity. "You can't put me out of my goddamn house. I'm not going no muthafuckin' where."

Out of his mind with blind rage and humiliation, his fist raised without him even realizing it. Chevonne was close to getting her head bashed in. She let out a helpless little whimper when his fist slammed into the door, right above her girlish ponytail.

Deep in his subconscious, he'd always felt that the rug would be pulled from under him. And that time had finally arrived. Like most of his male relatives, like all the young thugs he'd grown up with, Lincoln, too, was going to wind up in jail.

"Tell me that muthafucka's name," he bellowed. Spittle sprayed from his mouth. He was out of control and contemplating murder.

Chevonne covered her mouth in horror.

"Daddy!" Amir and Tori shrieked in unison. The fear in their voices jarred Lincoln into awareness, giving him a reason to hold on to his sanity...stopped him from killing their mother with his bare hands.

CHAPTER 7

Solay had only been asleep for a few hours when the alarm went off. Most mornings, she frowned at the clock, hitting the snooze button and muttering curse words. But today, warmed by the afterglow of last night's passion, she awoke wearing a smile. She should have been exhausted from the workout that Deon put on her, but she wasn't. His good sex had her feeling renewed and invigorated.

Ready to take on the day, she sprang out of bed.

A half hour later, she entered the bakery. The air was heavy with the scent of something that smelled like cinnamon buns. The combined fragrance of sugar and spice should have been pleasurable, but smelling that aroma wafting from her bakery was aggravating. *Here we go again!* None of her recipes required a heavy dose of cinnamon, so what was Melanee up to now? Sure, she'd given her assistant permission to be creative every now and then, but she hadn't expected her to whip up a new recipe the very next day.

I'm going to wait and see how many new ingredients she used before I flip out on her ass.

Solay pushed open the kitchen door, ready for a confrontation. But anger melted away when she noticed two baking racks filled with chocolate, vanilla, and red velvet cupcakes. "What time did you get in, Melanee?"

"Three-thirty. I wanted to get the bulk of the baking done before I put today's specialty in the oven."

Solay glanced toward the oven, and drew on an inner calm. "I told you that I don't have the money for extra ingredients."

Melanee gave Solay a sympathetic look that seemed to suggest that Solay was not keeping up with the competition. Ordinarily, getting that kind of look from Melanee would have infuriated her, would have pulled a bitter and cutting response from her. But still riding on a sustained state of sexual euphoria, Solay was unusually tolerant.

"So what's in the oven?" Solay said with a sigh.

There was a flicker of embarrassment in Melanee's eyes. "In keeping with the sex theme..." She was obviously uncomfortable about openly discussing anything of a sexual nature. She lowered her head and spoke. "I came up with a cupcake called Sexy as Sin," she said, pushing her sliding eyeglasses up the bridge of her nose. "It's a cinnamon bun cupcake, so I considered spelling sin with a 'C.'"

Solay imagined the spelling on her chalkboard, and shook her head. "No, I don't like spelling it that way," she said, asserting her authority.

"No problem, we can spell it the regular way."

"What ingredients did you use?"

"Nothing extravagant. I added cinnamon to our vanilla batter. I'm making a creamy glaze that will have cinnamon cake crumbles sprinkled on top. No extra cost. We have a ton of cinnamon on hand," Melanee said, pointing to the large containers of spices on the overhead shelf.

"Your ideas are really impressive."

"Thanks."

"But I don't understand why it's so important to you. I mean, all this extra work and having to come in so early. What's the point?"

"I need an outlet for my creativity. That's all."

"Well, as long as your ideas are cost-efficient, and as long as Vidal doesn't have to be pulled from the register to help out, then feel free to experiment." It was apparent that Melanee was not going to give up easily, and Solay was feeling too good to get into a heated debate. The customers had gone berserk over yesterday's specialty. She was curious to see how they reacted to the cinnamon bun cupcake.

Solay tied on an apron. "I'll start mixing up the frosting for the chocolate cupcakes."

"I'll pitch in as soon as I get the Sexy Sins out of the oven."

Sexy Sins. Solay smiled at the cute nickname for Sexy as Sin. For Melanee to be such a prude, she sure was jumping on sex themes with wild abandon.

"Oh, my God! That cupcake is so good…makes me wanna smack my mama. Hell, it makes me wanna smack your mama, too," Vidal exclaimed when he bit into one of the cinnamon bun cupcakes.

Melanee laughed. "Do you think it's as good as the Screamin' O?"

"Different, but just as good."

"Thanks, Vidal."

"You got skills, girl. You need to be showcasing your delectable treats on one of those baking shows."

"That would be so nice," she said wistfully.

"I'm serious. You should look into it."

"You're sweet, Vidal."

"Sexy Sin," Vidal said, smiling as he took another bite. "You give off a real innocent vibe, but lemme find out you're an undercover freak."

Vidal chuckled, and Melanee laughed along with him, seeing the humor in the notion of her having any kind of freaky ways. She realized that most people regarded her as being straight-laced and practically asexual.

Carrying a metal tray filled with Sexy Sins, Vidal returned to the front of the bakery. He would have choked on the cupcake he was munching on if he had even an inkling of how much of a freak, Melanee actually was.

The moment she was alone in the kitchen, Melanee wiped her hands on her apron and then pulled out her cell, checking the message again. *I might want you to eat some pussy tonight. Will let you know.*

Her heart fluttered as she waited for the ping of the next message. Fifteen minutes passed. Nothing. It was ridiculous the way she allowed herself to be treated. After an hour, she turned her cell off, sparing herself the agony of disappointment. Toying with her emotions was her lover's favorite pastime. Melanee was in a sick and twisted relationship. Trapped. Love-struck.

It was getting close to quitting time. Feeling hopeful, she turned her phone back on. No messages. Dejected, Melanee busied herself sweeping the kitchen floor. The sound of the text tone put a smile on her face. Grinning, she read the message: *My place. 8:00 sharp.*

She was aroused and so stirred up, she could have climaxed right there.

The very thought of being with her lover produced a level of excitement so high, she actually had goose bumps. After weeks of having absolutely no appetite, Melanee was ravenous with hunger. Before going home to get a quick nap, a shower and change out of her grungy work clothes, she stopped at Taco Bell and gorged on burritos, tacos, and a cheesy, delicious chalupa. She finished off the meal with a large limeade beverage. Her lover always complained when she let herself get too thin, and Melanee hoped she'd eaten enough to put on a few pounds.

CHAPTER 8

A t eight on the dot, she was at the front door. Melanee knew the drill. She rang the bell twice to announce her arrival, waited exactly one minute, and then let herself in.

Heart palpitating, she stepped into the entry, and then made strides down the corridor that led to the main room. And there he was. Her lover. Her master. The man she lived and breathed for.

Colden was sitting on the white leather sofa. Beside him was a plump white girl.

Melanee kept a straight face, though she wanted to frown at the sight of her lover's broad arms, wrapped around a fat white chick. He didn't acknowledge Melanee. His face was buried in the chick's bosom.

The white chick had on black panties and bra. The straps of her black bra dangled over her shoulders. The bra was still hooked around her back, but the cups were pulled down. When she noticed Melanee, her blue eyes sparked in frightful surprise. Then she let out a gasp and pulled away from Colden. "Somebody's..."

"Ah, our guest has arrived," Colden said as if Melanee's presence was an unexpected delight.

Guest! It was shameful the way she'd been downgraded to being a guest in the place that was once her home.

"Why is she here?" The fat chick tugged on her bra, attempting to pull it up and cover her naked breasts.

Colden stilled her hand, firmly covering it with his, leaving her ample breasts and large pink nipples exposed. "Brandy, I want you to meet Melanee. She's going to be joining us."

"Hi, Brandy," Melanee said, trying to put the white bitch at ease. She noticed that there was a cheapness about Brandy—tramp-like. Not like a paid prostitute, but more like the town slut who gave the goodies away in an unending quest for love.

She had a round baby face. Her blue eyes were decorated with a ton of dark mascara and eyeliner. And the way she spoke, well, Melanee could tell that Brandy hadn't gone very far in school. She was nothing like the classy women Colden usually went for. He had a penchant for beautiful and elegant women. Women who spent hundreds of dollars at the hair salon, and who were into high-end fashion, Pilates, and other forms of body sculpting. Women who put Melanee to shame.

For the first time since she'd begun her twisted relationship with Colden, Melanee didn't feel inferior. She felt a little sorry for Brandy. The naïve girl probably thought that Colden really had the hots for her. He didn't. He was kissing and cuddling right now. But those acts of affection were merely a ploy to reel Brandy in. Very soon, he would begin to break down her will and any sense of value she might possibly have.

In a way, Melanee felt lucky. Colden hadn't given her a false impression. He clearly defined their relationship, the moment he met her.

Melanee was earning extra money, working for a catering company. She met Colden while serving appetizers at a fundraiser that was held at the home of a married couple, who appeared to be morally upstanding citizens. It seemed to be a regular social gathering, but all of the guests indulged in an alternative, secret lifestyle.

Colden was flanked by two beautiful women when she approached, offering tasty tidbits from the silver tray she held.

The women declined, turning up their noses. Colden regarded her large glasses and bad hairdo and smiled. "You're an interesting-looking serving girl. I'm not hungry, but when you've emptied that tray, I'll allow you to service me." His female companions erupted in catty giggles.

Stunned and humiliated, Melanee scurried away. Her face burned with shame as she worked the room, offering the guests exquisite gourmet morsels. Though she tried to avoid any eye contact with the man who had ridiculed her, she kept sneaking glances. He had a commanding presence, and his crude words had ignited something strange inside her. Intrigued and inexplicably sexually excited, she sought him out after she'd finished serving the guests.

She had hoped to find him alone, but he was still chatting with the same two women. Afraid that he'd leave before she gave him her number, Melanee approached him.

"Um, excuse me. Can I speak to you in private?" she said, eyes lowered, her face aflame with mortification.

He looked at her as if her presence was offensive. "Give me a minute," he said. After making her wait five minutes, he walked a few steps away from his female companions.

"What can I do for you?"

"I want to give you my phone number," she said in a quivering voice.

"And why would I want your number?" he asked, and then let out a rumble of laughter. The two Barbie dolls sneered at her and shook their heads in disgust.

Melanee wanted to go through the floor. "Oh, I'm sorry. I thought—"

"What did you think?"

"That…you know…maybe you wanted to hook up sometime."

"I live in the moment. If you want to service me, then you can do it now."

Melanee looked around. People were mingling and socializing. The other catering staff was going about their duties. Maybe she wouldn't be missed if she slipped away to one of the bedrooms for a quickie. This man had a magnetic personality. He aroused her in a way that she didn't quite understand.

"Okay," she shamefully agreed.

In the midst of the party, he took her to an alcove—not a bedroom—he didn't even seek out the privacy of a bathroom. He pulled her into shadowy recesses of the large room.

He unzipped his pants and presented a large and venous dick. "Kneeling is the only way you're going to service me properly." He spoke to Melanee as if she were a dull-witted child.

"You want me to…" her voice trailed off as she looked around worriedly. "You want me to do it, right here?"

"Why not?" Amusement gleamed in his charcoal-colored eyes.

She had assumed that servicing him meant sexual intercourse. He was so confident and physically attractive, Melanee had been looking forward to getting a good, hard fuck. But Colden made it clear that he only wanted a blow job. And for some reason, she couldn't deny him.

On her knees, sucking a stranger's dick in a corner while the party was in full swing, Melanee was quite a spectacle.

Colden must have had some kind of pull because the hosts and the other guests looked the other way, pretending not to notice the debauchery that was occurring in the alcove.

"Swallow it," he demanded when he released a load inside her mouth.

As if caught up in some kind of love trance, she immediately obeyed. It took three gulps before she got all of his creamy mixture down. She wiped her lips with the back of her hand.

Colden didn't offer her a hand to help her up. With a hand pressed against the wall, she struggled to her feet.

Sucking dick on command was the most humiliating, yet insanely erotic thing that she'd ever done.

But while the attendees didn't appear offended, Melanee's boss, on the other hand, was irate and indignant. "You should be arrested for lewd and lascivious behavior," he told her after firing her.

Instantly hooked on sexual degradation, Melanee's life changed the night she surrendered her will to Colden.

"What do mean, she's joining us?" Brandy's confused voice brought Melanee back to the present.

Melanee patiently waited for Colden to bring Brandy up to speed. If the poor girl had been looking for love, she was in the wrong place.

"Are you trying to get me involved in a threesome or something?" Frowning, Brandy crossed her arms in front of her enormous breasts.

"Something like that." Colden cut an eye at Melanee. He gave her a conspiratorial smile, and she nearly swooned from the attention.

"I'm not into that," Brandy said with much distaste.

"How do you know you won't like it? Try it. It turns me on. Do it for me," he said in a placating tone.

"I don't want to."

"You don't have to do anything. Just open your legs and allow Melanee to eat your pussy."

"I don't know."

"I know it's your first time, but you don't have to be nervous. I'll be right here. Holding you, kissing you." His voice was velvet as he stroked Brandy's streaked hair. "You're my good girl, right?"

"Well, yeah, but—"

"Shh." Silencing her protest, he covered her mouth with his lips. Seduced her with kisses while his dark hands were busy, groping and squeezing her melon-like breasts as if checking for ripeness.

"Come over here, Melanee."

Given a direct order, Melanee crossed the room and stood before Colden and Brandy. Colden tugged on Brandy's arm, urging her to sit on his lap. Once she was in place, he gyrated on her wide rear end; his long finger rubbed her panty crotch.

"Melanee is going to be especially gentle with you," he said softly. "She's going to show you the pleasure of a woman's tongue."

Melanee yearned to taste the dick that was bulged inside Colden's pants. The dick that was pressed against the white girl's ass. But she had to earn the right to even touch Colden's private parts.

Brandy squirmed, uncomfortable with Melanee standing over her.

"Relax, love," Colden whispered. He held one of her hefty breasts, offering it to Melanee.

Kneeling, Melanee drew the big pink nipple inside her mouth. She wasn't attracted to women in the least, but if she expected to get the treat that she really wanted, she'd have to suck titties and lick pussy until the white girl was persuaded to bust a nut.

"That's enough." Colden nudged Melanee away from Brandy's titty. "Take her panties off and make her cum."

Obediently, Melanee worked the black panties over Brandy's hips. Brandy shivered as Colden pulled her thighs wide apart, presenting Melanee a close-up view of wet pussy.

Crouched on the floor, Melanee licked the pussy drippings that began flowing freely.

Brandy moaned when Melanee's tongue snaked inside her pussy. She wriggled in sexual excitement. "Oh, my God, this is so freaky!" Brandy exclaimed, sounding shocked that her body was responding to the caresses of a female's skilled tongue.

"Lick it, baby. Show me how much you love eating pussy," Colden crooned.

Motivated, Melanee lapped with pleasure, totally disregarding the fact that she wasn't really into women. She ate pussy for Colden's pleasure. And for the reward he gave her afterward.

Brandy moved her hips and moaned, caught up in the excitement of forbidden pleasure. And Melanee was so thrilled to be back in Colden's good graces, she moaned along with Brandy.

Brandy grabbed the back of Melanee's head, undulating and grinding on her face.

Colden tapped Melanee on the shoulder. "She's ready. Go for it. Suck the cum out of that pussy."

Lips locked around Brandy's outer lips, Melanee's tongue swirled around her clit. When Brandy began moving her hips and breathing heavily, Melanee then penetrated the woman's plush walls. It only took a few minutes for Brandy to begin vibrating; practically screaming when she climaxed.

Brandy panted, palm against the center of her chest, as if trying to slow down her heart rate.

"You okay, baby?" Colden asked, smiling with pride as if he'd made Brandy cum.

Melanee didn't like hearing him still being so affectionate with this newcomer. She'd done what he expected, and it was her turn now.

"How was it?" Colden asked, still focusing on Brandy.

"Oh, my God. So good. I can't believe I've been missing out."

"Not anymore. All you have to do is put your trust in me, and I'll introduce you to a world of kinky pleasure."

"I trust you," Brandy murmured, sounding exhausted and satisfied as she made herself more comfortable in Colden's lap.

Melanee was jealous. She wanted to get off the floor

and get some of Colden's affection, but she kept her feelings to herself. She would have to really behave if she wanted to suck Colden's dick.

She missed waking up and serving him. She was suffering—literally withering without him. Every day, she asked herself why she had ruined their relationship—being defiant and challenging his authority. Now he only saw her occasionally, and she missed him so much. Hopefully, the day would soon come when she had proven herself worthy and obedient enough to be allowed to return home.

"Brandy," Colden whispered.

"Hmm?"

"When you're with me, you have to learn to share."

Brandy frowned.

"It's Melanee's turn."

Brandy's eyes popped open. "I don't eat pussy."

"You will. Eventually." He patted her ass, urging her to move over to the other cushion of the leather sofa.

Melanee's lips replaced Brandy's. She whimpered in appreciation as Colden's dick glided along her tongue. Tasting him was like heaven; she could have cried from sheer pleasure. But Melanee knew better than to lollygag. She went to work on his dick. Worshipping it with her tongue. Sucking it slowly, pulling it in deeply until the head was practically down her throat. She cupped his balls reverently, giving them a light squeeze.

Colden's tempo changed, and Melanee cracked her

eyes open. She observed him as he motioned Brandy to join them.

Melanee wanted to keep Colden's dick sheltered inside her mouth, but knowing what he intended to do, she released the suction hold.

"Take over," he told Brandy as he eased his dick from Melanee's mouth.

Brandy looked confused. "Do you want me to finish blowing you?"

"No. Jerk me off."

Unsure of what Colden expected, Brandy took his dick and held it delicately.

"Jerk me off."

Brandy gripped his erection tighter, sliding her hand up and down.

"Aim at Melanee's face."

"Huh?" Perplexed, she looked down at Melanee as she delivered hand strokes.

Still on her knees, Melanee edged closer. With her chin jutting upward, she anticipated a splash of sticky fluid—the kind of facial that couldn't be purchased from a store.

CHAPTER 9

S napped back to a more rational state of consciousness, Lincoln scowled at his balled fist, regarding it as something foreign. Disgusted, he unclenched it. He heard Chevonne comforting the kids, reassuring them that everything was all right between Mommy and Daddy. She sounded convincing; lying came easily for Chevonne.

Lincoln grabbed a pillow and snatched the comforter off of the bed. The sofa downstairs was much more appealing than sleeping next to the enemy.

No, fuck that. Chevonne would love the idea of him being banished to the sofa. If she didn't want to lie next to him, then she could trot her cheating ass downstairs and sleep on the sofa.

Calm and resolute, Lincoln threw back the covers and got into bed.

Chevonne slept elsewhere. He didn't know and didn't care whether she was curled up in Tori's little twin bed or was tossing and turning on the couch. Knowing where he stood with Chevonne was liberating. No more inner turmoil. No more wondering why his wife rebuffed him.

For the first time in many nights, Lincoln got a good night's sleep.

"Good morning, Rachel." Lincoln forced his mouth into a tight smile. Rachel was a busybody and it was hard to like her. He would have passed her desk with only a slight head nod if he didn't have to pick up his messages from her.

She handed him a small stack of papers. "Did you hear the news?" Rachel's eyes glittered through the lens of her eyeglasses. The hot gleam in Rachel's dark eyes and her accelerated breathing was almost sexual. The woman got perverted pleasure from bearing bad news.

Right and left, coworkers were getting axed. Seasoned architects were being replaced with inexperienced, new college grads. Given the option of being laid off or accepting a pay cut, Lincoln had taken the latter, losing a chunk of self-respect along with decreased income. Still, a lower salary didn't guarantee job security.

Sifting through the pile of messages, Lincoln winced. Was he about to get axed? "What's going on?" he asked, dreading the response.

Rachel edged forward. "This is between you and me."

He nodded, eyebrows knitted together in seriousness.

"Mitchell got his walking papers an hour ago," she whispered.

Lincoln groaned. Mitchell had been with the firm for many years and was a highly accomplished architect. But these days, experience was more a curse than an asset. Lately, the firm was only interested in the young and savvy. At thirty-four, Lincoln was starting to feel like a dinosaur.

"And get this…" Rachel motioned for Lincoln to come closer. Ordinarily, he wouldn't give the gossipy receptionist the time of day. But these weren't ordinary times, so he drew closer.

"Mitchell's replacement is in the office with the boss. Fresh out of college. A bright-eyed girl from Mount Vernon, New York."

Lincoln shook his head.

"Guess who's in charge of training the newbie?"

Lincoln released a hard sigh. "Me?"

"You got it! Have fun!" Rachel chortled.

Lincoln took long strides to his office. Training college grads was a pain in the ass. Being at work was becoming as fucked up as being at home.

Frank, the owner of the firm, tapped on Lincoln's door and introduced him to Amber, the young college grad from upstate New York. Amber looked about sixteen. Lincoln smiled and welcomed her to the firm, all the while wondering where he'd find the patience to put up with another wet-behind-the-ears kid.

Hired as an apprentice drafter, Lincoln explained Amber's job description. He gave her a tour of the three-story, loft-style facility. He introduced her to her new coworkers. And after a couple of hours of bullshitting, he was ready to ditch the young woman and get some work done. He walked her to her work area. After instructing her to familiarize herself with the employee handbook, he excused himself.

Alone with his thoughts, he sat behind his desk. The bronze-framed family photo that sat on his desk seemed to mock him. He wondered if his wife had taken another personal day. Was she holed up in a hotel with her lover right now? Or was she boldly getting her fuck on in her well-appointed city office? The thought filled him with hatred. Divorce was imminent. Custody, child support, division of property—it was going to get real ugly before it was over.

Lincoln suddenly noticed Amber standing in the doorway of his office as he pondered his fucked-up life. "Yes?" He tried to keep the irritation from his voice.

"I want to make sure I understand my responsibilities. I'm…like…not gonna use my skills to design anything?"

Lincoln couldn't help from chuckling at her naiveté. "No, not for quite a while."

"That sucks."

"Hey, I'm an accomplished architect, but I spend more time on the phone, in meetings, and consulting with clients than actually designing or drafting plans," he explained, giving Amber the best encouraging smile that he could manage. He was groaning inside. Placating and babysitting was not in his job description. This shit was demeaning. He didn't appreciate having to take this kid under his wing.

"So what exactly will I be doing?"

"Getting familiar with the firm. Researching zoning and building codes."

"That sucks."

"Life sucks," he said firmly. He glanced at his watch. "It's lunchtime; why don't you go grab yourself a bite to eat, and meet me back here in an hour and a half."

The boss popped his head in. "I see you two are getting along. Good. Very good."

"Yes," Lincoln replied. "Amber's about to take a lunch break."

"Good idea," the boss said, and then looked at Amber. "Have you ever been on South Street?"

"No." Amber perked up a bit.

"Give her a tour, Lincoln. Show her the hotspots… places where the young people hang out."

It was an executive order. "Sure thing, Frank." Lincoln tried to look happy about being Amber's tour guide.

Lincoln would have preferred having lunch at Ms. Tootsie's but his young charge wanted to eat at Johnny Rockets. *Jesus!* Sitting in a hamburger joint was juvenile. Listening to a freckle-faced white girl chatter on and on about nothing was a colossal waste of time. When Amber finished her burger, Lincoln waved the waiter over, more than ready to get the hell out of the noisy place.

Trying to discourage Amber from dawdling and window shopping, Lincoln walked briskly along South Street. Amber stopped suddenly. She literally clapped her hands and squealed like a little kid when she noticed a baking establishment called Scandalicious. "Oh, my God! A cupcake place. I have to go in there."

Before Lincoln could reject the idea, Amber was already inside.

There was quite a long line at the counter. The snazzy-dressed guy that was working the cash register seemed a little overwhelmed. Lincoln took a seat on an out-of-the-way, velvet couch, collecting his thoughts while Amber stood in line. The cupcake bakery had a moody vibe that was seductive and appealing. Sort of reminded Lincoln of a French bordello—not that he'd ever visited one. Nevertheless, the sexy ambience and the enticing scents improved his disposition.

An attractive woman emerged from the kitchen, joining the young man at the counter. The line of customers began moving along more swiftly now that there were two people taking orders. While waiting for Amber, Lincoln slipped into deep thought.

"Are you okay? Can I get you something?"

Lost in thought, Lincoln hadn't heard anyone approach. He was surprised to find himself staring at the face of the nice-looking woman who'd been taking orders behind the counter. She was even prettier up close.

"No, I'm okay. Waiting for my young coworker to get her sugar fix." He nodded over at Amber who had made it to the front of the line.

"Okay, just checking on you. Making sure you weren't passed out or anything. I've only been open six months. The last thing I need is for a customer to keel over after eating one my cupcakes." Chuckling, she walked away, resuming her position behind the counter.

Lincoln was impressed that a young black woman owned the bakery. Rent wasn't cheap on South Street. Judging by the amount of customers, the sister was doing pretty good for herself. If he'd followed his heart, he would have his own architectural firm, instead of slaving for the man. But being married with kids required a regular paycheck.

CHAPTER 10

A never-ending stream of customers had filled the shop until closing. Money-wise, that was a good thing. But Solay's stress level was on overload. Her baking assistant had been distracted—not on top of her game at all. Last week, Melanee had been a passionate baker, creating new recipes that introduced bold new flavors, but she'd been pretty much useless today. Burning cupcakes, forgetting ingredients, and smiling blissfully off into space, like she was in the midst of an erotic fantasy. Melanee was a complete puzzle to Solay. She never talked about her personal life, she shied away from talk about sex, and Solay wondered if the dowdy, little wisp of a girl was still a virgin.

Dismissing Melanee from her thoughts, Solay focused on her own needs, and what she needed was some stress release. She called that "rent-a-dick" center. Though she preferred to see Deon again, she decided to try something new. A rep for the agency recommended an escort who went by the name, Spanish Fly.

Solay excitedly rushed to the door when the bell rang. Through the peephole, she examined her escort. Spanish Fly had chiseled features, olive complexion, dark wavy hair, and a powerfully built body. The handsome Latino looked like a promise of many hours of sweaty body slapping.

"Hey, Spanish Fly," she welcomed when she opened the door. Solay was looking forward to getting naked with this sexy Adonis.

"Good evening, madam. Please call me, Fly," he said with a sexy Spanish accent. Then he reached for her hand and delivered a soft kiss that sent delicious shivers up her spine. Sexy and suave, Fly seemed to be a good choice.

"Have a seat." Solay motioned toward the sofa, intending to chat for a few minutes before jumping in bed and requesting that her Latino lover talk dirty in Spanish.

"No, thank you. I want to get you in the mood," he said, as his tongue circled his lips.

"Okay, get me in the mood." She smiled, eager for some raunchy freakishness.

"I brought some music," he added with a wink as he pulled an iPod from the inside pocket of his jacket.

Hmm. Fly is kind of extra. Solay didn't need romantic music. All she wanted was a thick, juicy dick. Being polite, she accepted the iPod.

"I always do a performance. You know…to get your juices flowing." He removed his jacket, draping it over a chair.

Strange foreplay. "What kind of performance?" Feeling a bit uncertain about Fly, she set the iPod on a docking station.

Shakira's voice emerged from the speakers, singing "Hips Don't Lie."

Fly whipped off his shirt off and went into action. He flung his arms about as he swung his hips, shook his ass, belly danced, and even worked in some ballet twirls, all the while, licking his lips. One minute, he was working it like a stripper and the next moment, he was leaping and twirling. The routine was an embarrassment and hard to watch. Fly was over the top, and his dance style was way too sissified to get her juices flowing. No longer able to tolerate this shameful display of his true sexual orientation, Solay clicked off Shakira.

In mid-hip thrust, Fly froze. "Hey! Why'd you stop the music? Is something wrong?" he yelled, scowling in objection to the interruption.

"We're not a good match, Fly. But thank you for your time." If Solay were going out to a social event, Fly would have been fabulous arm candy. But he had too much sugar in his tank to fulfill her carnal needs.

"Are you serious?" he screeched in a high-pitched voice, totally releasing his inner girl. "I traveled all this way to spend time with you. I'm trying to give you a romantic evening, and just like that, you're kicking me out?"

"Sorry, but I'm not feeling that dance." She handed him the iPod, wondering if the agency would honor a last-minute request for Deon.

Fly snatched his iPod from her hand. "I was classically

trained at Juilliard. But you're not refined enough to appreciate—"

"Whatever!" she spat.

He pulled his shirt over his head and yanked his jacket off the chair. "You wasted my time, lady. I hope you realize that you still have to pay for my services."

Solay shrugged, knowing that she was going to call the agency, demanding Deon—or a refund. She'd pitch a bitch and threaten to sue if they insisted on charging her credit card for Fly's dancing ass.

Fly stormed out, slamming the door behind him.

Punk-ass!

Lips curled in dissatisfaction, Solay picked up the phone. *Those rent-a-dick shysters tried to play me. I requested a man that could put in some work in the bedroom, and they sent me a flaming ballerina!*

Surprisingly, the agency was apologetic and accommodating. Only problem—Deon was booked up until the end of the week.

"Greek Thunder is available tonight; he's a favorite," said the pleasant voice on the other end of the phone. "Would you like us to send him over?"

Solay pondered briefly. "No, I'll wait for Deon," she said, deciding against taking any more chances with unknown dick. Deon was tried and true. She liked the way he put it down.

Alone with her thoughts, she wondered if it was healthy to substitute a real relationship with paid escorts. *Hell yeah*, she responded. Relationships were all-consuming—bad for business. Once again, she assured herself that renting dick had to be healthier than allowing herself to become entangled in an emotionally draining and romantic situation.

CHAPTER 11

C olden had summoned her, demanding her presence at a dinner party that one of his wealthy friends was hosting. Colden had always kept her behind closed doors. He'd never invited her to any of the exclusive parties that he attended. Melanee was honored, but had no idea what would be required of her. The suspense had her tingling all over—made her panties wet.

At quitting time, Melanee ripped off her apron and raced out of Scandalicious. It took three buses and a fifteen-minute walk to get to the Montgomery County address that Colden had sent in a text. She didn't expect him to provide her with transportation. She'd gladly walk to the end of the earth to be with him.

By the time Melanee finally reached the lovely Tudor-style home, she was eager to become immersed in whatever sexual adventure Colden had planned.

Her pulse quickened with excitement as she lifted the heavy door knocker.

Colden answered the door. He looked dashing in a black suit and tie. "You're late! You missed dinner, and our hostess is infuriated."

"I'm sorry, Master. The buses were running late."

"Inexcusable." His whispered voice became a hiss.

Melanee felt heat prickling up the back of her neck. Fear as well as humiliation aroused her, causing her face to flush. "I'm really sorry. I tried to get—"

Colden held up his hand, silencing her. Melanee flinched.

His dark brown eyes bore into her. "Punctuality should never be an issue. You're nothing but a novice. If you can't manage time, then you're obviously in over your head."

"I'll do better."

"You're not ready for the lifestyle."

"I'm still learning."

He glared at Melanee, which caused her small nipples to grow taut. Colden was even more desirable when he was enraged. His smoldering dark eyes, the visible veins jutting out at the sides of his neck, the thin sheen of perspiration that covered his forehead—it all added to his sexuality and attractiveness. From the corner of her eye, she glanced at his muscular thighs inside custom-tailored pants.

She closed her eyes for a quick blissful moment, imagining Colden's strong limbs clamped securely around her head.

"If it were up to me, you wouldn't cross this threshold. But I've promised the hostess an evening of decadent entertainment. Don't fuck this up!" The controlled growl beneath Colden's words warned that a thrashing would be too good for her. And being exiled again—being denied the privilege of sucking his dick was more than she could endure.

Nodding grimly, Melanee moved toward the open doorway.

Colden blocked her path. He looked her up and down sneeringly. "The servant's entrance is in the rear."

"Oh." Having forgotten her place, she reversed her footsteps. She didn't dare ask what she would be required to do. She'd find out soon enough. Feeling both anxious and excited, she turned and hurried to the back of the house.

A pebble walkway led to the servant's entrance. Standing in the doorway was a large and imposing man, dressed in a butler's uniform. He had an abundance of kinky, silvery-gray hair that hung to his shoulders. His brown skin was unlined, youthful and taut—a complete contradiction of hair color that suggested a much older man. Stone-faced, the butler held the door open for Melanee. Ushered into the vestibule, she followed him into the kitchen.

He pointed to a door that looked as if it might lead to a basement. "Madam wants you to undress in there." The butler spoke in a pompous and affected manner, as if trying to sound British.

Who's Madam? Melanee wondered, but she didn't ask. Making inquiries of any type would imply that Melanee was untrained…wayward. And nothing was further from the truth. She was obedient and grateful for the opportunity to serve Colden and wouldn't dream of offending the gracious hostess.

Madam was no doubt a prominent member of the private society that Colden belonged to—a group of well-to-do people that gathered together to indulge their darkest and most deviant sexual desires. The man dressed as a butler was most likely Madam's sexual submissive. She figured that he was costumed as a servant specifically for this occasion.

Melanee was terrified of where the door might lead, but she'd do anything to please Colden. If he commanded her to descend into the bowels of a dark and torturous dungeon, then she had no choice—she had to do it.

She was relieved when the butler opened the door to a bright and well-organized pantry. Looking around at the stockpiles of food items, she wondered if she was expected to put on a maid's uniform and serve during the dinner party.

She scanned the room but didn't uncover a uniform or any other articles of clothing. "Where's my outfit? What does Madam want me to wear?"

"You won't be wearing anything. You are required to go au natural." The butler seemed insulted, as if he alone was worthy of donning a servant's uniform. With his nose turned up, he left the pantry, closing the door behind him.

As Melanee disrobed, a thrilling mixture of dread and excitement caused her to shake. She looked around for somewhere to hang her clothes. Finding neither a closet nor hangers, her first thought was to fold and place her clothes on a shelf that held canned goods. She thought better of that idea; Colden might not approve.

In keeping with her humble position, she tucked her pile of clothing in a corner on the floor—behind a large storage bin—hidden from view. Colden's friends had sensitive eyes, accustomed to the finer things in life, and Melanee didn't want to offend the hostess or anyone else with her cheap and wrinkled attire.

She'd lost so much weight. Would her thin body be offensive? She hoped the group would overlook her current appearance and judge her on her willingness to provide pleasure. As long as she remained in Colden's good graces, she'd have a healthy appetite. In no time at all, her weight would be back to normal.

Anxious, Melanee hugged herself as she waited for the adventure to begin.

The door pushed open, and a shudder rippled through Melanee's body when the butler walked in. "Madam will see you, now. Follow me."

He led her down the corridor; his back and shoulders were erect with self-assurance. He wore his butler gear with pride and confidence, as if he were wearing the decorated uniform of a four-star general. Padding along the corridor, Melanee's bare skin prickled; her steps faltered as she grew nearer to the sound of chatter and tinkling laughter.

Sensing her hesitation, the butler turned around. "Come, come. You must not keep Madam and her guests waiting any longer."

In a grand and spacious room, formally dressed men and women chatted and socialized while holding the end of a chained leash that bound their submissive mates to them.

Upon Melanee's entrance, all conversations stopped. The butler cleared his throat. "Madam," he said and then left the room.

"So this is the impudent little creature that belongs to Colden!" A snobbish voice of superiority emerged from the lips of a statuesque woman that Melanee presumed to be Madam. While all the other guests and their subs were scattered about the room, the woman, whose complexion was the color of molasses, stood in the center of the gathering—as if holding court.

High cheekbones complemented doe-shaped eyes. Her makeup was expertly applied, giving her dark complexion the look of silk. Her straightened dark hair was pulled back into a bun, and secured in a net of sparkling jewels. An off-shoulder, form-fitting, beaded white gown contrasted her skin and flaunted a toned and exquisite physique. She was regal, beautiful, and terrifying.

Tethered to Madam was a young man with a face that was almost as pretty as a girl's. The hair on his head was a lustrous crown of spiral ringlets—an abundance of golden curls. His bare chest and arms were rippled with youthful muscles.

He kept his eyes downcast as he stood beside Madam. Melanee noticed that all the subs—both male and female—were covered at the bottom, though their upper bodies were exposed.

Being the only naked person in the room was more disturbing than she'd imagined. Melanee felt lower than a peasant. Why was she ordered to strip naked and stand before these strangers, while the other subs were at least partially dressed? It was a cruel punishment. The heat of embarrassment flushed her face and then traveled downward, settling in her center. Her juices were so hot, they bubbled and overflowed. She squeezed her thighs together, attempting to conceal the heat of her arousal. Under such extreme circumstances, Melanee was not surprised that her pussy had become a dripping, clenching hot pool of desire.

Searching the crowd, Melanee sought Colden's face, hoping for guidance. Her questioning eyes found his, but were met with a glower.

Colden shifted his gaze to Madam. He motioned toward Melanee. "Tonight, she's all yours. Use her in any manner that gives you sexual pleasure."

Madam's eyes darkened with interest. As she scrutinized Melanee, her eyes running over every inch of her body, a frown formed on Madam's face. "She's a scrawny little thing. Completely unappealing."

"Madam Midnight," Colden addressed the woman formally. "My apologies for the girl's malnourished appearance. Unfortunately, she loses her appetite when she is denied my company. Should she pass tonight's try-outs; I plan to spend more time with her, taking her through rigorous and unrelenting training. I can assure you that with more meat on her bones, this girl is a delight to the eyes."

Melanee had no idea if Madam Midnight was the woman's true name or a moniker she used in the confines of this elite and secret society. She honestly didn't care. She was overjoyed to hear Colden publicly announce that he was going to take time with her and give her serious training. Her task was to make him proud in front of his fellow members.

Though the subs kept their gazes cast downward, the other people—the dominants—openly appraised Melanee. Their down- turned mouths conveyed their disapproval.

Nervous, Melanee chewed on her inner lip. She yearned to be accepted, and it was a struggle to remain calm. Mimicking the behavior of the better-trained subs, she lowered her head, fixing her eyes on the floor.

"Look at me, girl!" Madam spoke sharply. "I didn't give you permission to turn your eyes away from me."

Melanee's head shot up obediently. She forced herself to gaze into Madam's dark and contemptuous eyes. Melanee caught a whiff of her perfume; Madam not only looked like money, she even smelled expensive.

"What's your specialty—fellatio or eating cunt," Madam said bluntly.

"Both. I do both," Melanee answered quickly, cutting a nervous eye at Colden.

"Which…is…your…specialty?" Madam spoke through gritted teeth, putting space between each word.

"Fellatio!" Melanee exclaimed. She could tell that Madam had a quick temper. The last thing she wanted was to be on the woman's bad side.

Melanee hadn't noticed the large vintage bell that sat atop a table until Madam extended a long and graceful arm to retrieve it. With a slight and mysterious smile on her lips, Madam rang the bell.

The butler appeared almost instantly. "Madam?" he said with a slight head bow.

"This girl is going to entertain us with a demonstration. We're all eager to view her talent."

"I understand, Madam." The butler wore a somber expression. With a theatrical flourish, he began to unzip his pants. He palmed his flaccid penis, which he tenderly stroked until it swelled to an enormous size. The butler turned slowly, presenting each dominant guest with a showing of his massive erection.

When a great riot of applause erupted from dominant guests, a flattered smile formed on the butler's face. The leashed and collared subs were appropriately still and silent, showing no sign of being impressed by the butler's significantly enlarged penis.

At Colden's command, Melanee had licked lots of pussy, but she'd never been ordered to administer a blow job to any man other than Colden. She glanced at Colden questioningly.

Colden waved his hand, gesturing his permission. Though

his expression was stoic, a glimmer of warmth and pride was reflected in his eyes.

Encouraged by the promise of the reward she'd receive later, Melanee kneeled before the butler and drew his sizeable dick into her mouth, lathing it with her tongue, sucking as though it held the same sweetness as Colden's magnificent dick.

CHAPTER 12

The way his salary had been hacked, he only made a fraction of what he used to earn. Chevonne headed the Department of Tourism for the City of Philadelphia, and her salary put Lincoln's to shame. After his numerous pay cuts, she was responsible for the lion's share of the household bills.

Though he could barely cover his portion of the family's living expenses, Lincoln had thought about it long and hard, and had come to a decision. He couldn't stay under the same roof as Chevonne. Nor could he walk away from his children.

Sitting up in bed, her back pressed against the headboard, Chevonne stared at the monitor of her laptop and tapped the keys. As a department head, her responsibilities were tremendous. It wasn't unusual for her to bring work home. But after the discovery of her adulterous affair, Lincoln wondered if she'd been using the pretext of work to exchange sex messages with her illicit lover. He didn't put anything past her sneaky ass.

It incensed him that Chevonne had lain in bed beside him night after night, pretending to work, while possibly sending explicit pictures and emails to her secret paramour.

Lincoln recalled how badly he'd craved her body, forcing himself to try to focus on TV while waiting for her to finish whatever she was working on. But most nights, after she'd shut down her laptop, she would also shut her legs. Claiming to have cramps or a headache. Plenty of excuses and hardly any pleasure.

All too often, she'd turned her back toward Lincoln, denying him, leaving him no choice but to jack off as she lay sleeping beside him.

Every now and then, she doled out pity pussy. Lincoln cringed while recalling the occasions when he'd accepted pussy that was not given freely. Pussy that he was entitled to was reluctantly given with a frown and a long sigh of aggravation, as if Lincoln were a beggar or a hopeless charity case.

Bitter memories reinforced his animosity. "I'm leaving you, Chevonne." His hostile voice cut through the silence inside the bedroom. "I'm looking for an apartment."

Chevonne exhaled audibly. Before responding, she grabbed the remote, and turned on the TV. "I don't want the children to overhear us," she explained, in a hushed tone of voice.

Lincoln gave a snickering sound of sarcastic laughter. "You seemed to be an expert at keeping up a façade, but do you actually believe that the volume from the TV will disguise the dissension in our household?"

"I'm trying to protect Amir and Tori. They don't need to hear every detail of our marital problems."

Lincoln nodded, seemingly with understanding. Then he threw an unexpected, low blow. "Yeah, I can understand why you wouldn't want the kids to know that their mother is a slut."

"Sarcasm, name-calling, sulking. It's all so immature... and vicious." Chevonne shook her head pityingly, as if Lincoln's resentment was uncalled for.

"I'm not the spouse that cheated, and quite frankly, I didn't know that there were rules of etiquette in this situation. But since you're the one that was raised in a well-to-do family, why don't you school me? What's the proper code of behavior? What the hell is a civilized man supposed to do when he discovers that his wife is a whoring-ass bitch?"

"Is this name calling necessary? Can't you behave like a mature adult? What's done is done. All we can do is move forward now."

Lincoln gawked at her. "Move forward? Are you serious? Every time I look at you, I see a random dick sliding between your lips." He glared at her while his hateful words sank in. "Did you swallow, baby? Did you guzzle down that muthafucka's cum?"

Tears formed in Chevonne's eyes. Her distress gave Lincoln a small degree of satisfaction.

Chevonne wiped her eyes. "I was going to try to convince you to stay, but maybe a trial separation is a good idea. How can I fight to hold our family together with you constantly making snide comments? Go ahead and leave. Do whatever you want to do. I have to worry about our children—make sure that they're being raised in a healthy environment."

Eyes wide with incredulity, Lincoln pointed at his wife. "You destroyed our family. You poisoned this environment when you made the decision to drop your drawers for that muthafucka. Blame your cum-hungry pussy and your knob-slobbering lips, but don't try to blame me for destroying our family."

"Must you be so crude?"

"Tit for a tat. Your slut-bucket activities weren't exactly ladylike, you know."

She winced. "I'm sorry, Lincoln. You can't imagine how truly sorry I am. But how long do you think I'm going to tolerate your verbal attacks?" Chevonne said tearfully. "If this is the only way that you can communicate, then you need to go. I'll help you pack."

"Don't turn the tables on me. I'm not the bad guy. I'm the one who was duped. I thought I was married to a wholesome woman—a refined lady—with morals and family values. But I was hoodwinked. You're really no different than a two-dollar whore."

"I never presented myself as anything other than a human being. Educated? Yes. From a respected family? Yes. But you're the one that put me on a pedestal. And now you're trying to chip away at it—trying to tear me down."

Being from the 'hood, Lincoln had to claw and scratch for everything he'd gotten. Basketball was his ticket to college and his intelligence led him to what had started out as a promising and lucrative career. A classy chick like Chevonne would have never been within his reach if he hadn't pulled himself up by his bootstraps. Chevonne had been the ultimate reward—his trophy wife.

Now she was tainted. He gave her a look of repugnance.

Chevonne looked away from his condemning gaze. Eyes lowered, she asked, "Do you want to try counseling— as a last-chance effort? It might help."

Looking at his beautiful wife, repentant and beaten, he wished he could say something optimistic, but forgiveness was not in his heart.

"I wish you would have thought about counseling before you made that move. The trust is broken. How can talking to a counselor restore the trust that I had in you?"

"I don't know, but shouldn't we think about the kids and at least make an effort?"

Lincoln shook his head. "Like I said, I thought long and hard. I'm leaving. And Amir is going with me when I move."

Chevonne made a long, croaking sound, as if stabbed with a dagger. "You can't take my child away from me."

"We're over, Chevonne. Nothing can change that. But I'm not going to allow our situation to affect the close bond I've built with my son. If I fought hard enough—if

I paid for a high-priced lawyer, I could probably get Amir and Tori. But I think a girl needs her mother."

"Amir needs me, too!" There was a wild and desperate look in Chevonne's eyes—like she was capable of homicide.

"Amir needs me! I'll be damned if I'll allow my son to be influenced by the opinions and attitudes of a bunch of random dudes. Fuck that!"

Tears flowed from Chevonne's eyes. She sniffled helplessly. "I'm a good mother. I'd never allow my children—"

"A good mother thinks about her children's well-being before parting her skanky legs for some out-of-town dick."

CHAPTER 13

Tonight was the night! She was finally going to have Deon back in her bed. It didn't surprise her that Deon was in high demand. He put it on her in the bedroom. The extra bonus was his good looks and his thuggish swagger. That curved dick of his was well worth every dollar she'd put on her credit card.

"It's time for my lunch break," Vidal called out, his voice carrying to the kitchen.

Anticipating the hot night she was going to have with Deon, Solay wore a secret smile as she replaced Vidal at the counter.

"What's the weekly special?" a college-aged kid asked, squinting at the chalkboard menu. Solay recognized him as a regular who bought cupcakes three or four times a week.

"No special today," Solay replied. Though slightly aggravated that the student wasn't content with the regular menu, she managed a strained smile. "What would you like—chocolate, red velvet, or vanilla?"

The college kid scowled the menu again. "No, I wanted the special." He left the counter and skulked past the line of waiting customers.

Solay was flabbergasted. This was a first. No customer had ever left her bakery in disappointment. After the kid left, it seemed like every other customer was asking about Screamin' O's or inquiring about the weekly special.

She'd been thankful that Melanee was no longer mixing together expensive ingredients and slowing down the production of the regular list of options. Something was going on with Melanee. Her mind seemed to be off in the clouds. Miraculously, she'd fallen back into step with the way that Solay ran her business. Baking Solay's tried and true recipes only.

Now Solay was a little worried. With Melanee's specialties being so popular, Solay wasn't sure if eliminating them had been a good idea. Maybe she should to speak to Melanee; give her the green light to whip up some more delectable treats. But remembering how egotistical Melanee could be, Solay changed her mind. In the future, any specialty on the menu at Scandalicious would be something that Solay created. She'd be a fool to allow her temperamental baking assistant to have that much control over her business.

She checked him out through the peephole. Deon was a sexy sight. She flung the door open, welcoming him.

Solay felt seductive in black heels, a glittery, pale-blue thong and matching push-up bra.

Deon gave her a wide, appreciative smile. "You look gorgeous," he said and then hugged Solay tight, like they were long-lost lovers.

Her arms circled around his back, fully participating in the warm embrace. Being close to him felt good—too good!

If Solay didn't have a tight grip on reality, it would be easy to believe the male escort was really feeling her. Maybe he was...they definitely had good sexual chemistry, but that didn't change the fact that their connection was based on a money transaction. And Solay had no problem with that fact. As long as she was paying, she didn't have any expectations other than good dick and a powerful orgasm.

Deon cupped the back of her neck, his fingers plunged into her hair as he held her to him. With their hips pressed together in that lingering embrace, Solay felt his dick responding. She drew in a hard breath as she felt the shocking thickness of his dick as it lengthened beneath his jeans.

His lips brushed gently against hers. A soft moan vibrated in Solay's throat as she opened her mouth to him. His tongue licked against hers...slowly...teasingly, while his agile fingers unclasped her bra. His hands framed her breasts. He moaned in appreciation as his rotating thumbs brought her nipples to hardness.

Tearing his lips from hers, his mouth moved downward, latching onto one corkscrew nipple, and then the other; making Solay emit agonized moans of pleasure.

The last time they were together, Deon had relaxed her with a sensual massage. She had planned to return the favor, but their panting breath, and groping hands made it apparent that prolonged foreplay was not on the agenda tonight. It was also quite obvious that the heat between them was so overpowering, they weren't going to make it to the bedroom.

A few strides across her small living room, and they tumbled onto the couch. Hastily, Deon unbuckled his belt, unzipped his jeans and allowed the denim to fall past his hips. Like a cobra, his dick lay throbbing and coiled inside his boxer briefs. As if freeing a living creature, Solay yanked his drawers down, giving his dick ample room to stretch and swell to a full erection.

Deon was paid to pleasure Solay, but dual sensations overcame her. Her mouth watered and her pussy tightened at the sight of his masculine deliciousness. She didn't know whether to jump on the dick and ram it inside her moist walls or suck it like it was a big chunk of gourmet chocolate.

"Can I suck it?" She wanted to taste him so badly, her voice cracked with yearning.

"Hell yeah, you can suck it." Deon grabbed his dick and guided the head to her lips. With her mouth parted, Solay lowered her head. Deon thrust gently, feeding Solay increments of dick.

Careful not to nick or graze his smooth, even-colored

skin with her teeth, she drew in as much length as she could handle without choking. His dick had the sweetest flavor, like it was sugar-coated. Solay gulped in several more inches of the irresistible treat.

Deon groaned. "Daaaamn! I ain't know your head game was all like this! Slow down, girl. You 'bout to make me bust."

She didn't slow down. She didn't want to. Sucking off a big, curved dick was challenging, but also satisfying after she got it secured inside her mouth. Indulging her passion, Solay disregarded Deon's protests. She put a suction-hold on his dick that made him gasp.

"Stop, baby. For real. You gotta hold up—wait!" Deon tried to ease his dick out of Solay's mouth.

But Solay kept sucking. Slurping. Taking it all in. His dick was the ultimate pacifier and she refused to give it up.

Unable to hold back any longer, Deon cried out a warning. Solay didn't take heed. She wanted it. She closed her eyes blissfully as she swallowed bursts of white hot passion.

"That wasn't even fair," he said, his chest rising and falling as he tried to catch his breath.

Solay smiled and licked her lips in satisfaction. "Life isn't fair."

"True. True, but I gotta redeem myself." He shook his head, as if shocked by his lack of self-control.

"Would you like something to drink? You know, something with some kick that might help you recover?"

"Oh, you feeling yourself, now! But, yeah, I could use a lil' something."

"Henny, Patrón, Stoli…what's your pleasure?" Pushing her breasts back inside the cups, Solay readjusted her bra.

"I don't know why you fixing your bra. Them shits 'bout to come back off," Deon murmured. He kicked off his sneakers and came out of his jeans and shirt.

"I might as well show off my pretty lingerie until you're recharged," Solay said with a taunting smile. She stood and straightened her bra straps.

Solay was ready to leap on him when he stood up, looking edible in his Ralph Lauren briefs. That black tattoo that was draped over his right shoulder was crazy sexy. Deon was hot as all hell. Lawd! But she kept her cool. She was the one in control, and it felt damn good. Looking over her shoulder, she smiled confidently. "What do you have a taste for?"

Deon didn't answer her. He stared at her; his gaze held a hot intensity that made her heart flutter. The spark of lust between them was palpable, making her legs shake. His eyes penetrated, like a laser that ran from her face down to her breasts.

His serious expression wiped the cocky smile from Solay's face. Nervously, she moistened her lips.

Deon reached for her hand. "Where you think you going? Get over here, ma." He pulled her in front of him and his fingers began to tug on the strip of fabric that covered her crotch.

"Don't you want a drink?" she murmured, feeling her knees weakening.

"Fuck a drink," Deon growled. "The only thing I wanna taste is you." He pushed her onto the couch. Ripped the thin fabric of the thong. On his knees, he forcibly pulled Solay's thighs apart, situating her legs over his shoulders. With her pussy directly in front of his face, Deon burrowed his tongue inside her moist tunnel.

Her hips jerked. She clenched her teeth. Squeezing her eyes shut so tightly, her face was a grimace of sweet pain. What he was doing, the way he was licking her pussy, was giving her a feeling that was so intense, she felt like she could easily lose consciousness. Solay opened her eyes—wide—as she desperately fought to stay alert. But the pussy lashes he was delivering were too much for her. Her eyelids fluttered helplessly. The last thing she noticed before giving into blinding ecstasy were her sequined heels. Caught in a frenzy of sensations as his tongue lashed and stroked her to spasms, one shoe had fallen under the coffee table and the other had been kicked clean across the living room.

Hours passed.

"You got good pussy, baby. You da shit," Deon mumbled as he caressed Solay's breasts. "If you don't stop me, I'ma be on that ass all night long," he warned.

His words—the sound of his voice had Solay going wild. His touch was fire, and she loved the hot streaks that his hands made as they blazed all over her body. It was the beginning of another round—six—or was it round seven? Solay had lost count, and it really didn't matter. She and her sexy escort couldn't get enough of each other.

They got it in on the couch, in the shower and in a variety of positions—doggy style, standing up, missionary…like they were working their way through the Kama Sutra. With every sweet stroke that Deon delivered, Solay had yelled, "You're the best I ever had." It wasn't merely sex talk. She meant that shit.

Now they were in lying in bed. Chilling for a few minutes.

With his arms wrapped around her, her back was pressed against his chest. She could feel the beat of his heart, and it unsettled her. He cupped her titties, bringing her nipples to hardness with circling fingertips.

"You tired? Had enough?" Deon murmured.

"Give me five minutes," she whispered, realizing that she could use a short break. She closed her eyes, relaxing and enjoying the feeling of his touch that had cooled down from red-hot passion to soothing warmth.

She felt blanketed in emotional security, calmed by physical satisfaction—feelings she hadn't experienced in a very long time. She'd fooled herself into thinking that she didn't need a man, but having Deon so close—feeling his body pressed against hers was so relaxing—so calming. She was reminded of what was missing in her life. She let out a long sigh. Experience had taught her not to get too comfortable with this kind of pleasure. It was a shame that something as basic as having regular sex from a faithful man was as far from reach as the damn moon.

She turned around and faced Deon. Considering it a harmless fantasy, she pretended that he wasn't dick for rent—she touched his face and kissed him deeply. Their tongues lashed together—a prelude to another round of hot, sweaty sex.

CHAPTER 14

The door that bore the indentation of Lincoln's fist had been replaced, but the effects of his volcanic explosion still lingered in the household. For the past week, the children had been tense, watching their parents with anxious eyes.

Pretending that everything was all right, Lincoln and Chevonne went out of their way to speak in civil tones whenever Tori and Amir were within earshot. But their bedroom was the designated war zone. The marital bedroom was the place where Lincoln hurled unkind words and hurtful slurs.

It was past ten at night and Chevonne was lingering downstairs in the kitchen longer than usual. Lincoln assumed that she was hoping to escape the brooding atmosphere of their bedroom, trying to avoid another heated argument. She thought if she wasted enough time in the kitchen, Lincoln would be asleep when she turned in for bed.

She thought wrong. Lincoln brought his pissed-off attitude downstairs. He stood in the entryway, observing her as she unloaded the dishwasher. The emotional pain he was enduring hurt worse than a bullet in the chest.

The ragged hole in his heart bled without cessation. Pointing the finger of blame at Chevonne gave him temporary relief, but he realized that this was no way to live.

She turned to him, her expression weary. "Do you want to talk?"

"No. I'm tired of talking…tired of arguing; I want a divorce." Chevonne had committed the ultimate betrayal, and if he didn't leave her, he was going to wind up in jail for a crime of passion—a crime that in his mind was justifiable homicide.

Chevonne took in a sharp breath. "We can get past this…we have to."

He shook his head grimly. "My mind is made up. I've been looking for an apartment. As soon as I find one, I'm leaving."

Chevonne's eyes narrowed threateningly. "Amir is not going with you! You can forget that. I'm a good mother! I'll fight you in court over my children, and believe me, I'll win!" Her words came out in a rush of desperation.

Lincoln let her words sink in. Courts were reluctant to take children away from their mother…even when said mother was a whoring adulteress. Although Chevonne had recklessly gambled with their family's future, she would still be considered as the better parent in the court's eyes. A torrent of angry words came to mind, but Lincoln didn't say anything; he silently seethed.

"I don't want to fight you," she said quietly. "I want to work this out."

"Then you need to start telling the truth. Why'd you fuck him?"

Looking trapped and helpless, she shrugged. "I thought it would be a one-time thing."

"That's not what I asked. I want to know why you made a conscious decision to step outside our marriage and fuck that dude."

"We used to laugh and talk. We shared everything. You were my best friend. Then you changed. You became withdrawn and bitter—you know—after the pay cuts."

"I knew it!" He pointed at her accusingly. "In your mind, I became less than a man when my money changed."

"No, that's not what I'm saying. Your anger affected our relationship."

"Don't twist this around and try to place the blame on me. Own up to the fact that you tipped out on me during the worst phase of my life."

She nodded sadly. "I know that my actions have devastated our family, and I'm so sorry. But I really believe that time can heal this. We can at least try."

Lincoln shook his head. "I can't recover from this. As soon as I find a spot, I'm out. I love my children too much to disrupt their lives. I won't fight you for custody of Amir; I'll settle for visitation."

"Don't leave us, Lincoln. Me and the kids need you here. Why can't you find it in your heart to forgive me?"

"I wish I could, Chevonne."

"I don't expect forgiveness to happen overnight. We

can go to marriage counseling. I'll do whatever it takes to save our marriage."

Usually a vision of beauty, Chevonne's face was lined with worry. There were circles around her eyes and she looked noticeably thinner, and not in a good way.

He didn't enjoy seeing his wife at her lowest point, but since she was looking so terribly exhausted and defeated, he figured it was a good time to get the whole truth out of her; bully her into giving up the information that she had stubbornly withheld.

"You want me to go to counseling, yet you refuse to tell me who the hell you cheated with."

Chevonne gave him a pleading look. "Let's not go there. It won't help the situation."

"Who is he?" he persisted in a low, poisonous voice.

"You don't know him. Why is a name so important?"

"Tell me his fuckin' name!" Glowering, he waited for a response.

"Where'd you meet this out-of-town muthafucka?"

"I lied. He's from this area."

Lincoln braced himself. Was she involved with someone that worked for the city? He grimaced as he imagined storming into City Hall and confronting the mayor—punching the dude in his pompous face! But Chevonne and the mayor's wife were close acquaintances; she wouldn't stoop to that level of deceit, would she? *No*, he answered himself. This other cheater was probably some other crooked politician—someone on the state level. Maybe even federal.

"What's his fuckin' name?"

"Raheem! His name is Raheem Maxwell. We met... Uh...."

"Where'd you meet him?" Lincoln barked.

"We met at the BMW dealership—that's where he works."

He flinched as if he'd been slapped. "You let a slimy car salesman talk you out of your drawers?"

She swallowed nervously. "He doesn't sell cars. He's a mechanic—he worked on my car when I took it in for the state inspection." Though she spoke in a voice that was barely above a whisper, shame as loud as a trumpet was echoed in her confession.

Lincoln had a mental picture of grimy-mechanic hands touching his wife. He gave a rough sigh as he forced the image out of his mind. "You risked everything we've built over a goddamn grease monkey?"

"It's over between me and Raheem. I love you with all my heart. I'll do everything in my power to win back your trust...and your love."

As deceitful as Chevonne had been, Lincoln heard something in her voice—a note of honesty that touched him—brought him to the realization that leaving his family was not an option.

"You don't have to win back my love because I never stopped. But trust and forgiveness..." Lincoln's voice trailed off, knowing that he would have to dig deep to find the strength to get over his wife's betrayal.

Chevonne took quick steps toward him, embracing him

and murmuring how much she loved him. His arms encircled her, drawing her close as she wept bitterly. In an act of kindness, he wiped her tears, but his mind was on revenge.

In time he would forgive his wife, but there was no absolution for that mechanic muthafucka. That nigga had to be dealt with. He should have known that there were consequences for fuckin' with another man's wife.

CHAPTER 15

Though she was coasting on only three hours of sleep, Solay walked through the dining area with a happy strut to her walk. Under ordinary circumstances, sleep deprivation caused her to feel grumpy and mean. Thanks to the good sex and multiple orgasms from Deon, Solay felt refreshed and ready to take on the day. Deon was still asleep in her bed, and the image of him snuggled beneath her duvet made her heart flutter. *I'll check on him in a couple of hours.*

"Good morning," she sang out as she entered the kitchen.

Melanee was pouring batter into cupcake liners. "Morning," she muttered without lifting her head. Solay couldn't interpret Melanee's disposition, and she wasn't interested enough to try and figure out her if her baking assistant was in a mood. As long as Melanee got the job done, her temperament didn't matter.

Humming, Solay began mixing up a new specialty item for the menu. Influenced by sexy Deon, she felt a desire to express her feminine side. Creating on a budget, she blended packs of banana pudding into the regular vanilla batter. While the banana cupcakes were in the oven, she added strawberry extract to the butter cream, giving the frosting a soft pink color with the taste and fragrance of fresh strawberries.

Though Solay had chastised Melanee for deviating from the menu, Melanee didn't make any snide comments. In fact, she was so lost in thought as she went about her tasks, she didn't seem to even notice the delicious new scent inside the kitchen.

"Taste this," Solay offered Melanee a sliver of the banana-strawberry cupcake. "What do you think?" she asked.

"It's good," Melanee replied without much emotion.

"I'm gonna call them Pink Panties." Solay braced herself for Melanee to flare up in anger since the idea of adding specialty items to the menu had been Melanee's brainchild.

Surprisingly unperturbed, Melanee smiled faintly. "That's a cute name."

"Are you okay, Melanee?" Solay asked. Lately, Melanee seemed to be only going through the motions at the bakery. She'd acquired an odd serenity, and her mind appeared to be a million miles away.

"I'm better than ever." Melanee gave a faint smile and then went back to work, mixing batter.

As Melanee cracked and folded eggs into the flour mixture, Solay suddenly noticed identical red rings encircling both her wrists.

"What happened to your wrists?" Solay gawked at the angry red marks.

"New bracelets; they were too tight," Melanee said with a shrug.

Brows furrowed in confusion, Solay went into the dining room and added Pink Panties at the top of the menu.

The jingling bell announced Vidal's arrival. "Whaddup, people?" he greeted as he swung through the front door, his long hair bouncing with each jaunty step he took. With a face as pretty as a girl's and a man's lean muscular body, Vidal was attractive to men and women alike. He didn't seem to discriminate…at the bakery, he was equally flirtatious with both sexes. From snatches of conversations she'd overheard between Vidal and Melanee, Solay suspected that Vidal's personal life was a never-ending stream of wild parties and meaningless sex.

"Hey, Vidal," Melanee said when she came out of the kitchen with a large tray of cupcakes.

"Hey, Mel. What's good?"

"Nothing but cupcakes," she said with a chuckle. She set the metal tray on the countertop, leaving them for Vidal to place inside the bakery case, and then returned to the kitchen.

Vidal was much closer to Melanee than Solay, so she thought Vidal might have some insight into what was going on with her.

"Melanee has these weird marks around her wrists,"

Solay whispered. "Have you noticed how spacey she's been acting lately?"

"Not really," he responded absently as he squinted at the new addition to the chalkboard menu. "Pink Panties! That's cute. As long as she's getting her creative thing off, she'll be okay."

"That's not her creation; it's mine." Solay's eyes shifted away guiltily.

"Well, if she's into cutting on herself or any kind of mess like that, I guess you can take the blame for that."

Indignant, Solay frowned. "I didn't say she's cutting herself. I said she has some strange markings on her wrists, but why should I take the blame?"

Vidal's voluptuous lips twisted in contempt. "You shot down her fancy specialties." He arched a thick eyebrow toward the chalkboard. "Now it looks like you done stole her idea."

"I gave her an opportunity to continue making specialties. For your information, she declined the offer."

"Mmm-hmm," Vidal muttered dubiously as he began placing cupcakes inside the bakery case. His head shot up suddenly. He gasped. "Oh, my!" Vidal held one hand pressed against his chest as if holding his heart in place.

Solay followed his gaze. A surprised smile formed on her face. With his pants sagging low, his Yankees ball cap twisted to the side, Deon stood in the entryway that could only be accessed from Solay's apartment upstairs.

Mouth agape, Vidal looked from Deon to Solay, trying to figure out their connection. He didn't have to wonder for long.

Her eyes lit up and Solay hurried across the dining room. "Morning, sleepyhead." She beamed at Deon.

"Man, your bed is so comfortable, I could have slept 'til tomorrow. Hope I didn't overstay my welcome."

"Never that," she said with conviction.

He looked around at the sensual décor of Scandalicious. "Nice place. It's got a real sensual vibe to it. Your sexy flava is all over this place." His eyes settled on Solay. In an intimate gesture, he lightly touched her shoulder. "You working that uniform, ma." He moistened his lips.

Solay felt her face flush.

"You gotta wear that uniform for me one of these days, aye?"

She blushed and cut an eye over at Vidal. Craning his neck, Vidal gawked in their direction.

"I didn't mean to intrude on your work space or nothing, but I didn't want you to think that I was rude—you know—leaving without saying anything."

"Whatchu doing later tonight? You feel like getting together?"

Worriedly, Solay pondered her bank balance, wondering if she could afford a back-to-back session with Deon.

"This is off the books," Deon said in response to Solay's expression. "You wanna go out? We could check out a flick if you want to. Or I could take you to dinner."

Are you serious? What are we doing, Deon? An eyebrow

arched in puzzlement, but she dismissed her concern. "Okay, dinner sounds nice. I'd like that." Actually, she liked the idea too much and was worried by her eagerness.

"I'll see you tonight." Deon leaned in, his soft lips touching hers briefly. That gentle kiss had the impact of full-tongue penetration. Instantly hot, Solay wanted to steer Deon up the stairs to her apartment instead of walking him to the front door.

Vidal didn't even pretend to be working. Bending at the waist, he relaxed across the bakery counter. Propped up by his elbow on the counter, he cupped the side of his face as he studied Solay and Deon.

"Whaddup, man," Deon said, acknowledging Vidal with a courteous head nod.

"Hellooo," Vidal said with a breathless little giggle. He gazed at Deon like he was something delicious to eat.

Deon gripped the doorknob and then paused. "Eight o'clock?"

Trying to keep their conversation from reaching Vidal's curious ears, Solay spoke softly. "Eight o'clock is perfect. I'll see you tonight." Unable to resist touching him, Solay gently stroked Deon's hand as it rested upon the doorknob.

Another quick kiss and Deon was gone. Solay leaned against the door, her eyes closed wistfully. Her paid escort had changed up the game, and she didn't quite know what to make of it. *Enjoy yourself and stop trying to analyze the situation.*

"Where have you been hiding that hot hunk of male meat? Who is he?" Vidal squawked.

"Just a friend." Solay had no intention of disclosing personal information.

"I thought you preferred the suit-wearing, corporate type. I didn't know you were into thugs."

"I don't have specific type." *At least not anymore!*

"Mmm-hmm," Vidal murmured doubtfully. "So where are you and your cute thug dining tonight at eight?" he asked with a smirk.

Solay chuckled and shook her head. "Mind your business, Vidal." She went behind the counter and gave a sidelong glance at Vidal's lazy posture. "Are you bored… nothing to do?"

Vidal straightened up. "Dang, are you running a sweatshop, now? Can't a brother take a short break?" He finger-combed his lustrous hair and examined his glossy manicure.

Solay frowned at smudges on the countertop. "Wipe the counter." Then she waved a finger toward the dining area. "And make sure all the tables are spotless."

"I wiped everything off last night." Vidal folded his arms and twisted his lips in displeasure.

"Do it again," she said, reminding Vidal that she was his boss—not his equal. He had a lot of gall smirking at her and trying to be all up in her business. Smiling with satisfaction, Solay pushed open the swinging kitchen doors while Vidal huffed and puffed.

Melanee was slacking off, too. Solay caught her neglecting her duties and whispering into her cell phone. When Melanee noticed Solay, she nervously asked the person on the other end if she could call them back later.

Melanee was acting sneaky and suspicious. Solay wondered if her baking assistant was secretly upset about the Pink Panties addition to the menu. Was she plotting to leave Scandalicious? Solay could have easily flown into a full-fledged state of panic, but with all the baking she had to finish, she didn't have time for that.

Besides, she was too excited about her dinner date to worry about Melanee.

Suddenly her brows furrowed together in worry. What was she getting herself into? Sex with Deon was off the chain, but they didn't share any common interests. They were from entirely different worlds. *So what? I'm not looking for a husband; I'm having fun.* Deon was as safe or as dangerous as she allowed him to be. She told herself that she'd be okay if she kept her emotions under control.

Thank goodness Deon had decided to give her a freebie. He was not a cheap fuck, and her credit card was being absolutely abused.

CHAPTER 16

"**M**adam was pleased with you," Colden mentioned as he positioned Melanee's arms behind her back. The feel of the rope against her flesh sent icy shivers up her spine.

"Really?" Melanee had figured she'd made Colden proud. There was no other explanation for him putting in quality time. Just the two of them—the way it used to be.

"Are you happy?" he inquired in a low baritone. He could be such a loving dominant at times. Times like now…when Melanee deserved it.

"I'm very happy," she whispered. It had been so long since they'd engaged in rope play. Colden tightened the knot, cutting into her skin vengefully. "Oh, God," she uttered, wincing from the sweet pain. A wave of fear and excitement had her trembling violently.

"Your ass is getting plump. But not quite ripe for spanking."

Disappointment was palpable. She'd been eating everything under the sun. Killing the cupcakes at work; feasting on fast-food. "But I gained five pounds," she protested.

"I said your ass is not plump enough." His voice was stern.

Melanee pressed her lips together, trapping further protests inside her mouth. "I'm sorry, Master. So sorry that I'm not worthy." Aroused by that admission, her pussy throbbed, aching for attention. Yet Melanee had no idea if Colden would allow her release tonight. She never knew. That was the nature of their relationship. Trying to ignore her starving pussy's yearning, she closed her eyes and embraced the pleasure of the moment.

With her back turned to her master, she couldn't see his face. Yet being touched and handled by him—no matter how roughly— had not only caused her pussy to quiver, but a rivulet of sweat trickled between her small breasts. There was a tingling sensation around her nipples, coaxing them into sharp, sensitive protrusions.

Colden's hand stilled for a moment. He halted tying the intricate knots. "You're shaking. What's wrong?"

"Nothing's wrong, master." Her voice cracked with emotion.

He worked one hand around to her lower region and explored her moist pussy. "Don't lie to me."

"I'm sorry," she murmured, writhing from sexual agony.

Angry fingers traveled upward, large hands wrapped around her breasts. Then the tips of his fingers discovered nipples that were hardened with desire. Fingernails dug into the delicate tips, punishing them. Melanee squirmed and cried out in fiery pleasure. Each brutal pinch and twist of her nipples was received like a lover's caress.

Bound, she was completely at his mercy. "Harder. More. Please!"

"You're a glutton for punishment," he said mockingly and removed his hands. He resumed tying the knots. Colden enjoyed binding her with dozens of intricate knots.

Realizing that he was completely absorbed and would not be doling out any more pain, Melanee closed her eyes and enjoyed the heat of the rope that cut into her skin.

Finally finished with the knots, Colden gave her a sudden shove. Face down, she landed on his bed, her feet still planted on the floor.

Ass up, she hoped that Colden had had a change of heart.

Excited, she waited for the sting of his hand against her ass. If memory served correctly, the first blow would be harsh, taking her breath away and before she could recover, he would deliver a peppering of red hot smacks— one after another.

But he gave her something else altogether. Gently, he separated her butt cheeks. Melanee shuddered. Tenderly, a moistened finger caressed the tiny opening of her ass. When the front of his thighs touched the back of her legs, she gasped. But with her arms tied expertly behind her back, she was his captive.

He placed one hand firmly on the small of her back, pressing down hard as if uncaring of breaking her spine.

The other hand guided his swollen dick between her petite buttocks. She shouted into the thick coverlet on the bed as he forced his dick inside the impossibly small area.

She cried tears as her flesh was brutally torn. "You like this?" he growled.

She nodded vigorously. "Yes, sir!" Her words were muffled by the bed sheets.

He grabbed a hand full of her hair and yanked hard and cruelly as he anchored himself. Her scalp felt like it was on fire and her ass was being split in two. Now he released her hair, and used both hands to force her ass to open wider. With loving ruthlessness, Colden filled her with more inches of hard meat.

It was a whirlwind of agony…an eternity of misery. Finally, Colden's dick was completely buried inside her virgin ass, working up rhythm, and Melanee followed the tempo. This was a different kind of heaven. A feeling of euphoria that she had never imagined.

Her ass had been widened by the girth of his dick, allowing Colden to slide in and out with ease now. Something happened. A glorious sensation took her completely by surprise. While he stroked her ass, her pussy walls tightened and convulsed, bringing her to a surprising and magnificent orgasm.

She slid down to the floor. Her chest rose and fell as she struggled to catch her breath. Arms tightly bound, she lay uncomfortably on her side. He left her there. Her eyes followed him as he went into the bathroom and closed the door. She could hear the shower running; Colden was cleaning himself. Meanwhile, his secretions oozed down her inner thighs.

What was next? Would he leave her on the floor for the remainder of the evening? Or did he have another surprise in store? The anticipation—the unknown was exhilarating.

Colden came out of the bathroom but she could see only his feet and his calves as he approached.

"Master," she whispered worshipfully.

He didn't acknowledge her, he strode past her.

Melanee's shoulders slumped. "Master, didn't I please you?"

She wanted to spin herself around to keep him within her sight. She struggled to sit upright, but collapsed after a few moments of effort.

"No questions."

"I only wanted—"

"Don't you remember the rules? Do not speak unless spoken to."

She nodded briskly. There was the rustling sound of clothes as he got dressed. Colden left the bedroom. Was he going out for the evening? Would he leave her alone on the floor all night? Her heart thudded inside of her chest.

After an immeasurable amount of time, she heard him padding toward the bedroom. Her heart leapt with pleasure. He stood over her, watching. Obediently, she remained still, in spite of the awkward and uncomfortable position. Her muscles ached, her skin burned from the tightly bound restraints, but she didn't so much as twitch. Glorying under his gaze, she waited for his instruction.

The sudden flash of light startled her. "Do you know how beautiful you are—right now—like this?"

"Yes, sir."

Another flash brightened the room as he captured the image of her naked and fettered.

Colden bent down to her level. Gripping the strong rope, he pulled her to her feet, positioning her backward, so that the ropes could be fully viewed. Melanee was nothing more than a prop. The intricately tied ropes were the main attraction.

It took at least forty-five minutes for Colden to undo all the intricate knots. Free from bondage, the ropes fell to the floor.

As Colden held the camera, admiring the images of Melanee in bondage, she couldn't help from noting that he was becoming aroused. She licked her lips at the sight of the big dick that was clearly outlined inside his pants.

"Go ahead," he mumbled, focused on the pictures, not even bothering to gaze at her.

Melanee ignored the pain in her arms and her wrists. With Colden's permission, she unzipped his pants, retrieved his lengthy dick and feasted while he scrolled through the images in his camera.

CHAPTER 17

As planned, Lincoln walked into the BMW service center at ten minutes to four.

"Do you have a scheduled appointment, sir? We close at four," said a lean, young white guy, dressed in tan khakis, blue shirt and striped tie. He was sorting through a stack of yellow invoices as he stood behind the counter.

From the garage area in the back, Lincoln could hear the animated voices of laborers, loud and cheerful. Their work day was soon coming to an end.

"I didn't know that an appointment was necessary," Lincoln said. "I just stopped in to get a price on a part."

With furrowed brows, the service rep glanced up at the clock, not wanting to be left behind when his coworkers started heading home. His worried look quickly morphed into a courteous smile. "What part are you looking for?" His pleasant tone of voice and willingness to help, announced that this young man had been given excellent job training.

Wondering if he could pick his wife's ex-paramour, Raheem, from the group of mechanics, Lincoln leaned his head to the side, scrutinizing the fleeting silhouetted figures that moved noisily inside the garage. The men were becoming increasingly loud and jubilant as quitting time grew near.

A rugged-looking, dark-complexioned worker came out of the garage and sauntered up to the counter with paperwork in his hand. He added a couple of sheets of paper to the pile that was next to the computer. "You still working?" He turned his nose up at the young white guy, as if the idea of putting in an extra minute was a punishable crime.

"Man, they ain't paying you no overtime. You better cut that computer off and get ready to roll out." The man had an arrogant attitude and was throwing off a real bad vibe. Disliking the man instantly, Lincoln looked him over with a sneer. His body was somewhat husky—particularly around the shoulder area—like he pumped a little iron. Lincoln blinked in surprise when his eyes settled on the man's name tag. It read, "Raheem."

Hot anger rushed through Lincoln's entire system. He wanted to leap behind the counter, and choke the life out of that adulterous muthafucka.

"I'll check on that price tomorrow," Lincoln told the clerk with forced calmness. Being a civilized man, he clenched his jaws, controlling his primal urge to kill.

A few minutes later, sitting in his car with the motor running, he shuffled through CDs. But it was murder—not music—that was on his mind.

Raheem stepped outside and lit a cigarette, and then

strolled toward the parking lot. His slow, confident stride had a little dip, suggesting that the mechanic was feeling himself—walking through the lot like he owned the BMW dealership.

Lincoln watched the cocky bastard through his rear-view mirror. Raheem was laughing and talking with one of the mechanics, bobbing his shoulders side to side, fully engaged in a ghetto rhythm as he communicated. Lincoln was disgusted. Chevonne should have been disgusted, too. Everything about that clown should have been totally foreign and completely repugnant to a refined woman like Chevonne.

Lincoln had envisioned Raheem to be the quiet but strong, sensitive type that many women claimed that they were yearning for, but Raheem was nothing of the sort. From what Lincoln had observed, Raheem didn't have a sensitive bone in his body. He was arrogant, ignorant, and obnoxious. And he had a cigarette habit. Chevonne couldn't stand the noxious odor of tobacco, so how did she get so close with this dude?

Trying to fit into the business world and the architecture industry, Lincoln had gone through a severe transformation, changing his speech patterns, excessive gesturing, and rhythmic body swaying that was indicative of the urban culture. He'd effectively smoothed out his rough edges and was able to mingle in any crowd.

It was astonishing to discover that his wife had been sexually attracted to a common street thug. If Lincoln hadn't promised Chevonne that he'd move past her indiscretion, he would have picked up the phone and cussed her out. How the hell had she allowed a hood rat, ruffian to get into her panties?

What the hell? Mouth agape, Lincoln observed Raheem climbing into a brand-new Navigator. The truck had tinted windows and twenty-two-inch chrome rims. Apparently mechanics were earning more than architects. There was something horribly wrong with this picture.

Sitting behind the wheel of his five-year-old Dodge, Lincoln shifted into drive when he saw the red rear lights of the Navigator. Raheem glided out of the lot. Lincoln waited a few moments before pulling out of his parking slot. With no immediate plan other than to know all he could about the man that knew intimate details about his wife, Lincoln followed the shiny black Navigator.

Even with three cars between them, the big Navigator was hard to miss. Lincoln followed the mechanic to City Avenue, but kept a safe distance. He had to make a sudden left turn when his nemesis swung onto Monument Road, without bothering to put on his blinkers. *Inconsiderate fucker!*

Raheem parked in front of a bar called The Four Corners. Lincoln discreetly parked in the large Pathmark supermarket lot that was across the street from the bar. Hoping that Raheem wouldn't take too long, Lincoln sat in his car, letting it idle.

The sun had gone down, and the sky was gloomy.

Growing tired and irritable after waiting for forty min-utes, Lincoln was ready to call it a night. He'd pick up his surveillance activities at a later date. Right now, he wasn't mentally prepared to sit with cramped legs, while Raheem was having a good time shooting pool, listening to music, flirting with women, and chugging down cold beer.

The moment Lincoln shifted into reverse, Raheem bobbed out of the bar with that infuriatingly cocky walk of his. *Swagger* wasn't even the word for that nigga's strut. Lincoln envisioned himself using a baseball bat and giv-ing that wife-fucker a powerful blow to the knee caps. Picturing the mechanic hobbling and limping, a smirk formed on Lincoln's face.

Tenaciously, Lincoln tailed him through the streets of Philadelphia, while the mechanic made the rounds of various bars. It was after eight o' clock, when Raheem drove along Lancaster Avenue in West Philadelphia. He made another pit stop—this time he rolled into a small shopping plaza. In addition to the requisite Beauty Supply store, Footlocker and Dollar Store, there were a couple of food options—Chinese food, Popeyes Chicken and Subway—inside the plaza. It was an odd surprise when Raheem, strutting with his chest poked out, strolled into the Save-A-Lot grocery store. *Cheap bastard!*

He came out of the store a few minutes later, holding a skimpy, see-through, Save-A-Lot plastic bag, containing a gallon of milk.

Staying in the cut, Lincoln watched with amazement as the mechanic parked his big-ass Navigator on a run-down block that was so narrow, he had to park the monster-vehicle with two tires cranked up on the pavement. This was the only way other cars could get down the slim, one-way street. Raheem let himself into a decaying little house that Lincoln assumed was where Raheem lived with his wife and family.

Lincoln was appalled. Raheem drove a $50,000 vehicle, but he lived on a raggedy little block. This was drug-dealer mentality. Dude's priorities were all out of order. And Lincoln wouldn't be the least bit surprised if Raheem was hustling—using that mechanic gig as a front. Lincoln worked out an entire scenario in his mind: Raheem had most likely been locked up; he'd learned the mechanic trade while in prison. He'd gotten his current job through some help-a-convict program, but was only working to have proof of income for Uncle Sam.

The dude was criminal minded. Lincoln couldn't imagine what a refined woman like Chevonne had in common with a street hustler? She'd really gone slumming when she started fooling around with that joker.

Sure, Lincoln was a product of the ghetto. But dammit, he'd elevated himself. What the hell had Raheem done?

Lincoln had rejected the idea of going into couples' counseling with Chevonne, but now he was giving it some consideration. Not for himself; he didn't have any mental issues. But Chevonne… Lincoln sighed. His wife really needed some therapy. Chevonne had to be a little messed up in the head to have practically destroyed her family over the likes of a nigga like Raheem!

Over the next few days, Lincoln became obsessed with Raheem, staking out his house at different hours of the day: before work, during his lunch break and after work. He wanted to get a glimpse of the man's family. But no one ever went in or came out of the house except Raheem.

The more obsessed Lincoln became with his rival, the more passionately he made love to his wife, trying to make sure that he fucked that nigga's memory clean out of her mind.

CHAPTER 18

"**R**elax, baby. Lean with me," Deon reminded again as he turned a corner with his Harley-Davidson. Scared as hell, Solay's arms were wrapped tightly around Deon's waist, holding on for dear life. What the hell was she doing on the back of a bike? And the stupid helmet on her head was not only uncomfortable; it was ruining her hairdo.

Solay should have followed her gut instinct. She shouldn't have allowed Deon to persuade her to mount his Harley. The moment he'd shown up on his bike, she should have opted to take her own car and meet him at the restaurant.

"You can hang with this, can't you?" he'd asked, melting her reservations with a big smile that was pure temptation.

Trying to prove that she was down—pretending to possess the spirit of a daring biker chick, she'd agreed to this hell ride.

"Lean!" he instructed in a much more serious tone. Solay tried to, but her body wouldn't cooperate. Her back was as stiff as a board. She couldn't bear to see how close they tilted toward the ground every time Deon rounded a corner, and her eyes were shut tight in terror.

Basic turns seemed like extreme motorcycle stunts. Deon had cajoled her with the promise of a fun time, but a high-speed motorcycle ride on the expressway seemed to be as bloodcurdling as bungee jumping or parachuting. She promised herself that if she made it off of this death trap with life and limbs intact, she'd never, ever, get on a motorcycle again.

Off the highway now and traveling in regular traffic should have been less frightening, but Solay's nerves were terribly rattled.

Ready to jump in a cab and go home, she cracked her eyes open to determine how close they were to their destination. To Solay's relief they were only a few more blocks away from the Marbar/Marathon Grill on Fortieth and Walnut Street. The moment Deon came to a full stop, Solay planned to yank the dumb-looking helmet off of her head and flag down a cab. For real! She was not a thrill seeker. The only thrills she sought were in the bedroom.

Daredevil that he was, Deon could pop wheelies, do hand-stands, ride side-saddle, and engage in all the death-defying stunts that his heart desired, but Solay would not be joining him as he lived life on the edge.

Solay's legs were wobbly when she finally got off the bike. Rolling her eyes, she pulled off her helmet, no longer concerned if her hairstyle had survived the tight-fitting and unattractive headgear. An assemblage of scornful words were lined up on her tongue, but the words began retreating the moment Deon tilted his head and looked at her. His pretty brown eyes held a mixture of adoration and concern. "Aw, was my baby scared?"

"Terrified," Solay whined. Lips poked out and pouty, she melted into his embrace.

Comforting her, Deon patted her back. "Was this really your first bike ride?"

Lifting her head, she nodded. "My nerves are shot."

"Well, we're gonna have to do something about that. You like martinis?"

"Love them."

"Tell you what—I'ma make sure that you get the extra-large size to calm yourself down."

Solay felt an overpowering urge to kiss his lips—to caress and run her fingers all over his gorgeous face. Deon had a way about him—a suave self-assurance combined with delectable good looks, making him impossible to resist.

Solay completely changed her mind about jumping into a cab and leaving in a huff. She decided to wait— hop in a cab after she and Deon enjoyed their dinner and drinks.

The spectacular view at the Marbar Grill was perfect for people- watching and ideal for Deon to keep an eye on his Harley that was parked in front of the restaurant.

Solay had taken a two-hour nap after work and now felt revitalized. She took sips from a mega-size pomegranate martini; Deon nursed a glass of dark beer as they waited for their meal. Focused on getting lots of protein, body-conscious Deon had ordered steak and vegetables. Solay ordered fried jumbo shrimp and French fries. She was content with the natural curves of her body. Having youth on her side, she figured that she could eat whatever she wanted, at least for the next few years.

Their food arrived, and Solay pushed her mega-drink to the side and began pouring ketchup all over her fries and breaded shrimp. "How long have you been working for the agency?" she asked and then bit into a shrimp. She really wanted to know what had prompted him to become a male hoe, but she'd need a little more alcohol to ask such a bold question.

"Not that long," he responded, his head lowered as he meticulously cut the sirloin steak into small pieces. "I was doing some modeling in New York—"

"Oh, yeah? Print or runway?"

"Both. And I had a few acting gigs while I was out in L.A. Now I'm back home, making ends meet while I figure out my next move."

No wonder he was so concerned with his body image. "What's your passion? Acting or modeling?" Solay asked, eyeing him curiously.

"Acting," he responded with a faint smile. "But I've only done small parts, nothing that really showcases my talent."

"You've had training?" Solay leaned forward, waiting for his answer.

"Nah, not really. I had an acting coach for a minute,

but he couldn't tell me nothing; that was a waste of time. I'ma natural. True story." A proud, fleeting smile turned up the corners of his mouth. Then his expression turned serious. "But anyway, something big finally came through for me, but now the producers are talking about they got budgeting issues." He sighed and shook his head. "Shit is on hold…indefinitely. So you know—I do what I do. It's called survival, baby." He shrugged and became silent, indicating that he was through with the subject.

Solay couldn't picture Deon handling a major acting role. First of all, he wasn't particularly articulate. She didn't know much about the film industry, but she imagined that actors needed to have a strong command of the English language. As far as modeling…well, Deon had a body on him. Whew, Lawd! But still, she simply didn't peg him as a professional actor. Too many rough edges. Was he lying, making up an excuse for renting out that big, pretty dick?

She was on the verge of playing detective and asking him if he'd appeared in any movies that she might have seen, but when she glanced at Deon, his gloomy expression gave her a change of heart. It was obvious that his acting career was a sensitive subject. Solay thought it best not to pry.

It was none of her business, anyway. It wasn't as if she and Deon were making future plans. She was merely filling the sex void in her life…and having a good time in the process.

"You killing them fries," Deon said, ending the tense silence between them.

Solay smiled, relieved that Deon's somber mood had passed.

"Want some more?" he asked.

Before Solay could respond, Deon had beckoned the waiter. He motioned toward the few remaining French fries on her plate. "Get her some more of them joints. Refill her drink and bring her another order of shrimp, too."

The waiter nodded and whisked away.

Wow, Deon knew how to take charge. She liked that. Solay laughed. "As you can see, I can eat."

"Ain't nothing wrong with it. Your body is tight, ma. Filled out in all the right places."

"Thanks." She lowered her eyes, feeling flushed and tingly by the compliment—and the sexy sound of his voice. Deon was too smooth. He had her blushing and carrying on. Whether she wanted to admit it or not, she dug the shit out of him. Damn, damn, damn. What had she gotten herself into? Was there even a definition for their relationship? *Whoa*, she cautioned herself. She had to be careful throwing around the word, *relationship*… even if spoken only in her own mind. Whatever it was that she and Deon were doing, it was by no stretch of the imagination…a relationship.

I'm merely going with the flow. Grateful that I can have a good time without having Rent-A-Man run my credit card.

Shit, at the rate I was going, my card would have been maxed out in no time, Solay thought as she gazed across the table at Deon.

Deon put his arm around her when they left the restaurant. "It feels good having you next to me." When they reached his Harley, Deon kissed Solay's cheek. He handed Solay her helmet and straddled the bike. "Still scared?"

"Not at all." Being a little tipsy, Solay was suddenly fearless. Catching a cab was the farthest thing from her mind.

"Hop on, boo."

Solay climbed on the back of the Harley and clung to him—her boo.

This time, the ride on the expressway was exhilarating. The wind against her face felt good.

And when they arrived on the side street that led to her private apartment, she got off of the motorcycle and invited him in. Fuck the fact that she had to get up in the wee hours to bake and run her business. She couldn't deny it; Deon had her sprung and he could get it—whenever he wanted it!

CHAPTER 19

D eon sat with his back against the headboard; Solay sat between his outstretched legs while he massaged her shoulders.

"Your place always smells so good. I don't even have a sweet tooth, but when I'm here my taste buds start acting up, craving cakes and pies and all kinds of shit that I don't even normally eat." Deon and Solay laughed together.

"That sweetness that permeates the air is one of the benefits of living over top of my bakery," she said playfully.

"So how'd you get into the cupcake game? Did you have to take baking classes?"

"The women in my family—my mom, grandma, all my aunts—they're all great bakers."

"Oh, yeah," he murmured, applying pressure to her upper back.

"Uh-huh. I learned a lot from my family, but I'm like you—I have natural talent," Solay boasted.

He fell out laughing. "Ahhh, I hear the way you slipped that in. You tryna check my ass."

"I'm just saying—"

"It's all good. So how's it working out for you?"

"Having my own business is a dream come true. I was in the corporate world for three years after I graduated from college. I had this plan—work and save for ten years, and then strike out as an entrepreneur. But about eight months ago, I decided that it was time to take a risk and go after what I really wanted."

"I dig that. You followed your dreams and it paid off. That's whassup, baby."

"And I want more. I plan to branch out with bakeries all over the city. Actually, I want the name Scandalicious to be recognized on a national level." She'd blurted out her most cherished secret, and then ducked her head down, feeling a little foolish.

"Nothing wrong with having dreams."

"Yeah, I know. But I do get discouraged sometimes—"

He kissed the back of her neck. "Baby, I'ma be your motivation," he said, singing the lyrics to Kelly Rowland's song.

Solay and Deon both laughed. It was nice to talk to someone who was supportive. Her family all seemed to be waiting to say, "I told you so." Solay had the impression that her family would be relieved if she failed and went back to a nine-to-five like a normal person. They were all appalled when she quit her job and used all her savings to open a bakery. Solay had yet to admit to her family or friends that it was an enormous struggle to meet all her expenses. After paying the astronomical amount of money on rent every month, and after paying her staff, she barely broke even. She'd been faking it, pretending to be financially solvent. She really needed to figure out a way to make a bigger profit.

"You're real special, Solay," Deon said, breaking into her somber thoughts. His massaging fingers changed to a caress. The soft tone of his voice and his gentle touch began to put her troubled mind as ease.

His hands traveled to her breasts, squeezing them and stroking the sensitive tips.

"That feels so good," she murmured. "Too good. What are we doing, Deon?"

"Getting closer. As close as we can get."

Solay closed her eyes, enjoying the sensations that included Deon's touch and the sweet fragrance that drifted from the bakery.

"There goes that smell again. Now I'm feenin' for something sweet."

"Aw, do you want me to go downstairs and bring you a couple of cupcakes?"

"Nah, I don't need that artificial sweetness," he said, repositioning her body until she was flat on her back. "You got all the sugar I need." Deon pushed her thighs apart and buried his face between them.

The office at Scandalicious was actually a closet with a small desk, a phone and a computer. Solay rarely worked in the cramped quarters for several reasons. First, the level of noise coming from the kitchen and the dining area prevented her from concentrating. With Melanee banging around in the kitchen, Vidal yelling out orders at the front of the bakery, and the buzzing sound of customers' conversations created an outrageous cacophony. Secondly, closing the door of the claustrophobic little space was out of the question, and so Solay usually worked on the books upstairs in her apartment.

But when Vidal called out that someone from the City of Philadelphia was on the phone, Solay took the call in the tiny office. "Hello?" She hadn't violated any codes and wasn't in the mood for any bullshit.

"Hi, is this the owner of Scandalicious?"

Aw, shit. "Yes, this is Solay Dandridge. What can I do for you?"

"My name is Anita Blalock. I'm calling from the Mural Department, City of Philadelphia. We're co-hosting a charity event along with several major corporations to support mural art in Philadelphia."

"Okaaay," Solay said, mad that Vidal had called her to the phone for this. "I guess I can make a small donation, ma'am."

"No, I don't think you understand. I'm not calling for a donation. We've decided to jazz up our charity event with cupcakes instead of traditional cake. Lots and lots of cupcakes."

Solay stuck her foot out and closed the door. She needed privacy and was willing to endure a few minutes of claustrophobic misery. "How many?" The biggest order she'd filled had been for a hundred cupcakes, but she was definitely up for a bigger challenge.

"The students at the art school will make a huge cupcake display. Maybe two, if that what's necessary to showcase two thousand cupcakes."

Two thousand cupcakes! Solay gulped. Both scared and excited, her pulse quickened.

"Our event is next month, so I'd like to get the ball rolling as soon as possible."

"Oh, absolutely," Solay said eagerly as she wiped beads of sweat from her brow.

"I'd like you to come to your shop for a cupcake tasting and to work out the financial arrangements. What's a convenient time?"

Solay wanted to say tomorrow, but she had a big order to fill. "How about three o'clock Wednesday?"

"That works for me."

"Fantastic. I look forward to meeting you, Ms. Blalock." Solay hung up, yanked the office door open and screamed, "Oh, my God!"

"What's going on?" a customer inquired.

"Nothing major," Vidal replied. "That's how she gets when she tries out a new sex toy," he said, deadpan.

A chorus of chuckles erupted as Vidal did his thing, entertaining the customers at Scandalicious.

Solay was so happy—so shocked and amazed at her good fortune that she had another outburst. "Oh, my fucking God!"

On cue, Vidal remarked, "Well, folks, I guess that rabbit

gadget or whatever it is, really works. Ya girl's in the office experiencing multiple O's."

The crowd roared with laughter. "No, but seriously, folks. On some real ish, she just ate our newest addition to the menu…a new cupcake. It's called Multi-orgasmic."

"Is it for sale?" a woman asked.

"Not yet," Vidal, the consummate salesman, told the customers. Solay couldn't help from loving Vidal with his nosey-ass self. He always had her back. Vidal was her boy…flaws and all.

Still in awe, Solay remained in the little office, smiling as she tallied up figures on a calculator. From her tentative estimation, this job alone could get her out of the red. If she could rely on large, specialty orders at least once a month, she would finally start turning a profit.

Solay noticed that her outburst didn't prompt Melanee to come and check on her. The chick had always been a little weird, but she seemed to have gotten worse. She hardly ever conversed with Solay or even her buddy, Vidal. She kept to herself nowadays. Stayed busy with baking and she was always out of her apron and headed home by six o'clock sharp. Solay wondered it Melanee was rushing off to a second job.

Scandalicious had been swamped with customers for hours, but as soon as the crowd dwindled, Vidal sauntered away from the counter. He stood in the doorway of the office, giving Solay an amused expression. "Well?"

"Well, what?"

"Don't play dumb. Why were you in here screaming like your spot was getting drilled?"

"I landed an order for two thousand cupcakes—well, I think I did. The woman is coming here Wednesday for a taste test."

Vidal screwed his lips up. "What time. I hope she doesn't pop up during the lunchtime rush."

"No, she'll be here at three; is that all right with you?"

He shrugged. "Three is cool." He paused, but Solay could tell he had a lot more to say. "So what's my cut?"

"Huh?"

"What's my percentage of that big order? I took the call, after all. And you owe me for keeping the natives pacified and entertained while you were in here publicly masturbating."

Solay burst out laughing. "I was not masturbating and you know it. Those were screams of joy. I really couldn't contain myself."

"That's not the way it sounded to my ears. I heard sex sounds. I thought that hot thug of yours had slipped inside the office and was in here putting it on you. Seriously, you never close the office door. That was real suspect."

She shook her head. "It's a shame the way your mind stays in the gutter."

"You can blame that on this environment. Scandal-icious is corrupting me. I was a decent and morally sound young man before I started working in this cat house—oops, I mean bakery. It's hard to make the distinction when you look at the décor. Didn't you design this place to provoke thoughts of wild and decadent sex?"

Vidal had her falling out laughing. He was on a roll that you couldn't stop once he got started. "The theme is romance and sensuality."

"Mmm-hmm. Could have fooled me. This is some Moulin Rouge shit up in here; we should have 'Lady Marmalade' piping from the speakers." Vidal's eyes brightened. "Hey, that's a great idea. What do you think?"

"No," she said emphatically. "It gets noisy enough in here."

"So how's ya boy holding?" Vidal suddenly changed the subject.

"Huh?"

"How much pipe is your thug boo working with?"

Mouth agape, Solay stared at Vidal. She regained her composure and closed her mouth. "You're crossing the line when you ask questions about my sex life. Stay in your lane, Vidal."

He smiled sheepishly. Solay could never kick it with Vidal for more than two minutes without him overstepping his boundaries.

"Okay, I can respect what you just said, but I have to make one last comment."

Solay groaned.

"You've been awfully cheerful these past few weeks, and I'm really curious…is it thug loving that has you humming and smiling every day?"

Laughing, Solay threw a pack of Post-Its at Vidal.

"Ow!" Vidal rubbed his shoulder dramatically. "Okay, keep it up. I could use some time off with work-related injuries. I heard that Workman's Comp pays more than my paltry salary."

The doorbell announced another customer. "Oh, damn. Here comes another pest."

Solay sighed. "Here comes another customer, Vidal. We have highly valued customers; not pests," she said sternly.

"Umph. You stand out there and deal with those heathens for a few hours and then tell me what they are."

She couldn't help from snickering. When he wasn't being com- pletely obnoxious, Vidal could be hilarious.

"Melaneeeee!" Vidal shouted as he sashayed out of Solay's office "We're running low on red velvet, girl. Let's get it poppin'!"

CHAPTER 20

Snug inside her walls, he was still for a few moments. Chevonne was so tight, so wet and warm, Lincoln was astounded by the unbearable intense pleasure. With a deep breath, he lifted up and then thrust deeply, plunging into her hot depths. A familiar tremor reminded Lincoln that he wouldn't last much longer. But he wanted to. Chevonne wasn't ready. He knew her body, recognized the sounds she uttered. And she wasn't there. Not yet. He pulled out of the satin clutch of her body. He had to; otherwise, he would have climaxed.

"Lincoln!" She reached for him, grasping at his arm.

He looked at his dick, observed the thick sheen of her juices. He scooted downward, splitting her thighs with his chin. While not as deeply effective as his rock-hard dick, Lincoln's tongue would not betray him with an outburst of white hot lust. She trembled as his breath whispered through the dark patch of hair that covered her mound. Her body jerked when he kissed her pussy lips.

"Oh." The single word was breathy admission that she desired oral pleasure. Chevonne stretched her thighs farther apart, rolling her hips to meet his open mouth. He felt her hands on the sides of his head, pulling his face toward her glistening, hungry pussy.

He kissed her shiny pink folds again, paying homage to the pussy that he loved, giving it a French kiss as he separated the glistening, distended flesh with his tongue. Moaning in pleasure, Lincoln licked and sucked greedily, forcing from his mind the knowledge that another man's dick had enjoyed his wife's sticky pleasure.

"I love this sweet pussy, baby."

"It's all yours, Lincoln. I'll never give it away again." Chevonne's voice was high-pitched and quivering.

The topic of her infidelity was off limits during normal conversations. Lincoln and Chevonne pretended that it never happened. And in his normal state of mind, the thought of that mechanic touching his wife, was more than his mind and heart could stand.

But somehow, through some freaky agreement, that taboo subject was spoken openly, arousing them both to unimaginable heights whenever they fucked. Although Lincoln had initially agreed to counseling, he bristled at the idea of sharing his marital troubles with a stranger. *We can work this out ourselves*, he'd told Chevonne, in an unyielding tone of voice.

"I know you're not gonna give my pussy away again." He grasped her buttocks and brought her pussy directly to his lips. Determined that his wife would never stray again, Lincoln ran his tongue teasingly down the open crack of her vagina and then delivered one warm lick after another, lapping her sweet and sour nectar. Chevonne whimpered as she grinded against the mouth that threatened to devour her.

Switching it up, he inserted a spiraling finger inside as he sucked on her stiff clit. Her fleshy walls tightened around his finger, pulling it in deeper. Chevonne's breathing quickened and her hips engaged in a rhythmic rotation. Any moment now, he would taste her tart passion.

He didn't stop licking until he felt her shuddering violently as a giant crest of pleasure wracked her body. When her convulsion subsided, he deftly lodged his surging erection inside the slick, satiny passage. His dick slid in and out, gently at first. Then with an enormous thrust, he rammed brutally. "Did he fuck you like this?" The sturdy bed shook from Lincoln's vigorous thrusts.

"Nobody can fuck me like this. Only you," Chevonne said hoarsely.

"You gon' cheat on me again?" He pumped faster, harder.

"No, never. I love you."

Needing something else to focus on besides her tight damp pussy, he lowered his face to her breasts. His lips brushed against her skin, and he licked her breasts, heating her up more. Chevonne made a tiny scream. She wrapped her legs around his back as he drove his dick in and out creating hot friction.

"You gon' suck another man's dick?" Lincoln mumbled these words, as if too ashamed to speak audibly.

"No! Never again. I swear to God."

He drove deeper, filling her completely. Each surging, rhythmic thrust was a declaration of love. Hips swiveling, Lincoln pumped an iron-like hard-on into a pool of liquid heat, stirring his wife into a writhing, moaning frenzy, urging her to join him in that inner world of timeless bliss. They came together, bodies quaking as they shared the sweet yet almost painful intensity of that intimate moment.

Lincoln rolled onto his back, and lay immobile as he panted. After catching his breath, he lifted himself up and stared at Chevonne's beautiful face. Her eyes were closed, and there was a slight smile on her lips. She was still in heaven, unable to speak. He kissed her softly.

Her lips moved as she softly whispered, "That was so good, r—" She seemed to catch herself, and her eyes shot open in alarm.

"Raheem!" Lincoln said the name with disdain. A severe grimace distorted his face. "Did you fuckin' call me Raheem?"

Chevonne bolted upright. "No! I didn't call you anything. Why would I bring his name up at a time like this?"

"You were mumbling, but I heard you clearly!"

"I said, *'That was so good; real good.'* Baby, we've come so far. Let's not do this. Lincoln, please." Her dark eyes were wild with fear.

He was unwilling to let it go. But in actuality, she'd only made the sound of the letter "r." Chevonne could be telling the truth, and for the sake of his sanity, he decided to let it go. "You're right. I'm sorry, baby. I'm tripping," he said calmly, but his mind was all over the place.

Chevonne gave a sigh of relief.

Lincoln lay back and rested his head on the pillow. Looking off into the darkness of the bedroom, Lincoln shook his head, trying to clear it. Maybe he was hearing things because he hadn't totally forgiven her. Or maybe he was crazy. Whatever the case, something wasn't right.

CHAPTER 21

S olay mixed up batter for the cupcake presentation that was scheduled for three o' clock. Vidal was in the kitchen with Solay, doing busy work. The shiny, red Scandalicious boxes were delivered every month flattened in stacks. One of Vidal's duties was to structure the flat cardboard pieces into square shapes that were ready for packing. The boxes took up several long shelves in the kitchen, and some were stored behind the counter. Those boxes were a huge expense. Solay could have gone for something plain and less costly, but she loved the glossy Scandalicious boxes.

"Have you noticed anything odd about Melanee?" Solay asked Vidal in a quiet voice. Melanee had taken a break and would be back in fifteen minutes, but Solay looked around to make sure that she and Vidal were alone.

"She's always been a little weird in my opinion." Engrossed in inserting a flap of cardboard into a slot, he didn't look up. He always became quiet when involved in constructing boxes. That type of mindless, busywork was somewhat therapeutic for Vidal—like knitting or crocheting.

"Yeah, but something is going on with her. She goes through her day like a robot. No interest in her specialty items anymore."

"Well, you were the one crying poor-mouth about the ingredients she was ordering. I would think you'd be glad she got over that phase. The customers liked the specialties. You're slipping, Solay. That's good money you're missing out on. You should be all over that!"

"I know. But it's so much extra work. I really need more staff."

"You ain't gotta tell me. You got me doing so many different things, I feel like a rubber band, stretched to the max and about to snap! And when that happens…" Vidal shook his head. "Can't you afford to pay a part-time worker?"

"Not really," she said sadly.

"Umph! I find that hard to believe. Don't forget, I work at the register, and I'm aware of all the money that this place pulls in."

"Renting space in a tourist area is not cheap, Vidal. Yes, I do a killer business, but…" Her voice trailed off.

"But what?" he peered at her curiously.

"Nothing." She refused to give Vidal a breakdown of her profit and loss statement. "Anyway, I'm concerned about Melanee. Something isn't right. As far as you know, is she seeing anyone?"

"Melanee doesn't tell me anything."

"I thought you two were close. What happened?"

"We're okay. We're work associates. We didn't hang out at clubs or kick it on the phone or nothing like that. I don't even know her number. The only thing I know about Melanee is that she's on some sort of wild eating binge."

"Huh?" The conversation had just gone into left field.

"Girl, I'm serious. If you wanna keep this business afloat, you'd better hide your cupcakes and hide the frosting because I have caught her scarfing down cupcakes like they're peanuts—on numerous occasions. She's a sneaky eater. I have seen her literally stuffing her face with Double Chocolate Decadence and Red Hot Passion."

"What about Vanilla Kiss?" Solay asked with a chuckle.

"Nah, she don't seem to mess with them. But she's picking up weight. You can see it all in her cheeks and her arms and whatnot."

Solay shrugged; she hadn't noticed any weight gain. "It's okay if Melanee eats a few cupcakes. I've always said that you both were welcome to them—well, you know—within reason."

"Well, she's not eating them within reason. She's outta control." Vidal returned his attention to building boxes.

Solay didn't mind if Melanee ate a few cupcakes on the job. However, she found it curious that Melanee had developed a sudden craving for them. *I wonder if she's pregnant.*

There was no private area for cupcake tasting, and so Solay personally escorted Anita Blalock to one of the wrought-iron tables. Samples of the regular menu items along with three new additions—cupcakes that boasted bold ingredients and in-your-face flavors—were brought to Ms. Blalock's table on a silver tray.

"I think you'll find that each cupcake is a sensual experience," Solay boasted as she set the tray down.

Solay had expected Ms. Blalock to use the knife and fork that she'd provided to cut a piece of each cupcake, but she had her own way of sampling—a torturously slow way of cupcake tasting. She ate each individual cupcake, smiling and nodding her head as she chewed.

Solay noticed Vidal behind the counter, holding out his hands, gesturing. He was getting itchy, wanting to find out the outcome. Solay shrugged. So far, it was obvious that Ms. Blalock was enjoying the flavors, but she couldn't predict how this would turn out.

"Mmm, now what is that one called?" Ms. Blalock asked, after biting into a dark chocolate cupcake.

"That one's called The Sweetest Taboo; it's a mixture of Belgian chocolate and red wine," Solay said with pride.

"I love the names you come up with, and the flavors are out of this world. But this one..." She nodded her approval as she finished chewing. "The Belgian chocolate and wine was to die for." Ms. Blalock swayed a little, as if swooning over the taste. Solay felt encouraged. Her fingers were crossed; she didn't want to blow this opportunity.

"I love what I've tasted, but my only concern is that you won't be able to handle such a large order with only yourself and the one baking assistant doing all the work."

"Don't worry about that; we'll get it done," Solay assured her, wondering how in the hell she'd pull off such a monumental task without shutting down Scandalicious for a week.

"Would you like some more water?" Vidal came to the table with a pitcher of water. Ms. Blalock's glass was half-filled, and that was a good excuse for Vidal to mosey over to find out if Solay had sealed the deal.

"No, thanks. I'm fine."

"Milk or juice?" He wasn't giving up easily.

Solay gave him a dirty look, forcing him to skulk back to his station, leaving her in privacy to woo the potential big-money client.

"How far in advance will you have to bake them? I want them to taste as fresh as these." Ms. Blalock motioned to the empty cupcake liners and the crumbs that were left on the tray. "Will you have to freeze them? I don't like that defrosted taste." Her eyebrows were drawn together in concern.

Boy, this lady is a tough sale. "I would never serve cupcakes that weren't of the highest quality."

Anita Blalock stood. "Okay, young lady, I'm sold!"

Yay, hallelujah, thank God! Solay was turning cartwheels in her mind. They agreed upon a price—an astronomical amount—and Ms. Blalock gave Solay a check for the deposit.

Solay could be living on Easy Street if she could drum up this kind of business on a regular basis.

After walking Ms. Blalock to the door, Solay turned around, and grinned from ear to ear. "We got it!" She raised her hand to give Vidal a high-five, but he sucked his teeth, obviously brooding.

"Oh, now it's *we* all of a sudden. It was all about you a few minutes ago."

"I don't like your tone, Vidal."

"What's wrong with my tone? You don't like it when I speak my mind, cuz you know I'm right—expecting me to jump up and high-five after you gave me your butt to kiss."

"Vidal, you're so theatrical—blowing everything out of proportion."

"I'm not your friend," he said, sounding like a spoiled toddler. Sulking, he poked out his lips. He even folded his arms to punctuate his displeasure.

Having had enough of Vidal's brooding mood, Solay burst into the kitchen to share the news with Melanee.

"May I please be excused, Master? Thank you, Master?" Melanee whispered into the phone and then stuck it inside of her apron pocket. Wearing a pained expression, Melanee looked at Solay. "So, how'd the tasting session go?"

Startled into silence, Solay didn't speak for a moment. After regaining her composure, she found her voice. "Uh, the tasting went great. I got the contract." Solay tried to sound as normal as possible, but it was a struggle after those crazy words that had come out of Melanee's mouth.

Solay shook her head. She turned around and left the kitchen. She marched straight upstairs to the sanity of her own apartment. In the living room, she sank into a chair.

What the hell kind of freaky shit is Melanee into? It struck Solay that Melanee might be having phone sex, right there in the kitchen of Scandalicious. *Ew!*

CHAPTER 22

Melanee refused to feel embarrassed. Solay had overheard her speaking to Colden. She'd used Colden's appropriate title, and Solay looked appalled. Then her boss scampered out of the kitchen—getting as far away from Melanee as she could.

Initially, Melanee was going to make up a lie—tell Solay that she was only kidding around with one of her friends. But she changed her mind and kept her mouth shut. She didn't owe Solay an explanation. Melanee laughed to herself, imagining Solay's horror if she knew the actual truth about her lifestyle.

Solay thought love was about dinner dates and receiving flowers, but she didn't know shit. Love was total submission. Love was whips and chains. And intricately knotted ropes.

Ah! A swirling hot current moved between her legs. Weak in the knees, she reminisced about last night. Colden had spanked her with a miniature paddle. Pussy paddling was something he'd never done before. Melanee glistened with sweat, remembering the pressure and the sting of that small wooden paddle against her clit and outer lips. With each whack, pussy juice streamed out of her vagina. When she shouted that she was coming, Colden had lovingly inserted the rubber-covered handle of the paddle deep inside her clenching depths.

"What the hell is wrong with you?" Vidal demanded, catching Melanee with her eyes closed, and her head thrown back as she relived the moment.

She gasped. Her eyes popped open. "You scared me, Vidal." Melanee smoothed down her apron.

"You scared me, bitch!" Vidal scrutinized Melanee, looked her up and down sneeringly. "What were you doing? From your expression, it seemed like you were having an orgasm, but I don't know how that's possible since you didn't have your hand stuck between your legs."

"Vidal, please. Your imagination is running wild. I was lost in thought when you came in here." Shaking her head, she brushed past him. She gathered up cupcake tins, mixing bowls, measuring cups, whisks, spoons, and other utensils, and began stacking them into the dishwasher.

"Well, I'm no psychic, but I'm willing to bet good money that whatever you were thinking about had sexual connotations." He turned up his nose. "And nothing normal. You were thinking about some raunchy filth!"

Melanee's phone vibrated in her pocket. She didn't have time to go back and forth with Vidal. "If Solay comes down, tell her I'm right outside—taking a break." She raced out of the kitchen.

"This place is a nut house," Vidal said, following Melanee out of the kitchen. The customers seated in the dining area turned their attention to Vidal.

"Working here is like pulling down a shift in a mental hospital. If I stick around here, I'ma end up on medication. Y'all think I'm playing, but I'm serious as a heart attack." Though the patrons didn't know what he was talking about, they indulged him with tinkles of polite laughter.

Frowning in condemnation, Vidal observed Melanee standing outside of the bakery, her cell phone pressed against her ear.

He would have really had something to talk about if he'd been able to hear her delighted greeting when she answered her phone, saying, "Yes, Master?"

"Madam Midnight is going to give you another chance. She wants to see you tonight at nine. Don't fuck this up," Colden said sharply.

"I won't; I'll call SEPTA and get the schedule for the three buses I have to ride. I'll be punctual; I promise."

"You don't have to ride any buses this time. Madam Midnight is sending a limo to pick you up."

"A limo? Really?" Melanee smiled broadly. Madam had been upset by her tardiness, but the woman must have been impressed in some way. Otherwise, why would she offer Melanee such transportation? Melanee put great effort into the blowjob she'd given the butler. And the way he'd flooded her mouth like a tsunami proved that he liked it. No one could deny that her fellatio skills were on point.

Madam Midnight made her nervous and jumpy, Colden held the woman in high regard. It was her duty to represent Colden's training to the best of her ability.

With her brows drawn together in concentration, Melanee listened to Colden's instructions. From what she gathered, tonight would be a totally different scene than she was accustomed to. Although Colden wouldn't be there, Madam Midnight would be his eyes and ears, giving him a full report of Melanee's performance.

Melanee planned to coat her lips with a thick covering of lip gloss—for better dick glide-ability. This time, there'd be no question about her superb head-training.

Following Colden's precise instructions, Melanee dressed up for a night at the theater. The gleaming super-stretch limo seemed out of place in front of her humble apartment building. She felt like Cinderella when the driver opened the door for her.

The luxurious inside of the limo seemed larger than her studio apartment. She looked around in amazement. The amenities were crazy: butter-soft leather couches, a flat-screen TV, a fully stocked, mirrored bar, a mirrored ceiling, and a mirrored partition.

This was heaven. The only thing missing was Colden. Melanee sighed, wishing they could share this moment together. Their day would come. Everything in due time, Melanee reminded herself.

Colden had informed her that Madam Midnight was a very wealthy woman and an important business associate. Melanee was the key to improving his relationship with Madam. All she had to do was make sure that Madam was thoroughly entertained tonight.

The limo glided out of her neighborhood. From the backseat, she could see the admiring glances of pedestrians and other motorists. She wished that stuck-up Solay could see her in this glorious moment. She wondered if Solay and her boyfriend ever went to the theater. Melanee doubted it. From the conversations she'd overheard, their dates consisted of movies and dinners that featured Buffalo wings and burgers. Solay thought she was the shit. Owning Scandalicious had gone to her head.

Downtown Philadelphia was alight with activity. The limo parked in front of Walnut Street Theater—America's oldest theater. The area pulsed with excitement. Melanee hadn't thought about the name of the play she would be attending, and was a little disappointed when she read the marquee: *Little Miss Saigon*. She would have preferred something that featured black people singing—*Dreamgirls*, *The Color Purple*, Whoopi Goldberg's play, *Sister Act*.

She clutched her purse, waiting for the driver to get out and open the door. She wondered if she'd be seated alone or if she'd be joining Madam and her party in their box seats.

"Would you care to watch a movie or listen to music? And by all means, please help yourself to some champagne. Madam insists," the driver said from the front of the limo.

Melanee frowned in confusion; she checked her watch. "What time does the play start? I don't think I have time for a drink. I don't want to be late." She shuddered at the thought. There were dire consequences for turning up late at any of Madam's functions.

The driver looked at her with sympathetic eyes. "The play started forty-five minutes ago. Madam and her escort will join you during intermission."

"Oh." Melanee was surprised and very disappointed.

"We have a wide selection of movies, but Madam has suggested that you watch her own personal favorite."

"Oh, yes. Absolutely," Melanee said, as she popped the cork from the chilled bottle of champagne.

The movie was Asian with subtitles. Melanee scowled in disgust. She hated subtitles. But just in case Madam decided to give her a pop quiz, she'd better pay rapt attention to the storyline.

What the hell? The scene opened with naked women in a palace. Melanee leaned forward, suddenly interested. According to the words on the screen, an Asian princess was to be bathed and prepared for bed. The bath scene was sensual and erotic with six or seven naked maidens hand-bathing the princess.

The princess was lying in her regal bed in the next scene. Melanee's eyes grew wide as she read the words on the screen: the princess required one hundred and one tongue licks to assure a sound sleep. *What the fuck?*

Thoroughly engrossed and captivated by the erotic

movie, Melanee barely heard the driver say, "It's intermission; Madam will be arriving any moment."

"Uh-huh," she said distractedly, her eyes glued to the flat screen. A brawny Asian male with a ponytail trailing down his back had entered the bedroom and was crouched between the princess's legs. The close-up of his tongue stroking the princess's pussy had Melanee's face flushed with arousal. Her pussy was wet, and her nipples were so sharp and pointed, they seemed to be poking right through the cups of her bra. The tongue stroking on the screen was a turn-on that warranted another glass of champagne.

Melanee poured quickly, splashing a little bubbly on her hand. Then she remembered that the driver had said something. "Excuse me, driver…what did you say?"

"Madam is here," he said grimly and got out of the limo in a flash.

Oh, shit! Melanee didn't know whether she should get out of the limo and give Madam Midnight a full curtsey or what. Sidetracked by that freaky movie, and feeling a buzz from the champagne, Melanee couldn't remember all of the details of Madam's requirements. Colden was going to punish the shit out of her if she fucked this up.

Remembering her main purpose for being there, she removed the tube of lip gloss from her bag.

Madam and her escort entered the limo. Her presence was frightening. Extremely intimidating. She exuded power and dominion. "Ah, the girl is here," Madam said to her companion—the same strikingly gorgeous, pretty boy with the golden curls. The one that had been kept on a leash at the dinner party she'd hosted.

This time he wasn't showing off his bare chest. He was well-dressed in an expensive suit and tie. And Madam was a vision in her flutter, silver gown.

Melanee could feel her heart pounding in fear and anticipation. "Good evening, Madam Midnight." She bowed her head as if greeting royalty.

There were three separate little couches; Madam sat on the far end. The escort closed the mirrored partition and then joined Madam, leaving the middle couch empty.

Melanee took the liberty of scooting over to the middle seat. She had a service to perform and figured she should be close to Madam and her boy toy.

Madam and the boy toy were the oddest couple. Not only in appearance but in behavior. After sitting next to Madam, the boy toy wrapped both arms around her and lowered his head to her bosom. Then he closed his eyes as if trying to get some rest.

"Tired, dear one?" Madam spoke in a kind voice that Melanee hadn't heard her use at her dinner party. From her purse she withdrew a pacifier—a blue fucking pacifier with a curved nipple—and inserted into the boy toy's suckling lips. Then she embedded her long, jeweled fingers into his hair, and began stroking through his bouncy golden curls.

Okay, I don't know this routine. Colden didn't mention

anything about a pacifier. What am I supposed to do?
Melanee tried to keep a straight face, as though seeing
a grown man being given a pacifier was an everyday
occurrence. She'd heard of the fetish, called infantilism,
but had never seen it in practice. What was her role?
Colden hadn't mentioned that she needed to pack a
diaper bag or baby bottles. Or had he? Shit! She would
have remembered something like that. The fact was,
Melanee was unprepared, and for that transgression,
Colden would be unforgiving.

Madam caught Melanee's eye as she administered to
her…uh…baby. Melanee bestowed her with an endear-
ing smile and then said, "Aw, your little boy is adorable."
Unaware of the rules to this game, she didn't know what
else to say.

"He's uncomfortable around strangers," Madam hissed,
stroking the boy toy's hair with more fervor.

This wasn't going well. Not at all.

"Sweetheart, intermission is over. We have to go back
inside." Madam withdrew the pacifier. Boy Toy whimpered when she returned the object to her purse.

She turned cold eyes on Melanee. "You did absolutely
nothing to console him. I'm going to have harsh words
for your master."

The driver opened the door for Madam and her escort.
Outside of the limo, Boy Toy straightened his shoulders
and appeared to be once again, a normal, adult male.

"I could get in trouble if Madam found out that I shared

information with you. You seem like a nice girl, and if you don't mind I'd like to offer some sound advice."

"Please. I need your advice; I'm not sure of what I'm supposed to do."

"I've been with Madam for a long time, and I'm pretty much accustomed to her moods and her wide range of erotic pleasures. If pleasing Madam is important to you—"

"Oh, it is. Definitely." Wistfully, she envisioned Colden's pussy paddle and the sweet pain that it delivered.

"Well, if I were in your shoes, I'd take something from the storyline in that movie. There must have been a reason that she wanted you to watch it."

Finally, Melanee got it. And she wouldn't need any lip gloss.

CHAPTER 23

P eople began trickling out of the Walnut Street
Theatre. Melanee sat up straight when she spotted
Madam and the boy toy. Madam was such a cultured
and refined woman, Melanee didn't want to displease her
with slouched shoulders and poor posture.

When Madam and her youthful escort got into the
limo, Melanee could tell from his petulant expression,
that something was bothering Boy Toy.

Afraid to speak without being spoken to, Melanee sat
quietly. A trained submissive never looked a dominant
straight in the eye without permission, and so Melanee
kept her eyes cast downward, but managed to steal glances.

The boy toy wasn't cozied up with Madam, nor was
he being calmed with a pacifier. Looking pissed and
mumbling in discontent, he sat on a separate couch,
between Madam and Melanee, and Melanee wondered
if she had imagined the spiteful glares that he seemed to
be sending her way.

When Madam opened her purse, Melanee assumed it
was time to indulge the golden-haired boy. He was being
so fussy, Melanee half expected Madam to pull out an

actual baby bottle, replete with milk. Instead, Madam withdrew a key ring from her purse, with a single silver key dangling from it.

"Garrett won't be joining me at my home; please drop him off at the apartment on Green Street."

So his real name is Garrett, Melanee mused, as she took another quick look and noticed that Garrett's mouth was parted in shock and indignation.

"Start the film from the beginning," Madam instructed Melanee without bothering to look at her.

Fumbling with the remote, Melanee followed her orders. She kept her eyes glued to the screen. Though curious to see where Garrett was being ditched, she didn't risk missing a second of the film. For Melanee, *100 Tongue Strokes* was not to be viewed for entertainment; she had to study the film as though watching a training video.

After Garrett exited the limo, Madam and Melanee rode in complete silence for the duration of the ride. The limo glided to a smooth stop when they reached Madam's grand home, and when he opened the door for Madam, the butler was there to greet the woman of the house with a courtly bow.

"Good evening, Madam. Did you enjoy the musical?" the butler inquired. He sounded to Melanee like a character from a movie. He took his butler role way too seriously.

"It was divine; simply divine," Madam said, sounding

equally theatrical. "I want you to inform my assistant that I'd like to invite some of the cast to a private party."

She handed the butler the Playbill. "I've circled the names of the cast members whom I've found interesting."

Madam had it going on. She could summon actors to her home to entertain her. Melanee was certain that the actors wouldn't be obliged to sing or speak lines from the play; they'd be required to showcase other talents. Melanee was impressed with Madam's power.

Peering through the tinted window, she watched Madam being escorted to her front door by the butler, while she was left behind without any instructions.

"Are you supposed to take me back to my apartment?" Melanee asked the driver after Madam and the butler disappeared inside the house.

"No, I don't think so. More than likely the butler will be back for you," the limo driver replied.

Though Melanee tried to concentrate on the erotic, foreign film, the suspense was killing her, and she couldn't help staring out of the window.

Over an hour elapsed, and at the exact conclusion of the movie, the butler came outside. With his shoulders squared and his torso erect, he strode toward the limo. Each precision-step looked similar to a military march. When the butler approached Melanee's side of the limo, she jerked away from the window and refocused her eyes on the TV screen and the rolling credits.

The butler opened Melanee's door. "Follow me."

It was déjà vu all over again, as Melanee dutifully followed the butler along the path that led to the servant's entrance. She hoped she wouldn't be required to repeat her dick-sucking performance. But of course, she'd do whatever Madam required of her.

She stripped out of her clothes inside the kitchen pantry and folded them into a pile, exactly as she'd done before.

Naked, she followed the stuffy butler down the corridor, but this time, he didn't escort her into the grand room. Instead, he made a right turn, ushering her toward what appeared to be a secret staircase.

Midway up the stairs, the scent of roses filled the air. At the top of the stairs, the butler opened a door to an enormous and beautiful bathroom. Like the princess in the movie, Madam was soaking in a sunken tub filled with rose petals that floated upon soap bubbles. Lit candles surrounded the ledge of the tub, creating a relaxing ambience. It was a glorious sight. The room looked and smelled heavenly.

Madam's eyes were closed; her head rested on a plastic pillow. The butler cleared his throat, and Madam's eyes reluctantly fluttered open.

"The girl is here," he announced.

"I can see that; I'm not blind," Madam said in the snippy tone that she seemed to use most of the time.

"Shall I send the masseur in?" The butler gazed at his watch. "Will you be ready for him in an hour?"

Madam laughed. The sound was both wicked and lovely

at the same time. "I don't require strong hands to help me sleep tonight."

"Very well. I'll dismiss the masseur. Shall I set out your sleeping tablets?" he asked, his eyes wandering curiously from Melanee to Madam.

Melanee didn't dare speak without Madam's permission. She communicated her puzzlement to the butler by lifting a brow and shrugging a shoulder.

"This girl will lull me to sleep, using a much gentler touch."

The butler glared at Melanee with hatred. He bowed and then left the room.

Being left alone with Madam was an experience in terror. Madam gave a sigh and then closed her eyes again. While the woman's eyes were closed, Melanee explored her face. Madam was beautiful. Her bold features—broad nose and full lips looked as though sculptured. Her eyes traveled to the exposed body parts, her toned shoulders and her long and shapely legs. Twin nipples that were dark and beaded poked through the white suds.

She hadn't been given any specific assignment, but following the storyline, Melanee remembered that the movie began with a bathing ritual. She recalled that the female attendants had sat on the ledge of the tub while attending to the princess.

Melanee had never bathed a grown woman or anyone else. She would have loved to soap up Colden's hard body, but he'd never allowed her that pleasure.

Bathing a woman turned out to be a surprisingly

enjoyable task. She squeezed a minty bath gel onto the bath sponge and began lathering Madam's neck, shoulders, and arms. Imitating what she saw in the film, she set the sponge aside and dipped her hands into the warm, sudsy water, and tended to Madam's large beautifully formed breasts. Her soapy hands glided over mounds of luscious flesh, fondling and stroking, drawing a sigh of pleasure from Madam. Her thumbs played with the hardened nipples until Madam whispered, "Enough!"

Respectfully, Melanee withdrew her hands quickly. In her haste, she caused a splatter. "I'm so sorry, Madam," she apologized. She winced when she noticed clusters of white suds dotting Madam's exquisite, velvety skin. Using her finger, she delicately wiped soap from Madam's smooth brown face.

"Kiss me." The words were spoken without emotion, as if she were requesting Melanee to pass the salt.

She inhaled deeply, hoping that she didn't tremble while kissing this intimidating woman. As her lips met Madam's she was amazed of the soft and full texture; it felt like sinking her lips into a pillow. Soft and sensuous.

Not expecting it, she gasped at the sudden intrusion of Madam's tongue inside her mouth. But the taste of it was so appealing; she threw herself fully into the sweet kiss.

Without planning to, Melanee's hand broke the surface of the water, finding its way between Madam's firm thighs. She parted the satiny folds, moving the tip of her finger circularly around the entrance. Unable to resist, she prodded a finger into the tight sheath and began to thrust and probe—slowly and deeply, shocking a whimper out of Madam. Plunging as deeply as possible, she invaded Madam's pussy. She smiled when she felt Madam's pussy clenching around the intrusion.

Melanee didn't stop probing until her finger was drenched with dewy cream.

On cue, the butler knocked on the door and entered. He picked out a towel from the rack. "Madam, you don't want your beautiful skin to wrinkle. I think you should get out of the tub now."

Madam ignored him.

"For the sake of your beauty, please let me dry you off?" The butler stood at the ready, holding a big fluffy towel.

Madam opened her eyes. Considering the butler's words of warning, she pondered a bit. "You're right," she agreed.

The butler made quick steps to the tub, and helped Madam out. He shot an angry glance at Melanee. "Sit over there and wait," he said in a stern voice, and then pointed to a chair on the far side of the room.

Melanee was surprised by her reluctance to stop tending to Madam. She'd never felt so submissively connected to anyone other than Colden.

Banished from Madam's bath, Melanee watched with envy as the butler tenderly towel-dried Madam Midnight.

CHAPTER 24

◄═╦

All of Melanee's sexual liaisons with women had been performed while under Colden's dominion. She'd never had any intimate contact with a female until she'd hooked up with Colden, and all of those encounters had been acts of duty. No personal gratification for her.

Tonight was different. Even though she was following Colden's orders, her heart thrilled with pleasure at Madam's every erotic command. She hadn't expected to feel anything except fear and obligation. Now she wanted to fully experience being dominated by a strong, black female. Madam exuded power. Even Colden seemed intimidated by the beautiful, intriguing woman.

The butler was getting Madam ready for bed. He told Melanee to go down to the pantry and get dressed. He told her that he'd disarm the house alarm and walk her to the limo after Madam had retired for the night.

Melanee was burning with envy. She couldn't stand that self-important butler, and he obviously detested her. She snorted, recalling how she'd choked through and endured a mouthful of outrageously big, butler dick. She didn't hear him complaining about anything when she'd skillfully depleted him of a couple quarts of cum.

She should have had the privilege of pulling back the covers for Madam—not the butler, she thought, sulking. It should have been her giving Madam a gentle back rub. Or a foot massage. Or whatever the magnificent woman required to get a good night's sleep.

It had been a surreal experience to kiss, caress, and to finger-fuck Madam, and now she wanted more. For all the pussy licking that Colden had demanded of her, tonight was the first time that Melanee really wanted to taste a woman's spicy flavor.

Alone in the pantry, sitting on a stepladder, Melanee not only felt like a failure, but she also was afraid. She feared the consequences of not totally pleasing Madam. If Colden sent her away again, she'd be devastated. Sexually submissive by nature, Melanee needed to indulge her kinky desires. She preferred Madam over Colden, but common sense told her that the woman was out of her league. She didn't want to lose the only true dominant that she'd ever had. The day he met her while she was working for a caterer, he saw the dissatisfaction and the hunger in her eyes. Before Colden had taught her to submit, she'd only explored her sensuality in daydreams and fantasies. Colden trained her with a strong hand. The pain that he subjected her to, took her to sexual heights she'd never even imagined were possible.

But she wanted something more. In Melanee's opinion,

it was somewhat normal for a man to be in control, but to be under the dominion of a woman was so unusual and freaky, the idea made her pussy pucker and ooze.

She touched the dampened patch of her panties, debating whether or not she should make herself cum. No! That was forbidden by Colden; he required her to get his express permission to touch herself. Guiltily, she removed her hand. It was cruel the way he controlled her without giving her any satisfaction. A woman would be much more sensitive to her needs.

Madam Midnight, I need you, she screamed in her head. Moments later, the butler appeared. Melanee came to her feet.

"The limo driver has been dismissed for the night. Madam summons you to her bedroom." The butler wore a sour expression, as though each word left a bitter taste in his mouth.

"Really?" Melanee leapt to her feet, raring to go.

"Remove your clothing and your shoes," the butler said with disdain.

"Yes, of course. Absolutely." Melanee was so happy, she wanted to kiss the look of dissatisfaction off of the butler's face.

As if deliberately attempting to intimidate her, the butler didn't give Melanee any privacy as she undressed. Feeling no shame, she tore off her dress and underwear with such wild abandon, the butler lowered his gaze.

Impatiently, Melanee walked behind the butler. He

seemed to be moving at a snail's pace. Each step was ominously slow.

The butler was lucky Melanee didn't shove him to the side and make a crazy, running dash to Madam's bedroom. Actually, she didn't know where it was located and it was the only thing stopping her. The private bath was a vast, open area, with numerous corridors that led to who knows where. There was no telling how many doors she'd have to open to get to the paradise that was waiting between Madam Midnight's legs.

Good things come to those who wait! Melanee repeated the words like a mantra during the funeral procession style of slow-walking that the butler was forcing her to do.

Letting her imagination take over, Melanee thought about the many ways that she wanted to please Madam Midnight. She would prove herself to be a far better choice than that temperamental boy toy, Garrett. Melanee would be a worshipful lover and an obedient sex slave. Madam could do anything she wanted to Melanee, and Melanee wouldn't require a "safe word."

For far too long, Colden had been dispensing punishment in very small doses; Melanee yearned to be taken to the limit.

Moving agonizingly slow, they finished climbing the stairs. Melanee was getting the impression that the butler was stalling, hoping that Madam would fall asleep before Melanee could serve her. He was a selfish man.

They passed the bath area, and entered Madam's private suite from the corridor. He led her through a sitting room, and then opened a set of double doors. It was an amazing room, decorated with timeless sophistication. The heavy oak, four-poster bed with elaborate carvings that ran up and down the posts, made a dramatic statement. The room was filled with a brightly colored blend of various flowers; their fresh-cut scent lingered in the air. The room was majestic. It was fit for a queen.

In naked splendor, Madam was curled on top of a white, lace bedspread. With her eyes closed and lying perfectly still, she appeared to be asleep. Her ebony skin had been rubbed with essential oils and brought to a glistening shine. The high bun was loosened; the jeweled tiara removed, and her jet-black hair cascaded over her shoulders.

"She's here," the butler said in a bitter tone of voice.

Madam didn't open her eyes. The only indication that she was awake or had even heard the butler, was the swift dismissing motion of her hand.

With a brisk head nod, the butler took a few backward steps, and then grudgingly turned around, leaving Melanee and Madam alone.

As if Madam might break, she gently parted her shapely legs. She couldn't resist running her palm over the neatly trimmed pubic hair. Madam inhaled sharply at Melanee's tender touch. Using her thumbs, she delicately spread open Madam's flower, exposing her dark flesh.

Gently, she pulled the petals wider apart, and her mouth watered as she discovered the hidden, crimson-colored skin with the juicy, deep-gashed opening.

"Mmm," Melanee moaned, gazing at the secret tunnel. She marveled at Madam's clit as it become erect in response to the exposure and the sweet invasion of privacy.

With her nose pressed against the closely shorn mound, she slid her tongue deep into her opening. Holding her buttocks, Melanee surrounded Madam's rigid clit with her lips, swishing it back and forth with her tongue. Arching her back, Madam thrust her pussy against Melanee's face; her strong thighs clamped her head. Madam was not lying passively. She was in full control, permitting Melanee access only to her clit.

With a quick tongue swipe, Melanee was able to capture a few droplets of tangy sweet nectar.

"Stop!" Madam unclenched her thighs, sending Melanee into a little panic, thinking she had done something wrong and was being sent home.

"Lie down," Madam commanded in a throaty voice. Melanee did as she was told, her heart pounding with excitement as Madam Midnight mounted her, planting her pussy on Melanee's face and sliding it up and down, over her forehead, her nose, her mouth, and her chin. Melanee's tongue was not necessary for Madam's satisfaction. Madam gripped the headboard, and rode Melanee's face wildly. With hardly any air, Melanee was being suffocated by the woman's pussy.

She was engulfed in total darkness when Madam's thighs closed around her face. Deprived of oxygen, Melanee's arms flailed instinctively. She wanted to lie still and let Madam have her way with her, but it was a normal reaction of survival to try to push Madam aside as she struggled to breathe. But Madam ignored Melanee's signals of distress, and kept grinding and sliding her pussy all over Melanee's face.

"Please, stop. I can't breathe!" Melanee croaked out the muffled, indecipherable words and tried to wriggle free. Her pitiful efforts to suck in oxygen seemed to entice Madam to thrust and undulate more violently, completely cutting off her air passages.

At the point when Melanee thought she was going to lose consciousness, Madam began to groan and shake, shifting her weight and in a way that allowed Melanee to finally breathe.

In the throes of a shuddering orgasm, Madam toppled off of Melanee.

Choking…gasping, Melanee gulped in big bursts of air. She was shaken to the core by the near-death experience. She'd assumed that Madam had wanted a gentle love-making session; she'd been prepared to worship the woman from head to toe. What had just transpired had been rough and dangerous. Pussy asphyxiation was life-threatening.

As she lay next to Madam, trying to gather her thoughts and wondering what the woman expected of her next, Madam reached over and smoothed her hand along

Melanee's hipbone. *That feels nice*, she thought, seconds before the hand bunched into a claw.

"One hundred and one tongue strokes, girl," Madam hissed, digging her long fingernails into Melanee's skin. "Hurry, girl. Do as I say. I've decided to keep you. You belong to me now."

A smile blossomed on Melanee's lips. Though Madam had strange ways, she still found her intriguing and yearned to be enslaved by her. Obediently, Melanee sat up and scampered close to Madam. As if in prayer, she knelt between Madam's sturdy legs and bowed her head.

Madam's pussy oozed with fragrant juices. Melanee pushed her tongue into the hot depths of her new owner's pussy, coating her tongue with the sweet and sour cream—a unique blend of seasoning that was unlike any pussy she'd ever tasted.

She started off with slow strokes, building up a gentle rhythm. She lapped pussy in a leisurely fashion. It was heavenly. She moaned in pleasure as she licked the savory crevice with an agile tongue. She kept count in her head, at first. But intoxicated by the rare flavor, Melanee increased the tempo, losing track after tongue stroke twenty-nine.

The even breathing that emanated from Madam, hinted that the woman of the house had fallen asleep, but Melanee wasn't sure. She dared not stop until she'd reached one hundred tongue strokes, just like the princess required in the film.

Suddenly the set of double doors burst open. The butler stormed in; his hurried footsteps tapping hard against the marble floor. "Are you an insane person?" He grabbed Melanee by the shoulders and wrenched her away from her feeding place.

"Madam is asleep. Why would you risk waking her?"

"But…but," Melanee stammered, licking at the honey-balsamic film that covered her lips.

"The limo is here. Get dressed and get out! I don't ever want to see you again." Behaving as if he'd caught Melanee stealing, the butler yanked her by the arm and tugged her out of the bedroom. This time, Melanee walked in front of the disgruntled man. All the way down the corridor, the butler poked her in the shoulder with one white-gloved hand; and pushed against her back with the other, forcibly expelling her from the premises, and hoping to permanently banish her from Madam's life.

CHAPTER 25

For the second night in a row, Deon had stayed over. Solay woke up, checked the time and gasped. "Oh, no!"

Deon cracked an eye open. "What's wrong, baby?"

She threw the covers off. *I thought I'd set the alarm but I forgot.* She rushed around the bedroom, trying to quickly dress. "Your good loving is starting to get me in trouble."

He propped himself up on an elbow. "Whatchu mean?" He sounded insulted.

As late as she was, she took a moment to admire his bare chest. "Look at me! I'm losing it. Instead of getting my ass in gear, I'm gazing at you, wondering if I can squeeze in a quickie."

Deon flashed a smile. "Nothing wrong with that." He patted her side of the bed invitingly.

"That's the problem. You got me addicted. I have a business to run. And I'm seriously slacking up."

"Down, boy!" he instructed his privates that had risen at the mention of the word "quickie." He and Solay both laughed.

"Why is it so hard to balance a relationship and conduct business?"

"Is that what this is?"

"What?" she asked quizzically as she pulled a stretchy top over her head.

"What you just said; are we in a relationship?"

No, I didn't let the R-word slip out! "We're not technically in a relationship." She made air quotes. "You know what I'm saying."

"So what are we doing, Solay? Where's this going?"

She fell silent. The tables had turned on her. Asking where a situation was headed was normally her line. "Well, it's only been a few weeks and you know, I'm just playing everything by ear. Going with the flow," she said cautiously.

"I can dig it. It's all good. We don't have to put labels on nothing, baby."

"I know. Let's just live in the moment, and enjoy the time we spend together." Solay knew from experience that the minute she got too comfortable, the most beautiful situation could turn ugly. She had a string of bad romances, and so whatever she and Deon had going on was too good to mess up with labels.

"Damn, I don't wanna get outta bed, but I gotta piss." Deon threw his legs off the bed and stood up. Solay had to avert her gaze or she'd be all over him—stroking his curved dick while licking his sexy-ass tattoo. She squeezed her eyes shut.

"Why you closing your eyes like that?"

"If I look at you, it's gonna be a wrap." She sniggered.

"Look, don't put nothing else on. Stay just like that. I'ma piss right quick and then I'ma beat that pussy up."

"Nooo," she hollered as he walked past her.

He came out of the bathroom. "Ready?"

"We can't, Deon. I don't have enough time. I have a rush order. It's getting picked up in a few hours. My baking assistant has to handle all the other work by herself."

"Aye, I'ma get outta your way. I don't even know why I'm acting all stupid like I'm in high school. This ain't even my style."

"Well, I like the way you act, but I'm in a rush this morning. Okay, Deon?"

"Yeah, ma. It's all good." They smiled at each other for a long moment.

"Am I going to see you tonight?" she ventured to ask, feeling brave enough to deal with rejection.

"Do you wanna see me tonight?"

"Hell, yeah."

She had skidded around the kitchen, frantically trying to get the order ready for a birthday party at an adult day center. A 100th birthday celebration. Miraculously, Solay had pulled it off. Late nights spent with Deon was really starting to affect her productivity. She had to figure out a way to juggle her business and her love life. She could use some rest tonight, but she also wanted to be with him.

By three o'clock, the lunchtime rush was over and Solay was finally able to sit down for a moment and catch her breath. She checked her cell, looking for texts from Deon, but there weren't any. Disappointment hit hard. He usually texted at least three or four times a day.

She heard the jingle of the doorbell and sighed. Vidal would have to handle the trickle of late-afternoon patrons by himself. Solay didn't have an ounce of energy left.

"They're beautiful. For me?" she heard Vidal squeal.

"They're for Solay Dandridge. Can you sign here?"

"No one ever thinks about me," Vidal complained.

Solay looked at Melanee with questioning eyes. Melanee responded with a shrug and continued wiping down the counters and tables, puttering around the kitchen without any interest in anything outside of her inner world. But Solay was curious. She eased off the stool. Before she made it out of the kitchen, Vidal pushed through the kitchen door, carrying a huge bouquet.

"If thug loving gets you all this, I must be doing something wrong." Sighing, he placed the vase on top of a table.

Solay gaped at the gorgeous flower arrangement. She ripped open the tiny envelope and silently read the message inside. *Just a lil' something to brighten your day!*

"What's it say?" Vidal asked impatiently.

"That's personal." She tucked the card inside the pocket of her apron.

"Well, who sent 'em—a grateful client?"

"No, they're from Deon," Solay responded, breaking into a big smile.

"It's like that between y'all?" Vidal looked both surprised and somewhat miffed.

Beaming, Solay nodded her head.

Vidal fanned his face. "Whew, Lawd! Now I'm starting to become a believer of all those dire 2012 predictions. Any time ruffians have started sending elegant flowers, I know this world is about to come to an end."

Listening to Vidal had Solay's shoulders jerking with laughter as she texted her thanks to Deon. Vidal was such a comedian, even Melanee was giggling.

Tomorrow was going to be just as hectic. The woman from the mural event was coming to sample cupcakes... again! Through-out the day, Solay had debated whether or not she should cancel getting together with Deon tonight. Bone-tired and weary, her body was demanding a full night's sleep.

After she closed and locked up the shop, she called Deon. "Hey, I should have called you earlier, but I kept debating with myself. Listen, I have to cancel tonight. I'm sorry, Deon, but I'm really beat."

"Yeah, I feel you on that. I'm being selfish and not taking into consideration how many hours you have to put in."

"Thanks for being so understanding."

"I have to be. I gotta realize that it's not all about me and what I want. You calling the shots, baby. All you gotta do is let me know when...and I'm there."

"My sleeping habits are more like an older person than a twenty-six-year-old woman. I wish you could come over and just hold me while I go to sleep."

"I wish I could, too. Times like this is when a foot massage is necessary. I could do that for you and then lightly rub that ass 'til you drop off to sleep, but who am I fooling—I know I can't control myself. My dick gets stupid when it's around you—won't stay inside my drawers."

Solay laughed; she was flattered.

"My dick acts like it has adult ADHD. I be tryna keep it from wandering outta my drawers—I get it in a chokehold and I be like—'Yo, what I say? Settle down. Stop fuckin' with her.' But the minute I close my eyes, my dick is standing up straight, tryna start some shit. True story, baby. I'm innocent. My dick is crazy."

She laughed harder. "Oh, my God, you're so funny." Solay needed a good laugh.

Deon's voice took on a serious tone. "Next time we get together, I'ma make sure that I rock you to sleep by eleven o'clock. No more keeping you up until the wee hours. True story, baby."

"That's thoughtful." She wore a wide smile of appreciation.

"So get yourself some rest, okay, baby? And I'll talk to you tomorrow."

"Okay. Good night, Deon."

CHAPTER 26

B y nine-thirty Solay was calling it a night. She raised the window in her bedroom, letting in the chilled autumn breeze that would lull her into a peaceful sleep. Under the covers, she let her mind drift. A million fleeting thoughts filled her head, until her thoughts settled on Deon. She clicked on the bedside light to get one last look at the enormous bouquet of lilies, roses, snapdragons, and elegant tulips before she went to sleep. Set in the center of the dresser, the romantic flower arrangement faced her, promising a night filled with sweet dreams.

Solay rose a few hours before dawn, fully rejuvenated. It was a pleasure to go through her morning routine at a leisurely pace. All that skidding around her apartment in a race against the clock, had taken a toll. But the downside to feeling invigorated was that she missed Deon like crazy. She missed waking up cuddled next to him. She wondered how he felt having to sleep without his arm wrapped around her. She knew that he was knocked out cold at this hour of the morning, but before she could talk herself out of it, she picked up her phone and sent him a text with a heart emoticon before and after the words, *I miss you*.

She held her phone for a long moment, secretly hoping to hear the ping of a return message from him. *What am I doing?* Deon wasn't the kind of man a woman should get too attached to. His profession prevented that. For all she knew, he could be lying up with someone right now.

Furthermore, what would she tell family and friends about his occupation? There was no way to explain it. Since it wasn't possible to take their relationship to the next level, why was she putting in so much time and effort with him?

While she showered, Solay reasoned that it would be wise to put some space between her and Deon. It was time to start weaning herself off of him. They were supposed to be only fuck buddies, but something had changed along the way, and now she had to lay down some ground rules before one of them got hurt.

There was no joy in her heart as she went through her daily routine. She usually baked with a passion, but not today. Going through the motions, she whipped and blended ingredients, dreading having to tell Deon that whatever it was that they were doing, was over. Well, not over…but drastically changed. She hadn't signed up for a boyfriend when she'd called Rent-A-Man, and she only had herself to blame for confusing lust and passion for something that could evolve into a meaningful relationship. She started to call Deon and tell him what was on her mind, but that was an immature way to handle the situation. Acting like a mature woman, she texted Deon, telling him that she needed to see him tonight to discuss an important matter.

In her small but cozy living room, Deon set his helmet on the bookcase and then bear-hugged Solay. She tried to hug him with the same intensity, but didn't pull it off.

"What's wrong?" Deon asked, after releasing her. His expression went from bafflement to enlightenment. "I know you didn't ask me to come over here so you could tell me, deuces?"

"Not exactly."

"Aye, whassup?" He took a seat on the couch and looked at Solay intently.

It was extremely uncomfortable for Solay to voice her concerns; she had to force herself to be completely honest. "Deon, I know that we've been having a good time and everything. And I've caught feelings for you."

"Same here," he admitted.

"This isn't easy for me because I dig you. I really do. But I think we need to slow down, and think about what we're doing."

"I thought we were on the same page. What's wrong? Are you afraid of being happy…is that why you suddenly want to pump the brakes on us?"

"I did some self-analysis, and came to terms with the

fact that being young and female, it's in my nature to view the men that I get involved with as potential mates— husband material—father of my children." She laughed nervously.

"Wow! You took it there?"

"Yeah, I did."

"I gotta give you credit for keeping it one hundred."

"So, that's the dilemma I'm facing. We're getting really close. But there's no future for us." She paused for a beat. "You know, as a serious couple."

He scowled. "Why isn't there? I can have children; I'm not sterile."

"That's not what I mean. I mean…the man I get serious about should be someone that I can rely on. Someone who is career-oriented and financially stable. The kind of work you do, Deon… that's not something that I can tell my mother."

He moistened his lips and looked down. Solay had struck a nerve.

"I'm sorry, Deon. I wasn't trying to be hurtful."

"I know you're not. But what you don't realize is that I've cut back on the amount of clients that I deal with. The work I do with the agency ain't always about sex, you know."

"I know, you told me that you mainly escort career women to important events, but that's still not the kind of work that I can openly discuss with my family."

"Babe…" He let out a sigh. "I do other things. A lot of my money comes from personal training."

"How do you find those clients?" She hated putting him on the spot, and getting all up in his business, but it was best to learn all she could about Deon and his clients—now as opposed to later.

"Uh…to be honest, those clients are mostly the women that I've met through the escort service."

Solay grew quiet and thoughtful. As much as she dug Deon, this relationship was clearly doomed for failure. She was a planner; she had a five-year-business plan. Deon, on the other hand, was going with the flow of life. He didn't possess the kind of determination that she required in someone that she was serious about.

"Oh, yeah…I meant to tell you, I hired a new agent," Deon told her excitedly. "Yo, I'm about to go hard with my acting career."

It sounded like a farfetched dream. Dreams of fame were seldom realized, but not wanting to appear negative, Solay didn't share that thought. One thing was for certain; she couldn't tell her friends that were still in the corporate world that she was serious about an unemployed actor.

"My agent is on the ball. He may have an audition for me—for a commercial. I'll have to go to New York, but that's not a problem. Commercials pay good money… lots of residuals."

She gave a halfhearted head nod, unable to become enthused over a possible paying job. And even if he got it, he'd be forever staking his future on the next audition. Her future mate would have to have a tangible career. Sad to say, but Deon was nothing more than a gigolo with acting aspirations.

Deon leaned forward and grasped Solay's hand. "Baby, I'm not broke. I've been stacking the whole time I was dealing with the agency."

"My feelings aren't based entirely on the money you've acquired. I have feelings for you, Deon. But it matters to me what my family and friends think of my partner. I'd be so embarrassed if anyone found out about the way we met."

Deon laughed. "Do I make you happy?"

"Yes." She couldn't deny it; he definitely made her happy.

"Do I show you how much I care?"

"Yes, all the time."

"Do I treat you with respect?"

She nodded.

"Then why are you worried about what other people think?"

"That's how I was raised," she said, her expression pained.

Deon stood. "Well, I'm not gonna pressure you. I'm not tryna make a good girl go bad." He chuckled, but it had a sad sound.

Solay walked Deon to the door. He hugged her and kissed her cheek. She wanted him to kiss her on the lips. Keeping it real, she wanted one last bedroom adventure. But she realized that asking Deon for a farewell fuck would be terribly insensitive.

Priding herself on being level-headed, she let him walk out of the door. Now that that chapter of her life was closed, she could get focused and take her business to the next level. Her educated and career-oriented soul mate was out there somewhere, waiting to put a ring on her finger. If he wasn't wearing a suit—he was at least dressed in tailored pants and a dress shirt. Solay knew without a doubt, that her future husband did not wear sagging jeans.

CHAPTER 27

A suspicious mind knows no peace.

Back when Lincoln had first discovered that Chevonne was involved in an extramarital affair, he'd checked her cell phone records for the previous four months. He'd figured out which number belonged to her ex-sex partner, Raheem. Though tempted, he'd never called the number. But through his own detective work, he'd concluded that Chevonne and Raheem were no longer having a fling.

But after last night, he wasn't so sure. Sitting at his desk at work, he pored over the most recent Verizon Wireless bill, scrutinizing every number, searching for the ten digits that belonged to Raheem. There wasn't one call made to or received from Raheem's number in the past month.

Maybe Chevonne hadn't whispered Raheem's name in breathless passion last night after Lincoln had made love to her. Maybe she was telling the truth. *It was all in my mind*, Lincoln concluded. Chevonne wanted their marriage to work as badly as he did. Forgiveness meant letting go of the past and moving on.

His rational mind implored him to move on. But on

an emotional level, Lincoln knew that he couldn't—not until he'd dealt with the slimy mechanic.

Lincoln's brother Earl came to mind. Lincoln and Earl were as different as night and day. A womanizer, Earl had irresistible good looks and an aversion toward gainful employment. Lincoln, on the other hand, wasn't bad-looking. But he was very much, an average-looking guy. He had family values and a strong work ethic.

Earl still held on to that gang-banger mentality, so he'd be eager to put in some work for a couple of dollars. Trouble was, Earl moved from place to place. His last place of residence was with some chick that lived way out in the northeast. Lincoln scrolled through his cell phone, looking for Earl's most recent number.

All of Earl's relationships culminated in Earl and his few possessions getting tossed to the curb. *Damn, I hope my trifling brother didn't get kicked out yet!* Lincoln dialed the number and smiled with relief when Earl picked up.

"Hey, man, I guess you must be behaving yourself since your number hasn't changed."

Earl chuckled and then went silent. Lincoln knew he was inhaling a big burst of fragrant smoke. They say that marijuana isn't addictive, but Earl went through blunts like some people tore through a pack of cigarettes.

"Whassup, man? How's the family?" Earl finally said.

"They're good. Everybody's good. Yo, man, look, I gotta problem with this dude. A mechanic. He did some work on Chevonne's BMW." Lincoln could never admit to his brother or anyone else that his wife had been fucking and sucking another man's dick. It was emasculating, and since last night, he'd begun wavering between loving and hating his wife.

"Dude fucked up her whip?" Earl had an instant attitude.

"No, the car is all right. The mechanic bull did something shady, though. He charged Chevonne up on parts and labor. Taking advantage of her because she's a female. Man, he had my wife paying triple for what that job should have cost," Lincoln spat, lying through his teeth, though his indignation was real and from the heart.

"That's messed up. A white dude got her?" Earl commented with disgust.

"No, a brother."

"That's even worse. It's fucked up when niggas take advantage of their own people." Earl's mind was slightly muddled due to years of smoking marijuana; otherwise, he would have realized that a mechanic doesn't set the price at any car dealership.

Though Lincoln had never been much of a liar, the story he concocted, sounded convincing.

"You know how Chevonne is; she wants to go the legal route…handle this shit in small claims court."

"Nah, that ain't how we do it," Earl said, following his brother's train of thought. "Give me that muthafucka's info. I know you ain't tryna body dude or nothing, so whatchu got in mind?"

"He needs to be taught a lesson."

"Uh-huh. True dat…" Earl waited for Lincoln to continue.

"A beat down. You know…the kind of ass whooping he won't forget. No guns. No stabbing. Make it look like a robbery. I don't want anything to come back to haunt me."

"Aye, aye…I got this." Earl sounded annoyed about being told how to go about his craft. Back in the day, Earl was the muscle for the biggest neighborhood drug boy. He knew all about beating, maiming…and Lincoln suspected that Earl was no stranger to killing.

"There's a couple of dollars in it for you," Lincoln said, and then quoted a reasonable price.

"That'll work. When you want this done?"

"Soon as possible."

"Now that might be a problem, unless you let me hold ya wheel. My girl's whip got booted and towed yesterday. Too many tickets." Earl sighed in disgust. "Man, the city's a trip. Putting people's property on lockdown and shit—over a measly couple of tickets. It's crazy out here."

All the tickets on the car were no doubt the result of Earl's irresponsibility. Every time his brother hooked up with new girlfriend, Lincoln felt guilty for not warning the poor woman that she was about to be victimized.

"You can bring the car around tonight, and I'll drop you back off at your crib." Earl sounded anxious to get behind a wheel and start racking up more tickets. Lincoln had to think for a moment. Did he want his car anywhere near a crime scene? *Hell no!* "Can't you borrow a car from one of your friends?"

"Nah. But you could use one of your credit cards, and rent me one if you want it done ASAP."

Earl's driver's license had been revoked years ago. Lincoln didn't bother to acknowledge his brother's request. "How's your girl…uh, what's her name?"

"Michelle."

"Yeah, that's right. So, how's Michelle getting to work? Isn't her job way out in the suburbs somewhere?"

"Her car just got towed yesterday. I got in late last night, so uh, I guess she must have hooked up a ride with one of her friends."

"You guess."

"Yeah, man. I don't know all the ins and outs of how she's getting around. I know she's on the job right now. I was in a coma-type sleep when she left this morning. Shit, as early as she has to clock in at her job, I was probably just turning over good when she dipped out." Earl laughed, finding it hilarious that his girlfriend went to work while he was lying in bed.

It was that kind of self-centered laziness that always got Earl thrown out on the streets. But Earl would never change. He knew that there would always be another female that was willing to hand over the keys to her heart, her home, and her car.

"Watch yourself, man. Michelle's a good woman. You don't wanna mess that up."

"It's all good, Linc. So, what about the car rental?"

"You don't even have a valid driver's license, Earl."

"So what? That's between you and me."

"I'm not going to rent a car in my name, when I know you're liable to get pulled over for doing ninety miles an hour while you're blasting Rick Ross. Nah, man, I can't do that."

"Oh, you a law-abiding citizen whenever it suits you. It's okay if I break the law whipping that nigga's ass that you got beef with, but you gon' chump me over renting a whip? Come on, son. I know we better than that."

"Use that reverse psychology bullshit on your women. That shit you kicking doesn't work with me."

"Aye. It's cool," Earl said in a surly tone.

"You don't have any friends that own a set of wheels?"

"Yeah, my mans, Crowbar, might be able to help me out."

"Crowbar? How'd he get that name?"

"My mans used to be notorious for using a crowbar for breaking and entering."

"Damn," Lincoln muttered. Crowbar sounded treacherous.

"If I bring Crowbar into this, you gon' have to cough up a lot more paper. Times is hard out here. Y'ah mean?"

"How much more are we talking?"

The amount made Lincoln grimace and groan out loud.

Lincoln knew all too well how hard times were, yet he was willing to dip into his family's savings to buy himself some peace of mind.

CHAPTER 28

D eon was abiding by her wishes, and he was definitely leaving Solay alone. For three days, there had been no texts, no phone calls, no flowers…no communication. And the sinking feeling in her stomach was close to feeling like physical pain. She tried to stay occupied at all times to keep her mind off of Deon. But it didn't seem to be working. She was of a mind to change the easy listening that was piping through the speakers to some old-fashioned blues, to better suit her mood.

It was absurd for her to feel so down in the dumps when she was the one that had called it off.

Even so, cutting herself off cold turkey from good dick like Deon's had her going through something that felt like withdrawal. Her stomach was queasy; her hand shook whenever she tried to hold a measuring spoon steady. With all three ovens going, the kitchen seemed like it was as hot as hell fire, making her sweat. And Vidal was really getting on her nerves today with his loud-ass voice and silly antics. The world had been a kinder, gentler place when she had Deon.

She missed him, and not just the sex. She missed Deon the person—the man. And if she hadn't tried to live up to society's expectation, she'd be whistling like…like Melanee!

It suddenly dawned on Solay that Melanee was whistling, and the sound was aggravating. She tried to ignore her, hoping she'd stop, but Melanee just kept on whistling while she worked. The impulse to scream was so strong that Solay turned the electric mixer to high-speed to drown Melanee out. To no avail.

"Melanee," Solay said sharply. "What's going on?"

Mid-whistle, Melanee stopped. "Nothing's going on." She fixed her lips to start again.

"No, no, no! You can't whistle in this kitchen."

"Why not?"

"Because it's aggravating. I can't concentrate. You're not even whistling a real song. You're just making noise… giving me a headache. Stop it, please." Solay didn't care if she sounded like an unreasonable, psycho bitch.

Melanee heaved a sigh and shook her head. With her lips drawn tight in annoyance, she turned and scooped batter into cupcake liners.

Throughout the day, Solay tried her best to stay busy, sifting flour, cracking eggs, pouring milk—all the while, rolling her eyes at nothing in particular. She usually baked with love—not anger; she wondered if her cupcakes held a bitter taste today.

The hole in her heart was growing bigger by the hour.

By closing time, she was convinced that she'd been a fool to give up Deon. She missed him. She missed the intimacy that they'd shared.

Upstairs in her apartment, she wandered from room to room. She caught her reflection in the mirror in her bedroom; her eyes stared back, looking bleak and miserable.

She finally settled in the gloom of her living room, holding her face in her hands, so very unhappy. She couldn't bear the loneliness for another second, and though she feared rejection, she felt like she should at least make an attempt to get Deon back.

I know this is childish, and it seems like I can't make up my mind. But believe me, Deon...I miss you, she wrote in a text. Too distressed to try to come up with a mature and sophisticated way to convey how she felt, she gave it to him straight; telling him exactly how she felt.

She could scarcely believe it when the phone rang almost immediately after she hit SEND.

"Baby, baby, baby. I miss you, too!" The deep music of Deon's voice touched her heart and soul.

"I was wrong, Deon. I was listening to my head, but my heart knows what it wants."

"You can't even begin to know how good that sounds. I'm happy just hearing your voice, yo." She could tell that Deon was smiling. Tears were forming in her eyes but she was smiling, too.

"So, how you doing, Solay? How's my baby?"

"Terrible; I'm so miserable, Deon," she said, laughing a little, but getting choked up at the same time.

"We can change all that. You know what I'm saying? Do you want me to come through? Or we can go out somewhere if you want to. The Laff House is close by your spot…I could pick up some tickets. It's on you, baby—whatever you wanna do."

"No, I don't want to go out. I don't want to be around other people. All I need is you. I need to touch you, taste you, smell you. Oh, Deon, I've been craving you."

"Oh, you tryna blow up my dome; got me smiling and shit."

"I'm serious."

"Believe me, I know what you're saying. You ain't the only one; I've been feening like an addict my damn self."

She smiled faintly, somewhat satisfied that Deon had been yearning for her, too.

"Listen, I've been out riding my bike for hours, tryna clear my head. I have to take a shower and change, but I'll be there as soon as I can."

"Okay." He really didn't need to take a shower; she would have gladly given him a tongue bath, but she kept that thought to herself. *I'll show him how much I've missed him when he gets here.*

"See you in a little bit."

Though he could have chosen to let her squirm for a little while and suffer, Deon was too much of a man to play petty games. He was so easy to get along with. Low maintenance and drama-free. She must have been out of her freaking mind to let a fine-ass, good man like Deon get away. So what if he didn't fit the mold of her so-called perfect mate. He was loving and kind, and made her happy. Nothing else mattered. To hell with what people might say.

The minute she saw Deon's beautiful face, Solay started crying.

"What's wrong now?"

"Nothing. I'm just so happy to see you; I can't help it. Do you want a beer?" Solay asked, wiping her tears with the back of her hand, and walking toward the kitchen.

Deon followed her. In the kitchen, he pulled a napkin from the napkin holder. When Solay handed him the beer, he set it down on the counter. "Come here, baby," he murmured and began to dab the tears that dampened her cheeks. "This is a happy occasion, so stop crying, okay?"

Sniffling, Solay nodded. Deon dried the last of her tears. Staring at her, he broke into a grin. "There goes my baby; look at that pretty face."

He took her in his powerful arms, holding her so close, she could feel the bulge that was forming in his pants. "Damn," Deon muttered, releasing his grip on Solay as he shifted the hardened length of his dick to a more comfortable position inside his pants.

Solay was particularly horny. Se didn't need an orgasm

tonight, but she did have an overwhelming desire to lick and suck Deon's big and beautifully curved dick.

Her hand went for his zipper, which she unzipped swiftly. His bunched-up dick seemed to be bursting through the opening of his pants. She tugged his jeans down and then looped her fingers into the elastic waistband of his underwear, taking them down as well. His thickened dick stretched out and sprung into the air.

"I wasn't expecting all this," he said huskily as he braced himself against the kitchen table. Solay dropped down to her knees. Deon groaned uncontrollably; aware on some level, that he was about to get the hottest blowjob of his life.

She cupped his hard ass as she kissed the swollen head of his dick.

"Mmm, girl. You're making me weak." His eyes were half-closed. He licked and chewed his lips in anticipation. Then he let out a sudden gasp when Solay lightly scratched his balls. She stroked his dick with her cupped palm, as she licked the flesh of his nut sac. "Uhhhhh." The utterance of sexual arousal vibrated from his throat. She kissed his thighs, caressing his steely muscles with the sides of her face. "Damn, that shit feels good," he moaned.

Solay spread his legs wider apart, so that she could easily access his dick and balls. Now she alternated licking and kissing his inner thighs, making loud and erotic smacking sounds as she worked her way back to his dick.

His entire nut sac was inside her mouth. Deon's breathing picked up. She used her tongue to gently move his balls around, and his fingers became tangled in her hair. The pulling and tugging he was doing to her hair was making her hot—causing her to want to do more to please him.

She released his balls and with the tip of her tongue, Solay made a slippery path from the base of his dick up the sensitive underside, all the way until she stopped right under the head. Teasingly, she licked the ridges beneath the crown of his dick, and then switched directions, slowly licking her way back down.

Back at the root of his dick, Solay went so far as to lather his pubic hairs. She'd told herself that she wanted to give him a tongue bath and that's exactly what she intended to do.

Deon shuddered when she gripped his dick in her hand and puckered her mouth around the head, sucking on it like it was a lollipop. Fondling his balls, she took in the entire length of his organ and began to suck it in deeply. So deep, it touched the back of her throat. Quite suddenly, she stopped sucking and let his throbbing meat fall from her mouth.

"Why'd you stop? What's wrong?" he said, panting.

"Nothing's wrong. I want you to rub that dick that I've been feening for…rub it all over my face."

Sexually charged up, Deon groaned as he used the head of his dick like an oddly shaped paint brush, deftly stroking streaks of pre-cum and saliva all over Solay's face.

When he brushed the head against her lips, she drew him back inside the warmth of her mouth. As she swirled her tongue wildly around the smooth dick head, Deon's hips began to thrust his hips up and down. Swallowing so much thick dick had an almost strangling effect, making the blowjob wet and erotically messy as she continued to slurp and suck him off. The sounds she made were not only for his pleasure. Her pussy was completely drenched; she couldn't help from joining Deon as he moaned in pleasure.

Sweating now and sliding his dick in and out of her mouth like he was fucking a pussy, Deon increased the momentum. "I'm about to nut, baby," he warned.

Solay didn't rear back to avoid the outburst of cum. She took his warning as a cue to tighten her grasp around his length, keeping his throbbing manhood secured inside the moist confinement between her lips while bobbing her head up and down.

Deon's body jerked. His erection pulsed and flexed in her mouth. His pre-cum dripped like a leaking faucet, and Solay moaned with pleasure. Deon growled and cursed, struggling to hold back the intense rush of a built-up load.

He grabbed her shoulders, clenching them tightly as he involuntarily shot off a burst of hot lust. Savoring the experience, Solay captured every drop, smiling as she milked him dry.

Later in bed, Solay lay cuddled up in the curve of Deon's arm. She couldn't keep her hands off of his hard-as-granite body. Deon was still somewhat in a daze.

"So what was that?"

"What was what?" she asked, looking up at his face.

"What you just did to me—what was that—some type of voodoo blowjob."

"Why do you say that?" she asked, laughing.

"Because, man. That shit was intense. Tears were welling up in my eyes. I was like…whoa, man, you better not start crying like a bitch." He gave Solay a long look. "Lemme find out you working roots on me."

Shaking her head, Solay burst into laughter.

Deon clenched her chin and turned her face so that he could look her in the eyes. "I'm serious, though. You mean the world to me, girl. We need to talk things through the next time you feel like kicking me out of your life."

"There won't be a next time."

"We're not always going to see things eye-to-eye, Solay. I want you to always feel free to speak your mind. If you need your space—no problem, ma—you got it. I'll fall back; no pressure from me." His words sounded heartfelt.

She caressed his arm; loving the feeling of every sinewy muscle. "I was confused; blaming you because I was falling so hard…so fast."

"We dig each other; since when is that a crime? I heard everything you said about me not being the marrying type, and I'm not going to argue with you about your beliefs."

Solay lowered her eyes guiltily.

"All I can do is try to show you who I am. All sides of me. I can be strong when you're feeling weak, but I'm only human. And I'm not always on top of my game. What I just exposed was a vulnerable part of me." Deon's voice broke. And it was Solay's turn to comfort him.

She kissed his forehead, his eyelids, his cheekbones and then pressed her lips against his. She nudged him, urging him to turn onto his stomach.

"What are you tryna get into?" he asked, rising up and looking over his shoulder.

"Relax," she cooed.

"I can't. For all I know, you might be tryna do me with a strap-on or some kind of freaky shit like that."

"No, baby. That's not my style." She kissed the back of his neck, urging him to relax. Her lips moved to his shoulder blades; licking and kissing his skin.

Moving along the line in the center of his back, she proceeded to give him a tongue bath; concentrating on an area so sensitive, she noticed that his toes were curled.

CHAPTER 29

E very call to Earl's phone had been going to voice-mail. Lincoln had been trying to get in touch with his brother since noon. He realized that Earl wasn't a morning person, but it was two-fifteen in the afternoon. Any normal person would be up by now. Lincoln shook his head, reminding himself that his crazy-behind brother didn't live his life abiding by society's rules.

Lincoln had been on the edge of his seat all morning, waiting to hear about the visit Earl had paid to Raheem, the mechanic. The last time he and his brother had exchanged words, Earl told him that he and Crowbar were on their way to West Philly to holla at Raheem and leave him with a little memento. Lincoln had made it clear that the memento should not be life threatening; something minor like a knot on the head or bruised ribs.

Earl wasn't a morning person, but when it came to money, he had a way of dragging himself out of bed. Lincoln wouldn't have been the least bit surprised to find Earl and his partner in crime camped outside of his job when he arrived at work this morning.

There was something a little disconcerting about not hearing from Earl. *I hope Earl didn't do anything stupid last night.* He ran an anxious hand over his face. Suppose the plan had backfired—suppose something had happened to his brother?

The sudden ring of his desk phone startled Lincoln. He wasn't in the mood for work-related issues, but he reluctantly picked up.

"Hey, Lincoln," Rachel said. "Your brother is on the other line—"

"Put him through!"

"It's a collect call, but I went ahead and accepted."

Collect! Lincoln's heart dropped in his stomach. *Did Earl get arrested last night? Is he calling from jail?* "Rachel, I appreciate that you accepted; now would you please put the call through," he said impatiently.

"You're going to have to pay out of pocket when the charges show up on the company phone bill," Rachel informed, using a formal, business-like tone.

"Okaaaay!" Lincoln was two seconds from flipping out on the receptionist.

"Yo, Bro', that secretary that answered the phone is rude. She got issues. You need to get with her," Earl said, sounding miffed.

Hearing Earl's voice was a great relief. "Where are you, Earl? What happened? Please don't tell me your ass is locked up."

"Nah, ain't nothing like that. I'm good."

"Why'd you call collect on the work phone?" Lincoln was annoyed with his brother. Didn't Earl have a couple of quarters to drop in a pay phone? This was beyond trifling—even for Earl.

"I lost my cell during the melee last night," Earl said disgustedly. "All my contact information is in my damn cell. I had to call four-one-one to get the number to your job."

"Okay, man. I'm glad to hear your voice; glad that you're okay. So what's up—how'd everything go?"

Earl didn't answer. He was holding marijuana smoke in his lungs; that was always the case when he took a long time to respond. "Shit got fucked up, man," Earl said and then loudly inhaled on the blunt that he was no doubt puffing.

"What went wrong?" Lincoln had a horrific image of Raheem tagged up and lying in a morgue. That mental picture wouldn't be so bad if Lincoln wasn't involved. In the eyes of the law, Raheem's death would be considered a contract killing. *Shit!* He wiped sweat from his forehead. "What did you do, Earl?" Lincoln shouted. "What happened?" he said in a lower tone of voice when he noticed that his coworkers giving him curious glances.

"You didn't tell us that your boy was strapped. That nigga in the Navigator was tryna take us out!"

Lincoln's stomach began to churn. "Did anyone get hurt?" he whispered, eyes darting. He stood up to peer over at Rachel, to make sure she wasn't listening in on the call. Thankfully, she was chatting with the dude that delivered bottled water.

"I can't talk on this phone, Earl." Lincoln was pacing nervously with the phone pressed to his ear.

"Before you go, take down this information. I need you to send me that money by Western Union. I'm stuck in Atlantic City."

"What are you doing there?"

"Man, after we stepped to dude, that nigga started shooting. Bullets were flying everywhere. All over my head and shit. My whole life passed before my eyes. And my main mans, Crowbar—the bull that was with me—he's lucky he only got grazed. I had to get the fuck out of Philly for a minute after that shit went down. Gambling is relaxing—it's like a sedative. You know what I mean? I had to feel some dice in my hand to try to get my head together, calm down my nerves and whatnot.

"I'm broke, man, so I can use that paper you promised."

"All right, Earl. Give me the information, and I'll send you the money." After jotting down the details, Lincoln had to sit down for a moment and say a prayer of thanks. After composing himself, he strode past the reception desk, on his way to wire Earl some bus fare.

"Lincoln!" Rachel called out excitedly. Groaning inside, Lincoln stopped mid-stride. Rachel crooked her finger, gesturing for him to come closer.

Quite reluctantly, he leaned in close, braced for Rachel to comment that she'd "accidentally" snooped on his private conversation with Earl.

"I think the boss and Amber have something going on."

Relief washed over Lincoln, and he broke out in a big grin. If Rachel hadn't been gossiping with the water delivery guy, she wouldn't have been able to resist listening in on the "collect" call.

"No, not Frank," Lincoln protested. "He wouldn't get involved with a young girl like Amber," Lincoln said with a chuckle. The idea was ridiculous.

"I thought Frank was a straight-shooter, too. But I don't know…" Rachel shook her head. "Frank and Amber are getting awfully close. Keep your eyes and ears open." Rachel gave Lincoln a conspiratorial wink.

He nodded as if to say, "Sure thing." He hurried down the stairs and out the door. A million thoughts raced through his mind, and he concluded that Raheem the mechanic was a dangerous dude. How could Chevonne get involved with a man that accessorized his work uniform with a pistol stuck in his waistband?

Lincoln should have known better than to get his brother involved. Earl was a piece of work, and loyalty had never been a quality he possessed. If someone had gotten hurt or killed last night, Earl would have been quick to snitch—he'd have no problem pointing a finger at his own brother in exchange for a lighter sentence.

It had been a harrowing morning and afternoon. But it was over now. Thankfully, Lincoln wouldn't have to kiss his children, his wife, and his freedom goodbye. It was time for Lincoln to let shit go. His personal vendetta against the mechanic could have cost his brother's life. Miserable life that it was, Earl was still his blood.

From now on, Lincoln was staying in his lane; criminal activity was not his forte.

He drove to the nearest Western Union location and filled out the form. He handed the lady behind the counter fifty dollars. He was only giving Earl enough for bus fare and a couple dollars to get something to eat. That clown was crazy if he thought Lincoln was paying the full amount for a botch job.

CHAPTER 30

It didn't matter that his family rarely sat down to a home-cooked meal. What was important was that they were all together—Lincoln, Chevonne, and the kids—eating Chinese takeout.

"Mommy, can I get Dora the Explorer lip gloss?" Tori asked.

"You have enough lip gloss and nail polish. I refuse to buy any more," Chevonne answered.

Amir stuck his tongue out at Tori. Tori rolled her eyes at him.

Scowling, Lincoln looked at Chevonne accusingly. "Tori's only five years old; isn't that a tad early for her to be wearing makeup?"

"It's only lip gloss, Daddy—not makeup. All my friends wear it," Tori piped in.

"She's right, Lincoln. They market the stuff for kids now." Chevonne lifted one shoulder in a quick shrug. "It's harmless. I think it's sort of cute."

"Why does our daughter have to do what all the other little fresh-butt girls are doing? How long has Tori been wearing lip gloss?"

"Since September, when she started first grade." Chevonne's eyes were darting about nervously.

"Why wasn't I involved in that decision?" Now Lincoln was getting irritated. Tori had many years of childhood before she started the turbulent teens. There was plenty of time for her to start worrying about enhancing her looks. For the time being, all she needed to focus on was staying an innocent little girl.

"You're making a big deal out of nothing," Chevonne said in a sharp voice that urged Lincoln not to disrupt their family time.

The phone rang. Chevonne crossed the marble floor and answered it. "It's your brother." She mouthed the words to Lincoln.

I can't believe that fool is calling my house, trying to hustle me! "Tell Earl we're having dinner; I'll call him back," Lincoln said in a voice that was loud enough for Earl to hear. Earl knew damn well that he didn't earn more than the fifty that Lincoln had sent him. Earl had a set of balls on him!

Chevonne relayed the message to Earl and quietly listened to whatever smack Earl was talking. Lincoln was growing more agitated by the second.

"He says it's an emergency." Chevonne held out her hand in a helpless gesture.

Lincoln stared at Chevonne pointedly, trying to convey with his eyes that he did not want to talk to his nuisance of a brother.

But Chevonne walked over to the table, bringing Lincoln the phone. "Earl, he says that he lost his cell phone; there's no way for you to get in touch with him."

Groaning, Lincoln took the phone. The call warranted privacy, and so Lincoln left the kitchen and stood outside on the deck. Hot with aggravation, he welcomed the chilly autumn air. "What's up, man?" he barked into the phone.

"We got problems." Earl's tone was grim, and Lincoln got the distinct impression that this call was not about money.

"What kind of problems?" Lincoln swallowed, dreading whatever Earl was about to tell him.

"You could have at least warned a nigga that the dude you wanted me to handle was stark-raving crazy."

"Huh?" Lincoln felt the hairs rising on the back of his neck.

"Huh, my ass. That mechanic muthafucka is tryna come for me."

"He doesn't know you."

"Man, I dropped my phone, and that nigga got it! He's been going through my contact list, texting all the bitches that I fuck with, pretending that he's me! One of them broads gave up the tapes. Now that nut bull knows my name and where I rest my head at. This shit ain't cool."

Earl was right. This was bad. Real bad. Lincoln's mind went blank and his body went numb.

"Say something, man," Earl bellowed.

Lincoln massaged the top of his head, trying to encourage his brain to come up with some helpful information. "What exactly happened last night?" he asked, stalling because he didn't know what else to say.

"I ain't got time to give you a blow-by-blow description of events. I stepped to dude and he shocked the hell out of me when he pulled out a hammer. I'm lucky to be alive. The nigga tried to kill me and now he wants to finish the job. He called my mans, Crowbar, you know, the bull that was driving the squatter last night?"

"Uh-huh." Lincoln didn't actually know Crowbar, but he wanted Earl to go on.

"That nut bull told Crowbar that he was going to torch his hooptie. Then he told Crowbar to watch his back, cuz he was gonna stuff some dynamite up his asshole."

Lincoln uttered a sound of shock.

"Crowbar ain't know if the bull was serious or not, but taking a precaution, he parked his whip a couple streets over from where he lives. And guess what?"

Scared to ask, Lincoln muttered indecipherably.

"That nut bull turned around and called Crowbar again—using my muthafuckin' cell phone! He told my mans that his car was in flames and that his ass was next on his list."

Lincoln grunted in distress. What kind of maniac had his wife been fuckin' around with?

"Crowbar said dude got a real raspy voice, and be talking a lot of raspy shit. He said dude sounded like one of them terrorists, yelling out a long list of heinous crimes he was about to commit. The bull had Crowbar so convinced that he was gonna light his ass up like a firecracker; Crowbar was shaking like a leaf. My mans had got his hands on some pain pills for that bullet graze on his arm. After listening to those terroristic threats, my mans popped damn near a whole bottle of pills. He washed 'em down with syrup—you know, to relax his nerves and whatnot."

"Is Crowbar okay?"

"Hell, yeah. He's better off than I am," Earl said with a snort. "Having them drugs in his system is Crowbar's ticket out of Philly. He just got out of rehab last month, but now he's on his way back to the rehab facility. He's gon' check hisself back in and use it as a hide-out spot."

"Umph," Lincoln uttered. He was thinking that Crowbar had come up with a good plan.

"So my mans, Crowbar, is safe out in the boonies, but the nut bull is still coming for me!"

"Where's your crew—those killer dudes you used to roll with?"

"All them niggas is either dead or locked up," Earl said with disgust. "Ain't nobody out on these streets, tryna go toe to toe with a maniac that's into bombing cars and sticking explosives up a muthafucka's asshole. Man, I should have stayed my ass in Atlantic City. I'm not tryna be nobody's sitting duck."

"Okay, let's not panic. Listen to me, Earl—"

"Fuck you! I can panic if I want to. I'm not listening to shit else you have to say. You need to make peace with that lunatic bomber. Call his boss at the BMW place. Tell 'em they got a loose cannon working on people's cars. Call the police. Get Chevonne to make some kind of a statement about the shoddy work the bull did on her car."

"I can't involve my wife in this," Lincoln blurted. He was appalled at the idea of letting Chevonne know that he'd concocted a miserable plan of revenge that had backfired horribly.

"Well, you gotta do something, Lincoln. You the muthafucka that he got beef with. All he wanted from Crowbar was the four-one-one on who he was working for. Crowbar didn't know what to tell him, because Crowbar don't know anything about you."

"Okay, good. Give me a second. I'm thinking…" As petrified as Earl sounded, Lincoln was sure that his brother would give up his name in a heartbeat.

"Fuck that! My life is on the line; I ain't got time to be sitting around while you're thinking. Pay me the rest of that paper that you owe me, so I can be out."

"Where are you thinking about going?"

"None of your fuckin' business; I'm not telling you nothing. It's your fault that I'm all tangled up in this bullshit."

"All right, man. Look, meet me outside my job tomorrow around ten. I'll have the money for you," Lincoln conceded. He felt horrible for putting his brother in such a dangerous predicament.

"Can't you get the money tonight?"

"There's a four-hundred-dollar limit on the ATM. I'll get all the money when the bank opens in the morning."

"Can't we can drive around to some supermarkets… you know, buy some shit and get cash back?" Earl sounded desperate.

"I can't get a couple G's from a grocery store," Lincoln remarked sensibly.

"Aye, man. I'll holla at you in the morning," Earl spoke in a flat tone of voice. Lincoln was accustomed to his brother being overly aggressive, but all his fight had gone. It pained Lincoln to acknowledge that he had a hand in crushing Earl's spirit.

Later on that night, Chevonne came to bed wearing a sheer, red negligee.

"That's pretty, baby. Real sexy," Lincoln mumbled halfheartedly. He put his arm around her, kissed her neck, but he didn't go any further. He doubted if his dick would even get hard with the kind of problems that were heavy on his mind. And his wife was at the root of his problems.

Chevonne was a poor judge of character, getting involved with that lunatic mechanic. Then again, how could she not have known that her dick on the side was dangerous and demented? Maybe she had a dark side that Lincoln didn't know about.

He looked at Chevonne from the corner of his eye, wondering if he really knew her.

CHAPTER 31

⟊

L incoln brought his car to a stop when he spotted Earl. Earl had on a denim jacket. Considering himself going incognito, he wore dark shades and the beak of his cap that was usually twisted to the side, was pulled down low, concealing his face. Earl stood close to the brick exterior walls of Clemmons and Associates. Shoulders hunched, his hands stuffed in his pants pockets, Earl resembled a stereotypical junkie, looking for a fix.

"Get in, Earl." Lincoln motioned with his hand.

Looking over his shoulder, Earl slid into the passenger seat. "You got that paper?"

"Yeah, but I don't want to hand you a wad of cash in front of my job. Cameras are everywhere nowadays."

Earl grunted and nodded, and looked over his shoulder again, obviously making sure they weren't being tailed by the Navigator.

"Calm down, Earl. Why you so jumpy?"

Earl gave him a look of disbelief. "Why you think?"

"That fool is messing with your head, man." With all his bravado, Earl was surprisingly terrified.

"Well, his strategy is working. Last night, Crowbar's girl, Sharonda, came to the crib, pounding on the door—banging like she had a warrant for my arrest. I ain't know what the fuck was up, but my ass was ready to leap from the bathroom window. Dumb-ass Michelle ran to the door, talking 'bout, 'Who is it?' I was so mad…if I didn't have to look around for my sneakers, I woulda popped Michelle upside her head. But anyway, when I heard Sharonda call her name, I closed the window."

Lincoln slowed the car on Bainbridge Street. A car pulled away from a meter, opening up a spot. Lincoln swung into the space. "So what did Crowbar's girl want?"

"That ain't important. Give me that paper, so I can bounce."

"Bounce where? Do you know where you're going? Do you have a plan?"

The long sigh that escaped Earl's lips seemed to take all the life out of him; Earl looked deflated. "Nah, but having some money in my pocket will make me feel a whole lot better. The first thing I'ma do is get myself a new phone."

"What actually happened the other night? I thought you were going to sneak up on the mechanic."

"I did! Dude was in front of his crib, and he stood in front of his front door chugging down milk, straight out the container. Me and Crowbar had him—or at least we thought so. That muthafucka is like a ninja or something—seem like he got eyes behind his head, cuz before we knew it, he whipped around and bam! He hit Crowbar right in the face with the milk jug, and whipped out his burner in one second flat.

"Me and Crowbar took off running, but that nut bull was running after us, taking turns firing at both of us.

"Wow! That's crazy," Lincoln said while wondering what was up with Raheem and his penchant for drinking milk.

Earl glared at Lincoln. "You should have told me that I needed to bring some heat."

"I had no idea."

Earl sucked his tooth. "Fuckin' with you, I could have got myself killed."

Lincoln opened his glove box and took out two bank envelopes, stuffed with cash. Chevonne would have a fit when she discovered the withdrawal, but fuck it. And fuck her for getting him into this shit!

A million unpleasant thoughts tunneled through his brain in the few seconds that he held the bank envelope. "Here you go, man." He gave Earl the money. "Don't go on one of your gambling sprees."

"Now you tryna tell me how to spend the money that I earned. That's a lot of nerve, man," Earl snapped. He took off his shades and peeked inside the envelopes, and then thumbed the currency. Despite being troubled, a quick smile came to his lips

"So where are you thinking about running? And how long are you gonna be gone?"

"I got in touch with one of my jawns from back in the day. She lives out in Leiperville."

"Where's that?" Lincoln asked.

"Exactly! Ain't nobody ever heard of Leiperville, so that's where I'm gonna be laying low. You dig?" Earl grinned with pride at his clever scheme. "Now how long I'm out in the sticks depends on when you handle that nut bull.

"You shoulda been the one dealing with that crazy killa in the first place. Why ain't you go to the Better Business Bureau or some shit like that instead of dragging my ass into your personal problems?" Earl was looking real surly with his lips poked out.

Earl was absolutely right, and his words hit home. Lincoln should have personally dealt with Chevonne's lover immediately after she gave up his information. Ashamed that he'd taken the coward's route, Lincoln dropped his gaze. He wasn't scared of Raheem, but he was terrified of doing jail time. He was horrified by the idea of losing his job, his family, and his status. Going back to his roots—being just another broke dude in the hood had been a recurring theme in his nightmares. Maybe he needed some therapy, after all.

"So what are you going to tell Michelle?"

"Man, fuck Michelle. My life is on the line; I'm not worrying about her. I'm going to the crib to pack my shit while she's at work."

"That's cold."

"The world is cold. Say, man, can you give me a ride back to my crib, and then drop me off at the bus terminal?"

Lincoln frowned. "No, Earl, I'm already late for work."

Earl screwed up his lips and expressed his disgust with a long, whistling sigh. He slapped the shades back on his face, tugged on the beak of his cap. He looked around suspiciously before opening the car door. "I'll holla at you when I get a phone."

Lincoln pulled a business card out of his wallet and wrote his cell number on the back. "Don't call my job; make sure you use my cell when you contact me."

Earl grunted a response and then took off down Bainbridge Street.

CHAPTER 32

All afternoon Lincoln had been trying to figure out a way to get Raheem off of Earl and Crowbar's trail. As far as he knew, Raheem hadn't placed him on his hit list. Few people would believe that he and Earl were even related, let alone brothers.

He left work early, telling nosey Rachel that he had a dental appointment.

He drove straight to Bala Cynwyd to wait for Raheem. If Raheem's routine was anything like before, Lincoln was going to be tailing him for hours. But it didn't matter; his adrenaline was pumping. Raheem had to be stopped.

The baseball bat that his son, Amir, had allowed to collect dust, was going to be put to good use. The bat was secured between the spare tire and a tool box, inside of Lincoln's trunk.

With four cars between him and the Navigator, he followed Raheem with his jaw clenched and vengeance in his heart. This time, Raheem didn't turn onto Monument Avenue. He stayed on City Avenue, gliding along. City Avenue is an odd street. One side of traffic is considered to be Philadelphia, while the other side is

Lower Merion territory. A black man didn't drive on the Lower Merion side unless his shit was in order…license, registration, and insurance all had to be up to date. Those Lower Merion cops had nothing but time on their hands, and the only time they were spotted doing police work, was when they pulled a black man over for a traffic violation or any minor infraction of the law.

Abiding by traffic rules, Raheem turned on his blinkers and turned into the Bala Cynwyd shopping plaza. Keeping a safe distance, Lincoln followed. Parked next to a minivan, he watched while Raheem sauntered away from his truck. He appeared to be headed in the direction of the fitness center. Lincoln groaned. *Damn, I gotta sit out here while this dude pumps iron.* Lincoln sneered at the man's distinctive arrogant walk, and made a mental note to work on Raheem's knee caps after he slammed a home run on his head.

Lincoln brightened up a little when he realized that Raheem wasn't going to the fitness center. He was heading in the direction of Acme Market. *More milk, muthafucka?*

Lincoln cut his engine, and reclined his seat a little to get some leg room. That's when he was struck with a brilliant idea. Lincoln turned the key in the ignition. He cruised up to the Navigator and wrote down the plate number.

He left the plaza and cruised over to a gas station that was on the other side of the street—the Philly side. Using a pay phone, he made an anonymous call that would alert the Lower Merion police.

Where he was from in the hood, if you happened to see a dude that you had beef with—he could be filling his tank with gas or inside a mini market, buying a blunt—one way to get even was to call the po-po and tell them that a robbery was being committed. Nine times out of ten, that fool would have an unregistered gun on him, and even though he wasn't trying to rob anything, he'd get popped for the gun violation. Hood niggas always seemed to have open cases, and the gun charge would result in parole violation. Problem solved; nigga gets locked up for three to five years.

Getting Raheem off the streets was safer than risking getting shot up or hauled off to jail. He called 9-1-1 and claimed the Acme Market in Bala Cynwyd had just been robbed. He rattled off Raheem's license plate number and then hung up.

Wanting an up-close look at justice being served, Lincoln followed the police cars, with sirens blaring as they speeded to the shopping plaza. Blending in with all the shocked onlookers, Lincoln smirked when the Navigator was surrounded by cops.

He wished Earl could have shared the enjoyment of seeing Raheem stretched out over the hood of his truck, while the jug of milk he'd been holding, hit the ground with a great splatter.

Nodding his head in satisfaction, Lincoln smirked

when the police retrieved a gun from Raheem's waistband. *Gotchu, you milk-drinking predator!*

Raheem was carted off to jail, and Lincoln continued to watch the spectacle until the Navigator was chained and towed.

Lincoln checked his cell phone, wondering if he'd missed Earl's call. The only calls had come from Chevonne and Earl's girlfriend, Michelle. Michelle had left eleven messages. The poor woman was probably frantic, wondering why Earl had packed his belongings and left without warning. Lincoln didn't know what to tell her, so he didn't bother to return her calls.

Lincoln stuck his phone in his pocket, deciding to wait until tomorrow to get in touch with Michelle. In the morning, he'd be working with a clearer mind and be able to come up with a plausible explanation for his brother's sudden departure.

Michelle was a good and hardworking woman, but Earl needed to get away from hood life for a while. Being forced to live out in the sticks might be a blessing in disguise.

Chuckling to himself, he thought about Raheem's predicament. Nobody likes jail, and so even if Raheem was held for only a few days or a couple of weeks, Lincoln doubted if the dude would be stupid enough to come back on the streets, looking for trouble. If Raheem wanted to keep that job of his, he'd be wise to keep a low profile.

Never much of a drinking man, Lincoln figured tonight

was an exception. Instead of going straight home, he decided to stop at a bar and have a private, victory celebration. Feeling good after throwing back a couple shots of tequila, Lincoln headed home.

It was late, and the house was quiet. As he climbed the stairs, he caught a pleasant whiff of Chevonne's favorite scent. The sexy fragrance wafted from the bedroom, sending a signal to his brain and then down to his dick. Twitching and stiffening, his dick had an instant reaction. Smiling, he opened the bedroom door.

Candles were lit all around the bedroom. Chevonne was lounging on the bed, lying on her side. The mound of her ass was outlined by soft fabric. Once again, Chevonne was wearing that sexy red lingerie. Lincoln stood still for a moment and stared at his beautiful wife. She was a feast for the eyes. She gazed at Lincoln questioningly, silently asking if he was in the mood to make love tonight.

He didn't say a word; he didn't have to. His rod was trying to burst out of his pants. Moving his erection to a more comfortable position, he unbuckled his belt and unzipped his pants. Pants fell down his thighs and gathered around his ankles. He stepped out of them and kicked them to the side. His dick was so hard, it was jutting almost obscenely through the opening of his briefs. With his mouth slack, his gaze fixed on Chevonne's firm ass, he moved slowly toward the bed.

There wasn't a doubt in his mind that tonight he was going to tear that pussy up.

CHAPTER 33

"None of this makes any sense. Everything was going good between me and Earl. Why would he suddenly move out?" Michelle cried. This was the third time in ten minutes that she'd asked that same damn question.

"That's how Earl is," Lincoln said weakly. He wished he could think of more comforting words, but nothing came to mind.

"I mean…what else could he be looking for? I cook for him, I pay all of the bills. He gets good loving whenever he wants it," she said, followed by more mournful sobbing.

That was too much information. With growing impatience, Lincoln rubbed the back of his neck.

"What can another woman do for him that I'm not doing?"

"My brother has a wandering eye. He's always been fickle. I'm real sorry he ran out on you."

"Sorry don't ease my pain," she said with belligerence that seemed to be directed at Lincoln, as if she sensed that he'd played a part in Earl's mysterious departure.

"I just can't understand why he'd walk off like this. The only thing I can't give him right now is transportation… and it's not my fault that the car got booted and towed. You see, what had happened was—"

"Earl's not the most responsible person in the world," Lincoln cut in. He'd already heard Earl's account of that story, and though there was probably much more to it than Earl had admitted, he had no interest whatsoever in hearing Michelle's version.

Listening to the woman go on and on was becoming intolerable. He tapped his pen on his desk, wondering how he could hang up without appearing heartless.

"I don't see what another bitch can do for Earl. I mean… seriously…I pay for his weed, the porn he rents—and that chat line bill, whew!"

"Chat line?"

"Yeah, Earl is easily bored. So while I'm at work he gets on those singles chat lines just to have something to do. It don't mean anything. He likes being a fly on the wall, listening to other people's freaky conversations."

"Oh, I see," he said, while actually thinking that Michelle was an idiot and a glutton for punishment.

"Cable, rent, phone, gas, electric, weed, porn, chat line and gas when we had the car…I pay all that shit. Earl don't contribute to nothing!" she said fervently, working herself up to anger that would no doubt be followed by more tears.

Michelle shouldn't have been taking care of his brother—

enabling him to be a freeloader and allowing him to behave like a perpetual child. If he'd had an emotional investment in Michelle, he would have tried to counsel and suggested that she was a big part of the problem. But he didn't know her well and had no intention of including her in his inner circle, so he kept his thoughts to himself.

Lincoln sighed. Michelle was draining him with her sobbing and asinine reasoning. He didn't know what else to say. He stared at the clock. At the beginning of the call, she'd said that she was on her fifteen-minute work break. Hopefully, break time would soon be over.

Michelle sniffled loudly, but had apparently run out of words.

"Well, I have to get back to work," Lincoln said, using the lull in the conversation as an opportune moment to get her off of the phone.

As if he hadn't said a word, Michelle launched into another conversation. "Earl was acting weird the night before he split—real nervous and jumpy. Somebody knocked on the door and he jetted to the bathroom… pushed open the window and was about to hop out. I had to yell and tell him that it was Crowbar's girl, Sharonda, at the door, to keep him from leaping."

"Crowbar's girl?" Lincoln was suddenly very alert. Lincoln now recalled that Earl had deliberately avoided telling him why Crowbar's girlfriend had come over that night. "What did she want?"

"She was looking for Crowbar. He was supposed to be at the rehab place, but he never made it."

Lincoln felt a little queasy.

"Sharonda was fit to be tied. She was so mad with Crowbar for tricking her into giving him her last little bit of money. He told her that he needed the money to check hisself back into rehab. But when she called the facility, they told her Crowbar had never showed up. Sharonda asked Earl where and when he'd last seen her man. Earl started stuttering and stammering, and looking like he was scared."

A chill went down Lincoln's spine. Now he knew why Earl had been so desperate to get out of town. Earl suspected that Raheem had caught up with Crowbar before he'd made it out of Philly.

And now Lincoln was really worried. He hadn't heard from Earl since he got out of his car yesterday morning. It terrified him to think that Earl had met with foul play. He cursed himself for not insisting that his brother give him the phone number and address of the woman who lived in Leiperville. He didn't have any pertinent information—not even a name.

"I don't know where Earl is, but the minute I hear from him, I'll make sure that he gets in touch with you."

"You know what?"

"What?" he answered wearily.

"I'ma fuck Earl up when I get my hands on him," Michelle raged. "He's wrong as hell to put me through this. Why would he do this to me when everything between us was going so good? Just last week, we were talking about having a baby," she said wistfully.

Just when Lincoln didn't think he could take any more of Michelle's ridiculous lament, the call dropped. He didn't know if Michelle's break was over or if her battery had gone dead. Whatever the case, he was grateful.

Staring at the set of blueprints on his desk as if they held the secret of his brother's whereabouts, he asked in whisper, "Where are you, Earl? You know you should have called me by now!"

Confounded, Lincoln scratched his head.

His cell vibrated and Lincoln grabbed it, ready to shut it off. He wasn't giving Michelle another second of his time. But when he gazed at the screen, he saw an unfamiliar area code. "Hello!"

"This is my new number, so lock it in," Earl said lazily.

"Earl! Man, you had me scared to death. Why'd you take so long to call? Man, don't do this to me anymore."

"Why you bitching at me for? You need to check yourself, cuz you whining and crying like a female."

Lincoln laughed heartily. His brother's slur didn't bother him at all. He was so happy to hear Earl's voice, he didn't give a damn about any derogatory remarks.

"I just got off the phone with Michelle," Lincoln said in a serious voice.

"Man, I'm not tryna hear that."

"I know. But she said something that made me pause."

Earl went quiet, no doubt inhaling marijuana and hold-ing the smoke in his lungs. "What did she say?"

"She said that Crowbar never made it to rehab."

"Dang, I was just starting to feel a little buzz. Why'd you have to remind me about what happened to Crowbar?"

"Do you know what happened to him?"

"No, but if I had to guess, I'd say that the nut bull caught up with him and fucked him up with those explosives."

Lincoln shuddered. "Look, I want you to stay where you are. Forget about Philly for a while." Getting Raheem arrested was only a temporary solution. There was no proof that jail had purged him of the grudge he harbored.

"I'm straight. You ain't gotta worry about me coming back to town. I mean…it's not all peaches and cream. This chick has two bad-ass kids, but I'm dealing with the situation."

"Okay, good." Lincoln wrote down all of Earl's perti-nent contact information, and found out that his new girlfriend's name was Ivella Drummond. Thankful that his brother was safe from harm, Lincoln was finally able to relax.

Earl's life hadn't been going anywhere in Philly. The woman named Ivella already had two boys, and Lincoln could only hope that she wasn't looking to raise a third child. It was time for Earl to step up to the plate and act like a man. It was wishful thinking, but Lincoln could dream, couldn't he?

CHAPTER 34

M elanee didn't want to be at work today. The atmosphere in the Scandalicious kitchen was crazy and chaotic. Vidal, who loved to create drama, hadn't even arrived yet, and somehow Solay was managing to cause a disturbance all by herself.

Solay was getting on Melanee's last nerve. She was worrying aloud about fulfilling her promise to bake two thousand cupcakes for a charity event.

The way Solay kept repeating, "I don't know how I'm going to get it all done and still manage Scandalicious," was really aggravating. Had Solay asked Melanee's professional opinion, she would have told her that a job that big couldn't be done without a team of experienced bakers. But all Solay saw were dollar signs. She hadn't asked Melanee's opinion, and so Melanee didn't offer it.

And now she was running around like a chicken with her head cut off, acting clumsy—clattering and banging pans and she even dropped a whole carton of eggs.

Melanee turned her head away from the slimy mess, defiantly refusing to give Solay any assistance. She did not intend to involve herself in Solay's problems.

She was bored with making the same ole butter cream and cream cheese frostings, but Solay was too cheap to jazz up the menu. As she blended sugar and butter, she couldn't suppress a yawn. A good hour of sleep would be refreshing.

After being ejected from Madam's house, Melanee had spent the next few hours lying in her stuffy little bedroom as thoughts and worries jostled in her mind. The butler's contempt for her was apparent. His words, "I never want to see you again," stung like hell. Not that she cared to see him, either, but she was concerned that he'd be able to convince Madam Midnight that she was unworthy of serving her. That prick of a butler wanted Madam all to himself. Though Melanee was certain that she'd satisfied Madam, the butler seemed to have a great influence on the woman's decisions.

Reminded that Madam had clearly said that she belonged to her now, Melanee felt somewhat hopeful. She wondered if Madam would hold an official ceremony to declare Melanee as her prized possession.

She thought of Colden and sighed. She actually felt a little guilty for betraying him. But she had a right to be with the master of her choosing, and Colden was always too busy for Melanee. He'd never really taken control of her the way that she desired. Madam lived her role as a dominant twenty-four-seven and Melanee longed to be at her beck and call.

During her many troubled thoughts, she wondered if

Madam would contact her through Colden. She preferred that Madam contact her directly, but Melanee's feelings were inconsequential. Being an insignificant submissive, she had no say-so or knowledge in the manner in which dominants traded chattel.

All she could do was wait and hope that she'd hear from her new mistress very soon. Maybe she could quit this dumb job and bake for Madam—using only low-fat ingredients, in order to help Madam maintain her beautiful physique.

Racks and racks of cupcakes had cooled and were ready to be frosted. Piping bag in hand, Melanee stretched her mouth open and gave an enormous yawn.

At that exact moment, her phone jangled softly.

She dropped the bag of frosting and ripped the phone from her apron pocket. Colden was calling, and Melanee didn't know what to expect. Ignoring Solay's curious glance, she walked out of the kitchen and went into the dimly lit dining area to take the call in private.

"Yes, Master," she whispered, but even spoken softly, the words sounded hollow and false.

"Am I? I've been told otherwise," Colden responded in a chilly tone.

"What do you mean?" She feigned innocence, but her heart quickened in anticipation of news from Madam.

"I loaned you to Madam Midnight, but it appears that you two have been plotting behind my back."

"No, I'd never do that," Melanee lied. "She told me

that I belonged to her, and what could I say? I was under the impression that you gave me away."

"I did nothing of the sort. And it's completely inappropriate for Madam Midnight to claim something that doesn't belong to her. She's overstepped her boundaries."

Wow, this is not going the way that I'd hoped. Melanee pulled off one of the plastic gloves she wore while baking and anxiously nibbled on her fingernail.

"Do you want me to contact her, and tell her that she misunderstood?" Melanee sounded sincere, but she really wanted Madam's contact information so that she could plead for her to take her.

"No," Colden answered. "Madam Midnight is a powerful woman and very well connected. She is not the sort of woman that anyone wants as an enemy."

Melanee sighed in relief. Colden was going to relinquish her to Madam. She wished that she could leave work early, go home, and start packing. There was no doubt in her mind that she belonged with Madam Midnight.

While Colden was quiet, no doubt thinking of how to outwit Madam, Melanee was imagining going to bed each evening and waking every morning with her face buried between Madam Midnight's sculpted legs.

"I have an idea," he said, sounding peeved as he interrupted her sensual reverie.

"Yes, Master, what do you have in mind?" she asked in a shaky voice. Colden was a clever man, and she feared that he might have come up with a conceivable plan to keep her for himself. *Save me, Madam; don't let him keep me!*

"Madam Midnight bores easily. She never keeps her subs for very long. Only last night, she sent that blond boy packing. She shipped him to Toronto to work for her Canadian modeling agency."

Melanee was intrigued by the information, and terribly flattered. *Madam kicked Garrett to the curb for me!*

"You and I are going to indulge Madam's whims. Between you and me, I am your rightful owner, but until Madam replaces you with another, we have no choice but to go along with her wishes."

Melanee's lips spread into a broad grin. "What's next, Master? I don't know what to do. I don't have any experience serving anyone except you."

"She's an odd woman, with an odd way of doing things, so until she claims you, I want to spend as much time with you as possible."

"Yes, sir." The thrill of excitement gave her a cold shiver.

"Meet me at my place tonight. Unfortunately, it may be the last time we spend time together for a while," Colden said solemnly. It took Madam Midnight's interest in Melanee for Colden to realize her value.

One man's trash is another woman's treasure!

After hanging up with Colden, Melanee returned to the kitchen feeling uplifted. She couldn't help smirking when she noticed Solay mopping the section of the kitchen where she'd dropped the eggs. Solay had over-extended herself; now she was further delayed, having to do grunge work. It served her right.

"You seem to be going through it, sweetie. What's wrong?" Melanee asked, sounding genuinely concerned, while secretly taunting Solay.

"The charity event…" Solay rolled her eyes. "I'm going nuts trying to run the bakery and start preparing for that big event. It's next week and I don't know how I'm going to pull it all together." Solay lifted her forearm, and used the sleeve of her sweater to wipe sweat from her forehead.

Melanee pondered for a moment, wondering if she should lift a finger to help Solay. She had, after all, shot down Melanee's contribution to that boring menu, and then had turned around and had tried to steal her idea by adding her own specialty items. But that didn't last very long. Solay was too stingy and didn't like thinking outside the box.

What the heck? She'd be leaving Scandalicious soon, and catering to Madam Midnight's sophisticated and discriminating palate. It wouldn't hurt to help Solay out of the mess she'd gotten herself into.

"I can call the pastry school if you'd like. They could probably send some students over to help out."

"Are you serious?" The way Solay's face lit up, one would have thought Melanee had offered her a million bucks.

"Yeah, their labor is cheap. Costs next to nothing. The students need the experience; you know what I mean?"

She knew that Solay didn't know what she meant because Solay didn't learn the craft at a prestigious pastry school. She wasn't trained and knowledgeable like Melanee. She was taught to bake by her grandmother, for heaven's sake. It was a miracle or some kind of a fluke that Scandalicious was actually succeeding.

Solay propped the mop against the fridge. "This is the best news you could have given me. Oh, my God! You rock, Melanee." She rushed over and gave Melanee a big hug. Melanee stiffened in response, declining to return the gesture. Solay wasn't one of her favorite people. But with a pack of students baking those two thousand cupcakes, Melanee wouldn't have to worry about Solay hounding her to put in more hours.

CHAPTER 35

"How come you're not dressed?" Deon asked when Solay opened the door for him. She was wearing a pair of clingy, low rider sweats and a short crop top—showing off lots of bare skin.

"I had a rough day, thought we'd stay in tonight. I put this on just for you; don't you like what you see?" She ran both hands along the curvature of her waistline and around to her taut stomach. "I was thinking about getting a piercing, right here…" She touched her navel. "What do you think?" she smiled seductively.

"I think piercings are sexy as shit. But you're sexy already; you don't need none of that extra stuff."

Solay smiled at her man; he always knew what to say. She eyed Deon up and down, noticing that he was looking even hotter than usual. He was dressed so sharp, he could have been preparing to make an entrance down an urban-wear runway. His cap, shirt, and jacket were perfectly color-coordinated. His sagging jeans were of a high quality, appearing to have cost a whole lot more than Solay paid for her jeans. The new pair of boots on his feet did not come from Footlocker—they screamed

Neiman Marcus or Nordstrom or some exclusive, men's shoe boutique. Deon loved to dress, but he was looking a little too spiffy, being that he was about to come right out of that pricey gear.

"Put something on, baby. Don't you get tired of being stuck in the house all the time?"

"Not really." She didn't need the outside world as long as she had Deon.

"We're going out tonight. I'm serious. I'm not taking no for an answer."

"Okaaaay," Solay said reluctantly, thinking that the surprise she had for Deon would have to wait.

She went through her closet, and frowned. There were several hot semi-formal dresses and an undetermined amount of business suits from her corporate days, but she hadn't invested in too much casual chic attire. Scandalicious took up so much of her time, she rarely went shopping.

Solay finally found a cute pair of jeans that hugged her butt nicely, but the label wasn't impressive at all. *Oh, well!*

She put on a tight red cashmere V-neck with the jeans and admired herself in the mirror. But she concluded that she was going to have to step up her gear if she was going to hang out with such a fashionisto as Deon.

Although her business was on South Street and her residence was right off of South Street, it was rare for Solay to browse the famous tourist strip, or even eat in the numerous restaurants that lined the street. She was too busy running Scandalicious in the daytime, and she didn't feel safe to walk South Street alone at night. The out-of-town crowds and the Philadelphians were known to get drunk and out of control at night. Besides, Solay went to bed early. At this phase in her life, she had goals to achieve. Enjoying local nightspots and having an active social life was at the very bottom of her list of priorities.

Solay would have been perfectly content to stay home, order some take-out and watch a movie with Deon at her apartment, but he was pretty emphatic that they get out and have some fun. A healthy relationship required compromising and coming outside of your comfort zone, from time to time.

On their way to the comedy club, Laff House, they held hands, window-shopped, and stopped to smooch along the way. Deon looked fine as hell in clothes and buck naked, and Solay couldn't even get mad at all the women that gawked at him. But Deon wasn't paying those brazen females any attention.

You can look but don't touch, bitches!

Solay and Deon were approaching two teenage girls that were hanging out on South Street—both sporting visible piercings and tattoos. The taller girl made a lewd comment to her girlfriend: "Mmm. Now that's my type right there; I wonder how he's holding down there?"

"He needs to dump that corny chick, and come go with us," the other girl said. "Hey, daddy…the party's over here."

Stunned by the disrespect, Solay stopped walking. Her mouth dropped open. She looked over at the two teens, aghast. One girl was licking her lips invitingly, as if expecting Deon to drop Solay's hand and join her and her friend.

"Woof!" the other girl said, making a vulgar barking sound.

Solay looked at Deon, astounded. "When did young girls start acting so bold—making sexual innuendos and lewd comments to grown men?"

"They just acting crazy. Young and dumb. Don't worry about those silly girls, baby. We ain't gon' let nobody ruin our good time tonight." Gently but insistently, he tugged on Solay's arm. Smothering Solay with lots of affection, he put an arm around her, placing kisses all over her cheek. They walked the next block hugged up tight; something Solay hadn't done out in public since high school.

She felt so loved…so cherished, she soon forgot about the offensive girls. Deon was very attentive—behind closed doors and whenever they were out together.

The way he pampered himself with his extensive wardrobe, and horde of sneakers…the way he kept his hair and beard well-groomed, it would be easy to surmise that Deon was full of himself, but he was actually extremely humble. Very warm and giving. It was those traits that had endeared him to her. His cut-up and ripped body, his cute face and sexy ways were the icing on the cake for Solay.

It was tight inside the Laff House, with tables scrunched together. At first, Solay was worried that she wouldn't enjoy herself in such a crowded place. But by the time the comedians came onstage and started cracking jokes, she forgot all about the lack of elbow room. The great drinks and prompt service didn't hurt, either.

Between acts, Solay went to the restroom. When she returned to their table, she was surprised to see their waitress doing a little more than serving drinks. Grinning and preening, the hussy was all up in Deon's face. Hot anger felt like fire, and Solay was certain that her brown skin had turned several shades of dark red.

She squeezed past the flirty waitress and took her seat, then began to possessively caress Deon's hand. Without saying a word, she was sending the waitress a loud message: *He's taken!*

"Is everything okay?" Deon asked, turning away from the waitress and giving Solay his full attention.

"Yeah, I'm fine," she replied, smiling broadly, hiding her annoyance and jealousy.

"Just making sure. You took so long, I was about to come in there after you."

"No, I didn't," Solay said, laughing.

"It was too long for me." Deon leaned in and gave her a quick kiss, and Solay immediately felt better.

"Well, enjoy the show," the waitress said, frowning as if offended by the open display of affection.

That's right, keep it moving, bitch!

After the show, as they walked back to Solay's apartment, Deon said, "The way South Street is poppin' at night; I'm surprised you close up so early."

"Six-thirty is not early when you've been up way before the crack of dawn."

"But babe, look at all these people." He motioned to the droves of sightseers on both sides of the street.

"I'd have to hire evening staff that I could really trust to keep Scandalicious open late, and I'm just not there yet. Scandalicious is still growing. I don't want to bite off more than I can handle."

"I can dig it. I know you got it all figured out, because you got a good head on your shoulders. That's one of the things I really dig about you."

"Oh, yeah?" she said, smiling up at him. "What else do you like?"

"You ain't even gotta ask that; you know what I like." He reached behind her and grabbed her ass. "I like that booty, baby."

Solay laughed and blushed, and then gazed at him adoringly. "I have a sexy surprise for you tonight—something really freaky," she said, lifting an eyebrow suggestively.

"A ménage?" He raised both his thick brows and grinned devilishly.

"Not that freaky." She gave him a playful shove.

"Just kidding," he added quickly.

She'd seen a photo of a freaky dessert, called a banana-dick sundae, and she wanted to try it. She had the ice cream, cherries, whipped cream, and chocolate syrup. Deon's dick would serve as the banana—the featured attraction. She couldn't wait to get his curved dick on a plate with all the accoutrements surrounding it. Then she'd lap it all up, licking ice cream, whipped cream and chocolate syrup off his pretty dick until it was clean as a whistle.

The thought of it gave her a hot rush.

She'd expected Deon to press her for details of the kinky dessert, but he was surprisingly quiet as they turned the corner on the small side street that led to her apartment.

"Uh, I'ma have to pass on that dessert, babe. I got an audition coming up, and I want to go home and start preparing for it."

"Oh," she uttered, disappointment apparent in her tone of voice. "Well, we don't have to do the dessert thing. I can deal with a quickie every now and then." Solay hoped that she didn't sound desperate, but she was taken off-guard, and wasn't ready for the evening to end.

"I'm sorry, babe. I can't. That ain't even how we do it. With you, sex is more than just a physical act; I'm not tryna bust a nut and bounce. Nah, it ain't like that. I like to put my whole heart into it when I'm making love to you."

"So, uh, what are you auditioning for? Another commercial?"

"Nah, it's something big. I'm not up for a starring role; but it's a big part."

"Really? What is it, Deon? TV? Movies?"

"It's a low-budget film. Something independent. But for me, it's major." He looked slightly embarrassed. "I don't really want to talk about it. I'm sorry, Solay, but I just don't wanna jinx it." He touched his heart, and Solay felt compassion. Deon was showing her his vulnerability, and she appreciated that.

Though it was on the tip of her tongue to ask him if he needed help to rehearse his lines, she realized it would seem as if she were using a sneaky ploy for him to go along with what she wanted. She told herself to stop being selfish and insecure. They'd had a great evening, and he had a right to go back to his place to work on his lines. Now was the time to be supportive, and not a whiny nag.

Their kiss outside of her door was long and passionate. He pulled his lips away and stared in her eyes sincerely. "I'ma hit you up tomorrow. Okay, love?"

She nodded sadly as she placed the key into the lock. She didn't want him to leave her. He touched her cheek. She looked up, hoping he'd changed his mind.

"Sweet dreams," he said softly, and then bounded down the stairs.

Going inside her apartment while Deon went back to

his place seemed ridiculous. Inside, she slid the security chain in place.

Suddenly her life seemed a bit off-kilter.

Had the waitress slipped Deon her number? Did he secretly plan to get with one of those nasty girls that were cruising South Street, eyeballing men like they were raw meat?

No, Deon wasn't slimy like that. He got enough recreational sex working for that agency. Solay frowned and sighed. She was really starting to detest what he did for a living. She didn't want another woman touching him in any manner. Looking on the bright side, it was a good thing that Deon had an upcoming audition. It was time for her man to get out of the escort business and start a new career.

CHAPTER 36

V idal poked his head into the kitchen. "There's a girl from a cooking school on the phone. The phone has been ringing every fifteen minutes, with different people asking about a baking position."

"Are you serious?" Solay shot a look of surprise at Melanee.

Melanee looked unfazed. "We got so busy, I forgot to tell you that I was able to get you ten candidates. No pay. They all need the extra credit."

"Are you serious!"

Melanee gave her a look that said it was no big deal.

"You're an angel, Melanee. I can't thank you enough." Squealing with joy, Solay hugged Melanee for the second time that day.

Obviously in one of his prickly moods, Vidal sneered at the two women. "Umph, I hate to break up this 'Kumbayah' moment, but I'm feeling some kind of way. It would be nice if somebody would keep me abreast of what's going on around here."

Solay pulled off her gloves and hurried to her miniscule office and spoke to the student. She returned to the front counter and pulled Vidal to the side. "We're going to be getting a lot of calls from students; I'd appreciate you take down their names and make sure you get their numbers. I'm holding a group interview in a few days."

Vidal leaned way to the side. "Oh, now I'm your personal secretary! You got me holding down the front, entertaining the pests, wiping off counters, dealing with deliveries. God only knows what's next. I didn't sign up for all this. You need a personal assistant."

"I told you when I hired you that your job duties would change from time to time."

"Yeah, you did. But I thought working at Scandalicious was going to be a sweet gig, but this place is crazy. You should change the name to A Scandalous Mess!" he said and strode out of her office.

Solay shook her head. The only way to control Vidal's mouth was to erupt in an explosion of anger. And today, she was ecstatic over the free student labor to let Vidal upset her.

As if the day couldn't get any better, Vidal called out, "Solaaaay, ya man is here!" It was completely unprofessional for Vidal to yell in her bakery, but when she stepped out of her office and saw her golden delicious boyfriend, all she could do was grin. She should have been embarrassed for allowing the customers to see her blushing like a schoolgirl, but she wasn't. She had fallen so hard for Deon, nobody else mattered.

She was so happy to see her baby, she wanted to soar

over the counter and jump into his arms, but instead she walked around the counter. "I'm taking a quick break, Vidal." She motioned for Deon to meet her near the stairs.

"Mmm-hmmm, a break, huh? I wish I could pull off my gloves and get up outta here whenever I get good and ready. Some people got it made in the shade," he said for the amusement of the patrons. And the customers obliged Vidal with giggles and chuckles.

Growing bolder, Vidal pointed at Solay and Deon who were in the back of the dining area, locked in an embrace.

"I'm telling y'all, they don't call this place Scandalicious for nothing. Umph, umph, umph."

"Dude up front is off the chain," Deon commented. "He should go onstage on open mike night at Laff House."

"Vidal's a mess," Solay said, shaking her head. But Vidal and all his antics were the furthest thing from her mind. She was focused on the sexy man standing before her. *My man!* She shook her head, incredulous that she'd almost let such a good man get away, merely because he didn't aspire to fit into the mold of society's version.

Solay smiled. "It's good to see you. What a nice surprise! How'd your rehearsal go?"

"I'm feeling good about it. I'll find out when I audition. Anyway, I only stopped by for a quick minute. I know that last night didn't turn out the way you wanted, so I brought you a little something. It didn't feel right leaving you with that sad look on your face." He reached inside the pocket of his jacket, and took a small box, wrapped in shimmering gift wrap and tied with a tiny silver bow.

"Deon, you didn't have to buy me anything."

"I wanted to."

She accepted the small box. "Ooo, what is it?" she asked, beaming.

"Open it and find out. But since you asked, it's a love note."

"Huh?"

"Open it up."

She tore off the wrapping paper. Inside the little Tiffany box was a silver heart tag pendant with the words, *I Love You*, written in succession, in elegant script. "It's beautiful."

"It's called a Tiffany Love Note," he explained.

Solay gazed at the delicate gift for a moment, and then looked up at Deon. "This is so sweet of you; thank you, Deon."

"Welcome, baby." He drew her into an embrace.

She twisted herself out of Deon's arms, and arched an eyebrow. "So are the words true? Do you love me?"

Deon laughed. "Yeah, or something like that. If it's not love, then whatever I'm feeling is damn close to it."

He clasped her hand. "Have you ever been in love before?"

"A long time ago. In college."

"Did it feel like this?" he asked softly.

She shook her head.

"No? Daaaamn, you not only burst my bubble...you stomped on it and crushed it." He wore an expression of embarrassment.

"You didn't let me finish," she said, laughing.

"Oh, aye."

"That college feeling must have been puppy love, because it didn't feel anything like this."

Taken off-guard, Deon bit down on his succulent bottom lip and dropped his gaze, blushing.

"You're so cute when you blush."

Deon forced his features into a stern expression. "Does this look like I'm blushing?"

They laughed together.

Deon reached for the pendant. "Lemme put that on you."

"While I'm dressed like this?"

"Why not?"

"Because I look a hot mess." She frowned at her boring work clothes: old jeans, plain top, a flour-covered apron, and dogged, but comfortable, black Adidas sneakers that were decorated with dabs of cake batter.

"I'll put it on when I'm cleaned up and looking pretty."

Deon held out the necklace. "No, I want you to rock this necklace right now."

Solay turn around, while Deon gently placed the chain around her neck. He put his mouth to her ear. "You always look pretty to me, baby. And don't you forget it."

CHAPTER 37

H er palms were not clammy with nervousness. There were no butterflies in her stomach, no stirrings of anticipation. Willing to do whatever was necessary to be with Madam, she rode the bus to Colden's house and rang the doorbell.

He came to the door wearing a jacket. Instead of inviting her in, he came outside. "Come on," he said, taking long strides toward his Escalade.

She scampered behind him, trying to keep up. She'd never been inside his luxury vehicle…she'd never been allowed. As she climbed inside the spacious SUV, there was no rush of excitement, only curiosity. Was he driving her to Madam's house? Melanee didn't question him; she could sense that he was seething over something. Colden was always angry, and it had been her responsibility to service him in any manner that he required to improve his disposition.

Tonight, she didn't care about his foul mood.

Colden drove in grim silence. Melanee gazed out of the window, daydreaming about her life with Madam.

After twenty minutes, Melanee noticed a sign that read,

Bucks County. Why were they there? It was a nice area, but Madam lived in Montgomery County, and that's where Melanee wanted to be. Deflated, she slumped in her seat.

Colden turned off the main street, and cruised along a residential area that showcased big, exclusive homes. Whatever trick Colden had up his sleeve wasn't going to work. Occasionally, he took her with him to visit married couples that were in "the life," to give her the false hope that one day she, too, might earn the privilege of serving him twenty-four-seven.

Or maybe they were going to a private bondage party, being hosted in the home-dungeon of one of his wealthy friends. *Been there, done that,* Melanee thought with disinterest.

As they drove past one million-dollar home after the next, Melanee groaned inwardly. If she couldn't be with Madam, she'd rather be inside her dinky little apartment, alone.

Colden came to a stop. Sitting amidst the lovely homes in the prestigious neighborhood was a house in ruins. The big, broken-down house, with overgrown trees and shrubs, was quite an eyesore. As the SUV bumped along the cracked and crumbling driveway, Melanee gawked in shock.

Nose turned up, Melanee observed the unkempt lawn that was overrun with tall weeds, overgrown trees, shrubs, and hedges. It was an eyesore—a horrible blemish to such a beautiful neighborhood. "Who lives here?" She couldn't keep the frown off of her face.

"A recent acquisition," Colden replied. "I'm getting this property for a steal. A few repairs and this baby will sell for one-point-five million…maybe more."

"Oh," she muttered, indifferent.

He cut off the engine. "Come on inside with me. I want your opinion. I was wondering if I should stick to the original, elegant but old-fashioned interior, or vamp it up with a more modern style."

Melanee couldn't have cared less. She opened her door and followed Colden, who was dangling a key ring, looking proud as if he possessed the key to a castle.

"Oh, my God!" Melanee uttered when Colden opened the door. Her eyes were wide with shock as she surveyed the squalor inside the old, crumbling house. The place was in a shambles. There was an explosion of junk, spilling out of every room. There was so much crap blocking their path that Melanee and Colden had to step over mounds of scrap to get from the foyer area to the main room. Inside the would-be living room were old computers, shoes, bent-up boxes, turned-over chairs, lamps, picture frames, old phone books…you name it and it had been dumped there.

"What happened in here?" Melanee asked in a shocked tone.

Colden chuckled. "A crazy old man used to live here. He was a hoarder. He recently died and his daughter—

a friend of mine—wanted me to take this place off of her hands, and so I bought it." He smiled. "Lucky me!" Colden added, sounding as if he really felt the property was worth having.

"It smells awful," Melanee commented, hoping Colden would quickly come to a conclusion regarding the renovations.

"Let's see what kind of shape the kitchen is in." Colden began the tedious trek to the kitchen, edging along and climbing over objects.

The only thing that was clearly visible was the ceiling; it was difficult to observe the walls or the flooring, with so much crap all the place. Trying to hurry Colden along, she offered her opinion about the smelly, rotting dwelling. "I think you should stick with the original old-fashioned elegance of this place." *This place needs a wrecking ball*, was what she was actually thinking.

"Hmm," Colden said, considering her input. "I'll think about it," he said as he weaved past heaps of rubbish.

The kitchen was a nightmare. It was filled to the gills with junk. An odor of spoiled food lingered in the air. Growing nauseous, Melanee didn't venture into the hub of the mess. As if inspired by a task that would be daunting for a fully staffed cleaning crew, Colden wedged past upside-down cabinets, microwaves, old radios, and an impossible amount of trash. The kitchen table was piled high with a hodge-podge of insanity: a rusted toaster, magazines, piles of unopened bills, grimy bottles, mildewed clothes, and dusty electric trains along with broken tracks.

Colden pulled a pair of rubber gloves from his jacket pocket and began clearing the miscellaneous items from the table and tossing them onto the floor along with the many piles of scrap and trash.

Melanee gaped at Colden as he busily cleared an area on the table.

With a sinister look in his eyes, he asked Melanee, "How would you like me to fuck you on this table?"

Her eyes flicked to the filthy table. She recoiled with undisguised disgust. *You've got to be kidding me.*

Colden stared at her. His brown eyes held a spiteful expression.

She wanted to cry; her bottom lip trembled. She felt trapped and helpless.

"Yes, Master," she replied. She was panic-stricken, but was unable to refuse him. Colden still owned her, and Madam wouldn't want a defiant submissive.

"Why are you still standing there?" A sly smile snaked across his face.

Though she tried to pull herself together, she was shaking. And her body tremors were not from revulsion.

He knew her so well. Knew how to excite her. Knew all sorts of kinky ways to bring out her submissive side.

In her haste to get close to Colden, Melanee stumbled.

He laughed. "Clumsy slut," he said with a sneer. "Get naked," he ordered her.

Shivery tingles pricked her body as she pulled the soft white sweater over her head. Holding the sweater, she absently looked around for a clear space to put her clothes.

Impatient, Colden yanked the sweater from her hand and tossed it. Melanee watched her clean sweater float and then land upon a mountain of bizarre junk. Her bra, jeans, and panties, and ankle boots joined her sweater.

Standing barefoot in the midst of the disgusting rubble, she could feel something mushy on the bottom of her feet, and seeping between her toes. Melanee didn't look down; afraid to see the mess she'd stepped into.

Colden grabbed her by her hair and yanked her closer. She winced at the shock of pain as a few strands of hair were ripped from her scalp.

Roughly, he grabbed her by the shoulders and turned her around.

"Still not plump enough," he muttered disdainfully, and then smacked the ass that wasn't up to his standards.

Melanee flinched. He peppered her ass with a flurry of slaps; smacking one cheek with his right hand, the other with his left. Over and over, he slapped her buttocks until they were enflamed.

Her pussy was soggy with need.

"Get on the table," Colden ordered, with his dick in his hand.

She hopped her sore, bare ass up on the disgusting table.

"Lie down," he growled.

She obeyed. Her back and her naked ass became adhered to the cleared portion of the kitchen table, stuck by syrup? Jelly? Something sticky. She hoped like hell that the sticky substance wasn't glue!

She soon forgot the sticky situation the moment Colden started plowing his length into her, giving her the dick of life.

CHAPTER 38

"I'll be back in an hour." Chevonne stood on her tiptoes and pressed her lips against Lincoln's. "Can you order pizza for the kids?"

"Sure. Do you want me to order vegetarian for you?" Lincoln asked.

"I'm sick of pizza. I'll pick up a wrap at Chipotle after my workout."

"Okay, baby." Lincoln watched Chevonne's ass as she crossed the large kitchen floor. She was one fine woman and he could never get tired of looking at the sway of her ass.

With her gym bag slung over her shoulder, she was out of the kitchen door. Through the window, he watched her backing her Beemer out of the driveway. His heart sank a little. Chevonne's car was a constant reminder of that crazy dickhead she'd slipped up with. But what could Lincoln do: ask her to get rid of it?

Chevonne had no idea how much Lincoln knew about Raheem. Nor did she know that her psycho ex-lover had driven his brother out of town. Lincoln felt a small amount of self-satisfaction when he thought about Raheem being cuffed by the police. There was one less menace to society, now that the kook was locked up behind bars. At least temporarily.

Disgust over the whole situation put a sour taste in Lincoln's mouth. It was still a shock that Chevonne had picked a ruthless thug to fuck around with. The dude Raheem was pure, maniacal evil.

No matter how you looked at it, cheating was cheating. The pain of betrayal would not have been any less if his wife had been getting it in with a corporate executive.

It was the seven-year itch, Lincoln surmised. All married couples hit a bump in the road at some point. Things were still tense in their marriage, but their sex life had heated up like crazy. For him and Chevonne, sex was like a powerful narcotic. Once the effects wore off, the throbbing ache was still there. There were some wounds that only time can heal.

Lincoln had faith that in time, his wife's unfaithfulness would no longer be the running theme in his mind.

He pulled the pizza menu that was held in place on the fridge with a photo magnet of Tori and Amir. Gazing at the image of his kids' smiling faces was a reminder of one of the reasons he was fighting so hard to save his marriage.

He put the pizza menu back on the fridge. Now was a good time to start putting the family's state-of-the-art kitchen to good use.

"Amir! Tori!" he yelled. He made a sound of frustration, and trotted up the stairs. They were both in Tori's room, watching TV. It was blaring sky-high.

"Turn that thing down." He picked up the remote and pressed the volume, turning it down to a normal level.

"Aw, Daddy, we can't hear it," Tori whined.

"You both are going to go deaf."

"How can the volume of TV make us go deaf?" Amir gave him a challenging look. The kid thought he knew everything; he could be a real pain in the neck.

He pressed the power button, turning the TV off.

"Why'd you turn it off, Daddy?" Tori's face was scrunched in confusion.

"Because I want both of you to come downstairs and help me cook."

"Cook?" Both children squealed in unison, frowning as if their father was speaking a foreign language.

"Mommy said we were having pizza," Amir said sullenly.

"Don't you kids get tired of eating take-out food every night?"

"No!" Amir and Tori were in complete agreement. Their eyes darted longingly toward the blank TV screen.

"I could go for a good, home-cooked meal. Tonight, we're having a real dinner. Meat, green vegetables, and a starch."

"What's a starch?" Tori turned up her nose.

Lincoln's cell vibrated in his pocket. He checked the screen and smiled when he saw Earl's name.

"Yo, Earl," he greeted his brother. "What it do, man… what's good withchu?"

The kids giggled, getting a kick out of hearing their father speaking in dialect. Lincoln winked at them. "Hold on a minute, man." He tossed Tori the remote, giving her permission to turn the TV back on.

"Amir," Lincoln said, "go downstairs and get the pizza menu. Order the large size Buffalo wings for me, and get pizza or whatever you and Tori want." He wanted to talk to his brother and it was pointless to try to change the family's routine without Chevonne's support.

"Should I order a veggie pizza for Mommy?" Amir's mood had gone from morose to jubilant now that he wouldn't have to tolerate a cooking session with his father.

"No, she's picking up something else," Lincoln said as he walked out of Tori's room. No point in twisting their arms to eat regular food for a change.

"So how's Leiperville?" he said with laughter.

"Not bad. You ain't even gonna believe this…" Since Earl's tone was cheerful, Lincoln figured it had to be good news.

"Man, I got a j-o-b!" Earl said proudly.

"You got a what?"

"Man, I'ma tax-paying citizen."

"What fool hired you?" Lincoln joked, but was feeling hopeful that his brother might have finally turned his life around. "What kind of work are you doing?"

"Transporting."

"Transporting what—drugs?"

Earl chuckled. "Nah, my girl got me a job at this rehab center where she works."

"What kind of work does she do?"

"Office job. Something in medical records. Billing and coding…or some shit, fuck if I know. I know she had to go to school for that shit—community college!"

Lincoln was impressed that Earl's new girlfriend had a job that required at least a little bit of education. So far, she'd been a positive influence on his irresponsible brother.

"I transport patients," Earl continued. "Sick people that done went through surgery. You know, like hip surgery, knee replacements—shit like that. I have to push 'em around in wheelchairs…take 'em to their physical therapy appointments and whatnot. Those sick people love me. The workers, too. Man, everybody in that joint knows my name already—they call me Philly Earl." Earl sounded tickled.

"Does the Human Resources department know that they've hired a straight fool?" Lincoln asked, grinning.

"Yo, you should see…" Earl's voice trailed off as he indulged in his favorite pastime. "You should see the picture on my name badge. My eyes is half-closed. I was high as a kite when I rolled up in there to take that ID picture."

"Please don't go to work under the influence. You've got disabled people in your crazy hands. And don't be showing out, speeding around with those patients. Be careful, you know how reckless you can be. You don't want to knock those patients into walls or anything."

"I got this, Lincoln. I know what I'm doing. You fuckin' with my buzz with this corny-ass lecture."

"So, you and the new chick are doing all right?" Lincoln asked, changing his tone and the topic.

"Yeah, man. Ivella's cool people."

Lincoln nodded. "That's good, Earl. I'm glad to hear that."

"Any word on Crowbar?" Earl asked, his tone suddenly grim.

"No, I haven't heard anything. If Michelle knew something, I'm sure she'd tell me. She's been calling me pretty regularly, asking about you."

"Don't give her any info. She don't need to know shit!" Earl growled as if Michelle had broken his heart and skipped out on him. That's how Earl was—extremely irrational. That poor woman's only crime was to love Earl. Hopefully, she'd learn to love herself before she got involved in another relationship.

"You know I wouldn't give Michelle or anyone else your new contact information."

"Cool. Just making sure. I'm not tryna mess up what I got going on with my new dip. Ivella's got it going on."

Lincoln wondered how long Earl's new romance would last.

"I don't know what happened to my mans, but I hope it wasn't too painful. If the nut bull blew him up, like he threatened, I hope Crowbar went out real quick…and whatnot."

Lincoln was at a loss for what to say next, and he was kind of relieved when he heard Earl taking a deep inhale of marijuana.

The doorbell rang. "Pizza's here, Daddy!" Tori yelled.

"Okay, Earl. I'ma holla at you later. I gotta deal with dinner and the kids."

"Aye, man. Tell those two knuckleheads that Uncle Earl said, whassup."

"Okay, Earl. And try to stay employed…at least get through the ninety-day probationary period."

Lincoln and Earl shared a laugh before hanging up, but their laughter was hollow. Both were wondering about the fate of Earl's friend, Crowbar.

"I want to talk to you about something," Lincoln said when Chevonne came home from the gym, carrying the paper brown, Chipotle bag.

"Okay," she said, looking worried.

"Nothing to be upset about."

"That's a relief," she said, giving Lincoln her disarmingly beautiful smile. She unwrapped the foil around her sandwich. "I had a hard workout. So much stress on my job." She cut the wrap in half and closed her eyes as she took a bite. "Want some?" In an intimate gesture, she offered Lincoln a bite of her sandwich.

"No, I'm good. I had Buffalo wings."

She nodded as she chewed.

"I think I'm ready."

"Ready for what?"

"Counseling."

Chevonne leaned back in surprise. "Seriously, Lincoln? You're willing to go to couples' counseling?"

"Yeah, baby. It's time. I want to get to the real cause of what happened to our marriage. I know we're doing our best to try to fix what was broken. But it's not working. All we're doing is ignoring the problem."

Chevonne winced, taking aback by Lincoln's brutal honesty.

"I don't think that trying to bury my feelings is the solution to our problem." He looked at her intently. "I can't fake it, Chevonne. What you did is still bothering me, and I've got a lot of pent-up anger." He'd unconsciously balled his hand into a fist and was tapping anxiously on the kitchen table.

"Do you want me to start looking for a therapist?"

"Would you, babe?"

"Of course." She put her sandwich down, reached across the kitchen table and softly covered his hand with hers, defusing the impending violence of his restless fist.

CHAPTER 39

Deon was working for the agency tonight. He and Solay planned to spend time together later, after he'd finished with his escort duties. He told her to expect him around eleven.

Solay was not comfortable openly discussing Deon's escort itinerary, but he thought it was important to be open and honest about his job.

She couldn't deny the nagging awareness that at this exact moment, her man was getting spruced up, slapping on after shave, so that he could look and smell good for another woman. It made her a little sick to her stomach.

She fondled the "love note" that hung from her neck, and felt a thrilling little tingle that instantly brought her out of the dark moment that had briefly held her captive.

Having been up since five in the morning, Solay got in bed and curled under the covers. A two-hour nap would have her fresh and invigorated by the time that Deon stopped by.

It's funny how the mind works. The alarm on Solay's cell was set for ten-thirty, yet her eyes sprang open at ten-fifteen. Wanting to look sexy for Deon, she didn't waste any time hopping out of bed and heading for the shower. She checked her reflection in the bathroom mirror and frowned. Sleep had done a job on her face, leaving it puffy and tired...and looking irretrievably wrinkled. Gawd, she looked as if twenty years had been added to her age. Solay stepped into the stall, expecting a brisk shower to restore her face to its normal, youthful appearance.

After a refreshing shower, she wrapped a towel around her and wiped the fog from the mirror. She studied her image, turning her face at different angles. Nothing had changed. She sucked her teeth at the betrayal in the mirror. Her eyes looked tired and her cheeks were so puffy, they looked stuffed with marsh-mallows. Shit! What the hell had she been doing—fighting in her sleep?

It was unlike Solay to obsess about her looks, but with Deon constantly telling her that she was pretty, she wanted to feel remotely worthy of his compliments.

Makeup! Though, she hardly ever wore the stuff, tonight was a good time to try to work some magic. She raced to her bedroom, retrieved her makeup bag from the top drawer, and raced back to the bathroom, where there was better lighting.

Love! It was both exciting and scary at the same time. Love had Solay completely off balance, an emotional wreck.

She had it all together by the time Deon arrived—

music, candles, and sexy lingerie. Not to mention that the makeup had worked wonders.

"Wow, look at you!" he said appreciatively. "You got all dolled up for me; what's the occasion?"

"Nothing. I missed you, baby!" Solay fell into his arms as if she hadn't seen him for years.

She nuzzled his neck and sniffed, and was jolted by the smell of a woman's perfume. She could tell that it was something expensive, but on Deon, it smelled foul—really funky. Indignant, Solay wrenched away from him.

"What's wrong?"

"I can smell a woman's perfume, Deon!"

"For real? Aw, man." Deon rubbed his neck, as if he could wipe the stench away. "My client, she…uh, she hugged me when we said good night."

"Oh, really! What kind of good night was that?"

"Nothing serious."

"Her perfume is all over you. What the hell were you two doing, dry-humping at her front door?" Solay's voice was high-pitched and furious.

"Don't be like that. Do you want me to take a shower?"

"No," she said petulantly.

"Baby, you went out of your way to set up a romantic night…" He gestured toward the glowing candles that made a path from the living room to the bedroom.

"Suddenly, I'm not feeling very romantic. And who could blame me?"

Deon took his jacket off and sat on the couch. "I don't

wanna argue with you tonight. It's late, and I have an appointment with a client at six in the morning."

Scowling, Solay sat on a chair across from him. "How do you think it makes me feel to know, you have to rush from my bed to go spend time with another woman?"

He leaned back and grimaced. "Whoa, you're over the top with this. My client is a fifty-something-year-old woman. There's no reason for you to be jealous."

"Well, I can't help it…I'm jealous!" She folded her arms and glowered at him. "Why can't that old bag take her saggy butt to the gym? Why does my man have to be her personal trainer? If you weren't hot-looking, I bet she wouldn't be paying for you to stretch her out like Bowflex."

Deon laughed. It was light and easy.

"You're laughing, but I'm serious. I don't like this shit, Deon." Solay poked her finger, stabbing at the air in an angry gesture.

Deon went silent; his mouth drawn tight in frustration.

"Don't you have anything to say?" she snapped.

"Wow! You really spazzing out over this!"

"Don't act like I'm some crazy bitch, worked up over nothing. This is hard, Deon." Solay's voice cracked; tears spilled down her face. "I thought I could deal with it, but it's a lot harder than I thought. Now you've started telling me all about your escort assignments, like that's something I really want to hear about."

He blinked in confusion. "I thought you'd appreciate

it if I kept it one hundred with you. I wouldn't have shared that information if I thought it would hurt you. That's the last thing that I want to do."

Solay sighed heavily. "I don't know, Deon." She shook her head. "Knowing what you're out there doing…it's a whole lot to handle."

"But I'm not doing anything. I swear, I'm only doing my job…being an escort. That's it!" Deon held his arms out.

"A male whore! I should know what you are; I paid for your stud service!" Solay shouted. "And being a personal trainer to middle-aged woman sounds like prostitution to me!"

There was dead silence for a few moments. Deon looked at her, bewildered, and then rubbed his forehead, his hand moving circularly. "So we're back to that same ol' shit again," he said through clenched teeth, voice low to show his restraint. "I thought we'd moved past it. I thought we were all right."

"How can we be all right? Accepting what you do for a living is awful…it's demoralizing. I want a real relationship, Deon. One that's exclusive."

"We are exclusive. I'm not seeing anybody else. I'm not making love to any other woman."

Wiping tears, Solay shook her head.

"Think of it like this…if I was making a movie, and had to do a love scene, would you consider that as cheating? If I had to do a naked love scene that required twenty takes or more…would you think of it as male prostitution?"

"But this isn't a movie. It's real life, and you're delusional if you really think you're going to have a film career. That's nothing but a pipe dream. The only way we're going to make it as a couple is if you get a real job, making a regular salary."

There, she'd said it, and Solay had no regrets. Deon had thought that cutting back his days would solve the problem, but it hadn't. The fact remained that Deon was in intimate situations with too many women. He was supposed to be hers and hers only. Sharing him with a pack of desperate cougars and other horny bitches was taking a heavy emotional toll.

"You're the only woman that I ever had sex with on the job."

Solay held up a hand. "Deon, please."

"For real. The agency said that you just wanted to stay home. My intentions were to give you an erotic massage or some kind of romantic fantasy. I was going to play it by ear, since I never had a client that wanted to stay home before."

It seemed like he was speaking from the heart, but she wasn't sure, so she kept her head down, biting her lip, stubbornly refusing to meet his gaze.

"There was this chemistry between us…instant attraction," Deon went on. "One thing led to another and we ended up in bed. Think about it, Solay."

Finally, she raised her head.

He tapped his chest. "I know what's in my heart. I could have kept it strictly business between us…but I'm not that dude. No matter what you think, I'm not a male hoe."

"I don't like behaving like this…acting jealous and resorting to name calling. It's ugly…and I apologize. All I want is the reassurance that I'm the only woman in your life. and it's hard to feel that way if you're out with another woman on your arm."

"I can dig it. I'd feel the same way, if it was the other way around." He pondered briefly. "Tell you what…let's slow down. We can fall back for a minute. That audition that I was telling you about is coming up in a few days. I'll be in on Wednesday, and I'm staying over until Thursday. If I don't get it, we can go our separate ways."

Solay cringed at the idea of them splitting up for good. She merely wanted Deon to realize she couldn't put up with him escorting or personally training women.

"I don't want this to end. You know that, but I don't like seeing you upset like this and looking so unhappy."

"So, what you're saying is…that the future of our relationship depends on an acting job?"

"Pretty much." With his fingers intertwined, Deon nodded his head. "Yeah, that's what I'm saying. You want a man with a job and a regular pay, but acting is my passion, and there are no guarantees in that profession."

If she didn't know any better, she'd think Deon was

simply crazy, thinking that he could go to New York and get an acting job just like that! She loved him, and she wanted to believe in him. But being realistic, his chances seemed slim.

Deon stood up. "It's been a long night, and I have to get up early, so I'ma bounce, baby." He walked toward the front door.

Solay was right behind him. He turned the doorknob and stood with the door cracked open. "I wanna say that I'll hit you up tomorrow, but we need some distance—some time to think and get our minds right."

Solay nodded. "Call me when you get back from New York, okay?"

"I love you, Solay. I mean it," Deon said softly.

"I love you, too."

"We'll figure something out," he said.

The women's fragrance that lingered on his clothes and on his skin put a barrier between them, and Deon didn't try to kiss Solay. Instead, he kissed two fingers and held them out to her, before he closed the door gently behind him.

CHAPTER 40

With the assistance of an army of students, two thousand cupcakes were baked, frosted and carefully packaged. The gorgeous and scrumptious cupcakes were picked up by a city employee and placed in a city-owned van, and then delivered to the venue.

Anita Blalock called Solay to thank her and to also invite her to the event. "The media is going to be in attendance, and from one sistah to another, I don't want you to miss out on a photo op."

"Oh, thank you for the invitation. And thank you for selecting Scandalicious for your event." Solay hung up and smiled. She had a big check from the city and now another blessing…possible promotion.

She'd been so busy managing the students and getting two thousand cupcakes baked, that it hadn't occurred to her until this moment, that she hadn't spoken to Deon since the night he'd left her apartment. No phone calls and no texts. She'd never gotten around to telling him about her opportunity to showcase her cupcakes at a huge charity event. She wished he could share this moment with her, but he was in New York, right now, auditioning for a part. He was obviously giving her some space to analyze their relationship.

She didn't want to attend a semi-formal occasion without a date, but what could she do? Hmm. Pretty boy Vidal would make a perfect escort.

"Are you free tonight?" she asked Vidal as she stocked the bakery case.

"Depends." He scowled as if expecting Solay to ask him to work overtime.

"I've been invited to the mural event and I need an escort. Do you have a suit?"

Vidal's eyes lit up. "Of course I have a suit—I have a collection of suits: Armani, Marc Jacobs, Gucci, Prada—"

"Great," she interrupted. "Can you meet me at the Radisson downtown at seven-thirty?"

"Okay, but can I leave early?"

"No, I need you out here working the front."

"Listen, I have to get my hair and nails done." He suddenly smoothed the silky hair of his eyebrows. "Oh, Gawd, I need my eyebrows waxed, too! I can't show up at a high-profile event looking any ole kinda way."

Solay sighed. "How early do want to leave, Vidal?"

"In order to catch my hairstylist, I'll have to be out of here…um…no later than three."

Solay sighed again…this time, long and loud. There was no getting around it. She had to give Vidal his way or got to the mural event alone. On second thought, she could call Rent-A-Man. Nah, she didn't want to come off of all that money for a hired escort. Also, calling Deon's employer didn't sit well with Solay—she'd feel like she was cheating on Deon. Vidal was the perfect escort. He would enjoy the black-tie affair. Mingling with artists and ritzy corporate people would be right up his alley. He'd also take pleasure in seeing those two-thousand Scandalicious cupcakes that he helped create, prominently displayed.

While most women planned and shopped and took forever to prepare for an important event, Solay had always been low-maintenance. She wore minimal make-up, her hair was styled in a basic wrap, and she maintained her own nails, filing them neatly and applying one coat of clear polish. Tonight she wore a basic black dress, understated jewelry, sensible heels, and a black clutch. Though the end result looked spectacular, it actually took less than an hour for Solay to pull her look together.

With their arms linked, Solay and Vidal entered the grand ballroom of the Radisson. With his long hair flat-ironed to silky perfection, Vidal was catching the eye of both women and men, and he reveled in all the attention.

The well-heeled guests mingled and gazed at the art-work that was hung, but the real show-stopper was the cupcake display. A gigantic Plexiglas case that was shaped like the Liberty Bell dominated the ballroom.

In awe, Solay and Vidal approached the cupcake exhibit. "This is amazing," Solay murmured.

"Our cupcakes look like little works of art," Vidal commented as he gazed at the array of colorful cupcakes. "Let's get some pictures before the vultures swoop down on our edible art."

Alongside Vidal were professional photographers, snapping away. Dressed casually, the photographers stood out from the black-tie crowd.

"Are y'all from *The Philadelphia Inquirer*?" nosey Vidal asked.

"I'm with *Philadelphia Magazine*," said a man wearing Dockers and a T-shirt and had an awful, scraggly red-gold beard.

"We baked all those cupcakes," Vidal said proudly, motioning to himself and Solay.

"Oh, are you the owners of Scandalicious?" the bearded man wanted to know.

"I am. My name is Solay Dandridge." Solay stepped forward and extended her hand.

"Jack Grover…*Philadelphia Magazine*. I'd like to get a picture of you with the display if you don't mind."

"I don't mind at all," Solay said, smiling broadly.

"Umph, just knock me out of the way. I guess you don't need me to baby-sit you any longer," Vidal said huffily. "I might as well go mingle." He skulked off, mumbling discontentedly.

As Solay posed, the photographer asked a million questions about Scandalicious. "Maybe we can do a separate story featuring your shop in our Christmas issue." He gave her his card and merged into the crowd.

Now Solay needed a drink to steady her nerves. One amazing thing after another had been happening for her. She couldn't believe her good fortune. Taking a risk, along with hard work, was really starting to pay off.

After ordering a martini, she caught up with Vidal on the other side of the huge ballroom. He was sipping from a martini glass that was filled with a blue concoction. He seemed to be engrossed in a conversation with an artsy-looking guy. Though he had on a suit and tie, the young man Vidal was talking with was wearing a pair of sneakers. His long locks were tied in two ponytails. *Interesting.*

"Excuse me, can I speak to you for a moment, Vidal." Vidal frowned, aggravated by the interruption.

"He'll be right back," Solay assured the man wearing sneakers as she pulled Vidal away.

In private, she told Vidal everything about the possible magazine feature. "Vidal, can you believe it? Can my life get any better?" She realized that she sounded full of herself, but she was too over the top with happiness to tone it down.

"Your life may not get any better, but it looks like somebody just got upgraded." Vidal nodded his head toward the right. When Solay looked in that direction, she gasped in surprise and nearly choked on her martini. She stared across the room in silent horror for a few moments, refusing to believe her own eyes. Among the illustrious guests was Deon, handsomely dressed in a black suit and tie.

"Mmm, look at your man. He's wearing the hell out of that suit. I like his swag," Vidal murmured.

As if Deon's presence wasn't shocking enough, hanging on his arm was a black goddess—a forty-ish woman with a complexion so flawless it looked like dark silk. She was stunning and every eye was on her. Her hair was in an elegantly twisted bun and surrounded with dazzling jewels. She was blinging like crazy with diamonds sparkling around her neck, her wrists, and her fingers. A black lace, curve-hugging gown with a short train was the show-stopping dress of the evening. She had a long and graceful neck, long arms and legs for days. And the fluidity of her movements gave her the presence of a prima ballerina. *Black swan bitch!*

Solay felt utter and passionate hatred for the elegant vixen. Deon had delivered a sucker punch to the gut that was staggering.

"There's something so appealing about a thug in a suit." Vidal was being extremely mean-spirited, going for the jugular. "That diva that's hanging on to him is dripping in diamonds. She must be loaded; I wonder who she is." With his chin resting upon his palm, Vidal stared at the mystery woman.

"I don't know who she is, Vidal. But it really doesn't matter. Deon and I are not exclusive. We both see other people," Solay said as calmly as she could, trying to hold on to her last shred of dignity. Pretending to be disinterested, she stared into her drink, putting a lot of effort into stirring it with its cute little stick.

"I didn't know you were seeing other guys, Solay. They must be imaginary friends," Vidal said with a taunting chuckle. He was paying her back for pushing him out of the picture at the Liberty Bell display, she presumed. *Touché!*

Though she made a great effort to not look in Deon's direction, Solay caught another glimpse of him and his date. The bejeweled diva and Deon were deep in conversation. When Deon bent and whispered something in her ear, the woman touched his face in a very intimate manner. Solay felt her heart rate speed up when she noticed Deon slide his hand around the woman's waist. She felt faint. Sick to her stomach. It was too much to bear; her heart couldn't take any more.

Vidal noticed her miserable expression, and mercifully let up on the cutting remarks. "You should get in his face and cuss him out. Go make a scene, girl. Embarrass his cheating ass. Believe me, you'll feel much better."

Solay shook her head. "I'm okay," she said weakly.

"Do you want me to go stroll over there and accidentally spill my drink on Miss Thang's beautiful dress? Just say the word, girl."

"No, I don't want any trouble." After the adrenaline rush of baking and decorating so many cupcakes, Solay suddenly felt worn out.

There were so many people in the room, Deon hadn't yet noticed Solay. Solay stared at Deon from the other side of the crowded room. It hurt her to the core to see him being so attentive to another woman.

All the air seemed to have left the ballroom. It was absolutely suffocating, and she had to get out of there. "I don't feel good," she moaned. Frowning, she flattened her hand against her stomach.

"Well, turn your head; don't vomit on my Armani suit." Grimacing, Vidal took several steps backward.

"If you feel like you're gonna get sick, you should make a trip to the ladies room, Solay. I know you don't want the photographer getting a shot of you retching your guts out." Vidal turned up the corner of his lip. "That's not a good look. Real bad for business." Vidal wasn't being mean; he was being brutally honest.

She ducked out of the ballroom, but instead of going to the ladies room, she retrieved her wrap from the coat check, got on the elevator, and rode it down to the hotel lobby. Outside, she pulled the shawl around her shoulders as if to warm herself from the cold, cruel world. She was so choked up, she could barely get the words out to let the doorman know that she needed a cab. It was bad enough that she had been subjected to Deon's infidelity, but Vidal witnessing her humiliation made it feel ten times worse.

Why would he lie to me? I accepted what he does for a living. I've been really understanding. I don't like the way that he earns his money, but I sucked it up. I dealt with it. After all my kindness and consideration, Deon still couldn't be honest. He pretended that he was auditioning in New York—why'd he have to lie to me?

Solay wondered if the whole acting story was nothing more than a ruse—a made-up story to justify being a male hoe. Anger, jealousy, and suspiciousness invaded Solay's mental state. Deon seemed awfully comfortable with that black swan woman, grinning at her like they had a special relationship.

Like Solay, his date tonight had probably started out as a client, until Deon decided to take it to another level. What kind of sick game was he playing?

Relationships! No matter how hard a woman tried to guard her heart…no matter how many concessions she made to keep things running smoothly, a man could never be satisfied. Those bastards always ended up doing something foul. Solay should have never fallen for Deon's lines. She should have kept her options open and continued renting dick.

She texted Vidal, telling him that she'd left the hotel and was on her way home.

Distraught, she couldn't hold back the tears. Sitting in the backseat of the cab, Solay started sniffling. The cab driver cleared his throat. "You okay, ma'am?"

"I'm fine," she wailed, though she was clearly suffering.

"If you say so." The driver fixed his eyes on traffic while Solay gave into a storm of sobbing.

CHAPTER 41

S olay cried as she paid the cab fare. Blinded by tears, she stared unseeingly inside her purse, and then wiped her eyes as she searched for her keys. She kicked off her heels and changed from evening wear into pajamas, sobbing inconsolably. Once the deluge of tears had finally passed, Solay was left feeling beaten down.

Out of sheer weariness, she fell asleep immediately after dropping into bed. The quiet buzz of her cell seemed as loud as a chainsaw, startling her awake. Rubbing an eye that was puffy from crying and blurry with sleep, she picked up the phone with her free hand and squinted at the screen. The text was from Deon.

I'm sorry, baby. I can explain. Can we talk? The message was followed with a heart emoticon.

Hell, no, you can't talk to me, you fucking liar! No one had the right to make her feel this kind of misery. No one! She banged the phone down harder than she'd meant to and quickly picked it up, making sure she hadn't broken the screen.

Playtime was over. No more men interfering with her life.

Vidal and Melanee could talk behind her back; they could call her a cranky, sex-starved bitch. She didn't care what names they called her. One thing was for sure, love was for suckers and Solay was tired of repeating the same old part.

Over and over, she'd been made to regret having handed her heart to someone that stomped all over it. Men always wanted you to listen to their excuses after they did their dirt. *Why?* So they could squirm their way back into your life and finish demolishing your heart! She'd had enough. Men were sick puppies and she was even sicker for thinking that there might be one decent man in the bunch.

Telling me he had an audition. Pretending to be an actor. Hmph! Actor my ass! The only acting that Deon had done was in her bedroom, putting on great performances between the sheets—pretending that he really cared. *Why hadn't he simply let her remain a paying client? I didn't ask him to get into a relationship—he came at me!*

If she hadn't willed herself to be strong, Solay would have given in to another crying jag. But she refused. Resolute, she pulled the covers up to her shoulders. Deon had broken her heart. She didn't want to hear any more of his lies. End of story.

Solay and Melanee had been hard at work for a couple of hours when Vidal burst into the kitchen door, holding a steaming Styrofoam cup of coffee. He set the cup on a metal table and untied the designer scarf that was draped around his neck.

"News flash: I got the dirt on Deon's sugah mama!"

Solay rolled her eyes and sighed. "You can keep that information to yourself. I'm not interested." She cut an eye at Melanee, and was grateful that her assistant seemed to be absorbed in mixing ingredients, paying no attention to Vidal's news report.

"You're gonna want to hear this…" He smacked his lips and twisted his neck for dramatic effect.

"No, I don't." Solay shook her head vehemently, but Vidal chose to ignore her.

"The diva is a married woman," he exclaimed.

"I don't care!" Solay was livid. She didn't want to hear anything about that bejeweled, ballerina bitch! Vidal didn't have an ounce of decency. He knew that her heart was broken. Instead of coming in with drama, first thing in the morning, he should have had some consideration and allowed Solay to grieve in peace…in private.

"Girl, listen. She's married to one of her servants— her butler! But she didn't upgrade dude. He's still the damn butler. He wears a uniform…gloves…the whole shebang! And word is, he doesn't even call her by her first name. The butler calls his own wife, *Madam!*"

Taking a sudden interest in the conversation, Melanee stopped stirring and gazed at Vidal, her eyes wide with curiosity.

Solay glowered at Vidal. *Come on, Vidal. Damn, what's*

wrong with you? This is not cool, running your big mouth all crazy. Any fool knows that a woman who's been publicly humiliated wouldn't want to openly discuss it the very next day. Why are you putting me on blast? She glared even harder at Vidal, trying to make him read her mind, but he deliberately ignored the signals she was sending.

"Ya boy deserves a big congratulations. He came up! Last night, Deon was arm candy for one of the richest black women in the Philadelphia area. Her name is Quintouria Stevens. She owns all kinds of shit: weave bars, real estate, a limo service, and a modeling agency." He shook his bouncy hair. "I should take some headshots and send them to her agency," Vidal said thoughtfully. "I'd make a fabulous model." He began strutting through the kitchen, walking like Naomi Campbell.

Solay was sickened by Vidal's lack of sensitivity. She had no idea how he'd acquired so much information, nor did she want to know. She envisioned herself choking the black swan's neck as she squeezed the piping bag, angrily frosting row after row of chocolate cupcakes.

"I don't have time to listen to gossip, Vidal. I have a business to run. Start packaging the office party order."

"What office party?" Vidal's expression turned sour, as if earning his salary was completely beneath him.

"A company called Clemmons and Associates. I think it's an architectural firm. They're sending someone over to pick up the order at eleven. Three dozen. It's a mixed order—equal amounts of chocolate, red velvet and vanilla.

I need you to get those cupcakes boxed up before the morning rush starts."

Vidal picked up his coffee cup. "You're a trip, Solay. Would it kill you to let me get a couple sips of coffee into my system before you start barking out orders?" Driven out of the kitchen with the threat of work, Vidal sashayed to the front counter to drink his morning coffee, undisturbed.

Solay was glad to be rid of him and his big mouth.

"What was Vidal talking about?" Melanee softly inquired.

Nooo, not you, Melanee! Solay screamed to herself. *Does anyone around here mind their own business?* Melanee hadn't expressed any interests beyond her own weird little world in a long time. She and Vidal used to be really tight—at least while on the job, but Melanee had a secret lifestyle; she kept to herself now. When Melanee had offered to get Solay student workers, she'd spoken more words than Solay had heard from her in months. When Melanee wasn't baking, she was sending text messages to her secret lover—her mystery Master.

Though Solay suspected that Melanee was into some weird sado-masochistic scene, she hadn't questioned Melanee. Melanee was an adult, free to live her life any way she chose.

And that's what really irked Solay. For someone who was as guarded about her own personal life as Melanee, she sure had a lot of gall trying to get all up in Solay's private business.

"Deon and I broke up," Solay reluctantly admitted, and then released a sigh.

"Really? You broke up last night…at the mural event? What happened? Did you two have a big fight?" Melanee peered at Solay, eager for information.

What's up with this chick? Why is she probing me for details? "It's a sensitive subject. I really don't want to talk about it. Um…to be honest, I don't even want to hear his name. I hope you can respect that."

"Okay." Melanee gave a disinterested shrug, but her gleaming eyes told a different story.

Solay left the kitchen, deciding to have a talk with Vidal.

Vidal was sitting on a stool, drinking coffee. "I'm gonna box up that order in a minute!" he said sharply when he heard Solay approaching from behind.

She stood next to him. "I want to talk to you about Deon."

He turned and faced her. "The mayor came through and he introduced the rich chick as a major contributor. While she was giving a speech about the importance of murals in the inner city, I sidled up to Deon and let him know that you were in the house. At that point, I hadn't realized that you'd dipped out. Anyway, he wasn't surprised since the cupcake display featured the Scandalicious logo."

"How did he act…what did he say?" Solay hated herself for wanting to know.

"He asked me where you were. We searched the crowd for a few minutes and then I noticed your text, and I told him that you were so upset that you bounced."

"I actually came out here to ask you a favor."

"You need me to escort you to another event?" Vidal was all smiles.

"No, not any time soon. But I really appreciate your support last night. I'm sorry for hogging all the attention at the display."

Vidal twisted his lips at the memory. "That's okay. I wasn't tryna steal your shine."

"Anyway, this break-up with Deon isn't easy. So would you kindly stop mentioning his name?"

"Okaaay. My bad." There was annoyance in Vidal's tone.

"And don't talk about that rich woman, either. Please, Vidal. I'm in a lot of pain."

"Solay, I know you're my boss and everything, but you out of pocket, trying to tell me what I can and cannot talk about."

"As a friend, Vidal. Please."

"Oh, all right," Vidal conceded. "I suppose I can respect that." He picked up the coffee container, and finished off his morning brew.

CHAPTER 42

A surprise blow job from Chevonne was a special thanks now that Lincoln had agreed to go to marriage counseling. His wife had turned up the heat several notches in their sex life. She didn't stiffen at his touch anymore. In fact, she often initiated sex. Feeling desired by his spouse was a good feeling. This morning, after swallowing every drop of his passion, Chevonne kissed and whispered that she cherished his love.

Lincoln was on top of the world and nothing could dampen his spirit. Not even being sent on a cupcake run with the new kid, Amber. Having a happy home life made being treated like a damn gopher—like he was some kind of a chump—almost bearable. The office party idea was Amber's idea. She had complained to the boss that the vibe at the firm was tense. She thought the place could use a dose of cheerfulness, and suggested an impromptu lunchtime meet-and-greet, to give the old staffers an opportunity to get to know the new employees.

The young newcomers had a cockiness that was hard to stomach. Fat chance that a meet-and-greet office luncheon would warm the hearts of the embittered remaining staff.

The boss went along with Amber's silly idea, and that surprised Lincoln. After all, Frank's actions were the reason for the discontent—replacing experienced professionals with obnoxious, wet-behind-the-ear kids.

A real family man, Frank had been happily married for over ten years, and had three sons that he bragged about constantly. If Lincoln didn't know better, he'd swear that the boss was smashing Amber.

In truth, he liked being inside the cupcake joint. He slid into the same cushy seat that he'd sat in the last time he was here. While Amber transacted business with the young gay man at the counter, Lincoln took in the surroundings. He felt a giddy sense of excitement, like a schoolboy who had snuck into a whore's boudoir. The place screamed naughtiness. Being that sex sells, the concept was a great idea. Maybe he was in the wrong profession. He chuckled to himself.

While he was enjoying the atmosphere, he noticed Amber peeking inside the shiny red boxes.

"This is not McDonald's drive-thru. You don't have to check behind me; your order is perfect. I packed it myself." The gay guy's slim body jerked in irritation. He rolled his eyes at Amber as she continued to inspect the contents.

"I asked for sprinkles to be added on all the Vanilla Kiss cupcakes."

"I ain't get that memo! You musta wrote it in invisible ink!"

Laughter erupted from the waiting customers as well as those that were seated in the dining area. The young man was very entertaining.

"I know what I ordered…can I speak to the manager," Amber whined.

"Solaaay!" the fellow with the long hair yelled. He rolled his eyes at Amber. "Who's next?"

A nice-looking woman immediately emerged from the kitchen, wiping her hands on her apron. Lincoln smiled with recognition. She was the owner. She'd introduced herself and forced a cupcake on him during his last visit.

"What's going on?" the owner asked, her forehead creased with concern.

"She claims she asked you to put sprinkles on the Vanilla Kiss order. She must have imagined that crap. I told her we don't mess up orders here at Scandalicious!"

"Okay, Vidal. That's enough." The owner turned her attention on Amber. "I'm really sorry for the mix-up. I'll take care of it right now." She picked up the red box and disappeared into the back area.

Five minutes later, she returned with the red box and another smaller box on top of it. "I gave you an extra half-dozen of Vanilla Kiss."

"Ooo, thanks," Amber squealed. "That's really kind of you."

Lincoln met up with Amber at the counter. He stacked the boxes and said hello to the owner.

"We meet again," the bakery owner said, remembering Lincoln. "It appears that you've developed a sweet tooth, after all. My secret ingredients can be addictive."

He laughed. "No, I'm the muscle. Only here for pick-up. But you do have a cult following. Our coworkers weren't interested in spending lunch together until Amber here, mentioned Scandalicious cupcakes were on the menu."

"Aw, thank you," the owner said sincerely. "Take a card. Take several cards and give them to your coworkers.

Lincoln's hands were occupied with the three red boxes. Holding only the smaller box, Amber took the business cards.

After the three larger boxes were secured on the floor of the backseat of his car, Lincoln maneuvered out of the tight parking spot. "Nice lady at the cupcake shop," he murmured absently.

"That trick always works," Amber responded, running her fingers over the top of the box.

"What trick?"

"Complaining about stuff gets you freebies. I call and complain about products that I use all the time. Like shampoo, my favorite frozen dinner, even toilet paper. Manufacturers will send you a ton of coupons."

He waited for her to explain. When she didn't, he said, "And? What are you trying to say?"

"They didn't mess up the cupcake order. I just said

that—and look!" She proudly held up the glossy red box. "But these extras are for me; I'm not sharing them."

Lincoln gave Amber a sidelong glance. She was a pretty young woman—a little too chatty for his taste, but he'd considered her to be normal. Now he knew better. Amber was a nutjob. A petty thief and a liar. He was of a mind to give her a stern lecture, but changed his mind. She wasn't his goddamned daughter, so fuck it! He hoped for the boss's sake that he wasn't screwing around with Amber. But then again, after the way the boss had screwed over his staff, having a twisted little crook like Amber in his life was exactly what he deserved.

Lincoln decided that he'd go back to Scandalicious after work and pay for those stolen cupcakes. He felt responsible for bringing a con artist into that hard-working, young woman's shop.

He shot another glance at Amber. She was looking out of the window, a half-smile on her lips, obviously very pleased with the trophy on her lap. He peered at her warily and made a mental note to keep his desk locked. His favorite pen had gone missing a couple of days ago. Last week his stapler with the wood grain design grew legs and walked away. Now he wondered if Amber was the culprit. He picked up speed, anxious to get her out of his car.

Rachel had to handle the phones during the lunch-time get-together. Being a gentleman, Lincoln brought a plastic plate piled with wing dings, potato salad and a soft roll to the reception desk.

"Wow, thanks, Lincoln. I would have made my own plate, but Amber hasn't shown up to relieve me. She told me she had to set out the cupcakes...what's she doing; baking them?"

"She and Frank were talking the last time I saw her."

"I'm keeping my eye on that one. She has the boss wrapped around her finger. This little shindig was her idea, you know."

"Yeah. Bridging the gap between the old staff and the newcomers." Lincoln gave a sardonic chuckle. "Oh, I forgot to bring you something to drink. What would you like; Coke or Sprite?"

"Diet Coke." Rachel beamed. "There aren't many more gentlemen like you. At least not here at Clemmons and Associates. Your type is a dying breed. Those dot-com-era kids are taking over this firm. The boss says they're going to bring cutting-edge architectural designs to the firm. Hmph. Those young bozos don't even have decent manners. They're all disrespectful and really rude," Rachel said bitterly and then bit into a wing ding.

Lincoln took the stairs to the top floor of the three-story office building and quickly returned with the Diet Coke and two cupcakes on a festive-colored paper plate.

"Oh, how pretty," she said, smiling as she accepted the cupcakes. Two seconds later, she was scowling. "Young people and this cupcake craze is really something. There's really nothing new under the sun, you know. My grandmother made cupcakes all the time; it was no big deal. Now with all these fancy flavors, people treat them like they're a novelty."

He nodded, intent on Rachel's face, wondering if he should warn her that Amber was a thief. No, he'd keep that information to himself. Rachel gossiped too much and the last thing he needed was to be accused of spreading malicious office gossip. Rachel would discover in due time that there was a thief among them.

Trying to park on South Street during rush hour was ridiculous. Lincoln circled the block five or six times before giving up on finding a spot. Exasperated, he pulled into a lot. His brows shot up in disbelief. *Sixteen dollars for the first half-hour!* It was highway robbery, but he didn't have a choice. He'd have to pay for those cupcakes in a hurry and then hustle back to his car before the half-hour lapsed.

It ate away at him that Chevonne had to cover more than her share of the household expenses; money was too tight for him to be throwing it away on parking.

Standing outside of the business premises, Lincoln took a moment to absorb the colorful Scandalicious sign that was positioned above the door. *Nice.* The owner was about her business, and he admired her drive.

There was a different vibe inside the bakery with the after-work crowd. Though all the seats were taken, and while there was a cluster of people waiting to be served at the counter, the pulse of the bakery had slowed down. The atmosphere had changed from frenzied to peaceful. Lincoln noticed that the clientele were all from different walks of life. It surprised him to see three mature businessmen grouped around one of the Parisian-styled tables.

The owner, Solay, was taking the orders, and that might have accounted for the calm that permeated. Mr. Fancy Pants—the gay dude—exuded a lot of frenetic energy. Lincoln wasn't a homophobe…or at least he didn't think he was. But he did have strong opinions about a man wearing female hairstyles, man-scara, and lip gloss and gesturing in an expansive, feminine way. That kind of behavior seemed rather "extra."

Lincoln got in line, hoping it would move swiftly. He didn't want to spend a fortune on parking while doing a good deed and paying for the cupcakes that his psycho coworker had swindled from the bakery.

When he reached the front of the line, Solay smiled. "Oh, it's you again! Well, hello. I guess you're a converted cupcake lover, now."

"No, I'm still a French fries and cheese curls type of guy." He cracked a smile as he pulled his wallet from his pocket. "I wanted to pay for those extra cupcakes that you gave my coworker."

"Don't be ridiculous. Those were on the house." She waved her hand dismissively.

"My, uh…my coworker made a mistake," he stammered, uncomfortable with the wording. What his coworker had actually done was lied and cheated this industrious young woman simply for fun. "You didn't mess up the order. She realized when we got back to the office that she hadn't asked for any sprinkles." He felt ridiculous talking about sprinkles and it was rather silly to go out of his way to pay for some extra cupcakes. But it was a matter of principle. He was like that—a stand-up guy.

"Aw, I'm touched that you went to so much trouble. But I can't accept your money. We all make mistakes sometimes. I had extras, anyway. It was no big deal. Seriously."

"Are you sure?"

"Absolutely." She smiled, but her eyes were sad. Lincoln wondered why.

"Everyone at work raved about the cupcakes, so while I'm here let me grab a half-dozen."

Solay arched a brow.

"Not for me! Since I'm here, I might as well pick up dessert for my kids," he added with laughter.

She laughed with him, but there was something wrong. Behind her smile was pain. Raw pain was apparent in her eyes. But it wasn't any of his business, and so he paid for the cupcakes, gave a hand wave and left.

Having squared away business with Solay, his conscience was clear. Checking his watch, Lincoln walked briskly, eager to get his car out of the expensive garage.

CHAPTER 43

"It looks like the deal isn't going to go through," Colden told Melanee.

"What deal?" Melanee asked, feeling slightly nervous.

"The deal with Madam."

"Oh." Melanee's breath caught in her chest.

"She's a fickle person. She's going to be traveling back and forth to Toronto. She said that she doesn't have the time to train you."

"I see," Melanee said, with a tiny smile.

"Madam Midnight has her hands in everything. Her latest interest is the film industry."

"Is Madam starting an acting career?"

"No. She's producing movies. But it's just a phase. Like everything else, she'll grow bored with the film industry. Residential and commercial real estate is her real bread and butter. Every-thing else is just a hobby."

Though she'd pretended that she didn't really want to go to Madam, she suspected that Colden had known all along that she was infatuated with the enigmatic woman. Madam mesmerized everyone, which was why she had a revolving door of willing submissives.

Melanee could tell that Colden had been secretly jealous of her infatuation with Madam. That jealousy had prompted him to become a more attentive master.

Melanee was relieved that she had rediscovered her fierce desire for Colden before she went traipsing off to Madam's house. What would she have done if she'd lost her precious master? The night that he'd decorated her ass with his hand prints, had been a turning point in their relationship, bringing them closer together—making them both realize they were perfect for each other.

"With Madam out of the picture, there's no reason for us to be apart."

Melanee's heartbeat picked up. "There isn't?"

"No, I think you've learned your lesson. Do you think that you can be obedient around the clock?"

"Yes, Master!"

"Pack your things; you're coming back home tonight."

"Thank you, Master!" Melanee shouted. Her mind was spinning with delightful visions of being spanked, leashed and collared, and tied up for hours.

It was a half-hour until closing. Both Melanee and Vidal had already gone for the day. Behind the counter, Solay observed the customers that were seated throughout the dining area. Couples. Groups of friends. Coworkers unwinding after an eight-hour day. The harmonic tones of the intermingled conversations reverberated around the room. Pleasant chatter, and scatters of easy laughter from happy people, seemingly without a care.

Solay envied her customers' peace of mind—their satisfaction with their lives. Her life was shit. Love was the worst thing that could happen to a woman. Love was disruptive, all consuming, destined to end in heartache.

Deon and that woman. He'd been lying to her all along. On the verge of tears, she was jolted back to her professional demeanor when a patron approached the counter. "Two Red Hot Passions," a pretty blonde-haired woman requested.

"To go?" Solay asked hopefully. She was ready to close up shop, and acquiesce to another round of self-pity and mournful sobbing.

"No, they're for here. The vibe here is amazing."

"Oh, thank you." Solay forced a painful smile as she placed the cupcakes on two small, red paper plates.

"I'm on a blind date—an Internet hook-up," the woman added, nodding over to her table where another female sat. "I have to tell you, the ambience is terrific—sensual and kinky…I love it."

Solay was surprised to see that the blind date was a woman. She found it particularly curious that the date was also thin, blonde, and pretty—a darker blonde version of the woman at the counter. And judging from her dreamy expression, she was pleased with the hookup, too.

What was going on in the dating world? Women were hooking up with women who bore a close resemblance to themselves. Was it so hard to make a heterosexual relationship work that women were turning to their virtual clones for intimacy?

The last few customers left at six-thirty—a half-hour before closing. It had been a long day; Solay wasn't in the emotional shape to exchange pleasantries with any more patrons. She put the "closed" sign in the window and began straightening up.

She wiped off the tables in the dining room, holding back tears as she rushed through the task. She'd been coping with an aching heart all day, masking her pain as best she could as she interacted with patrons and staff. Now she yearned to mourn in private. In the solitude of her little apartment, she could freely shed a rivulet of tears.

Before turning off the lights, and going upstairs, she checked the kitchen, making sure that it was in pristine, clean condition. She heard the bell jingle, and sucked her teeth. *Pests!* she said to herself, picking up on Vidal's expression. Despite the "closed" sign in the window, someone was trying the doorknob, causing the overhead bell to jingle a refrain. Her first thought was to hide out in the kitchen until the pesky customer went away.

But the bell sounded again. Solay sighed, and stalked out of the kitchen, hoping she could keep a civil tone when she turned the customer away.

Her heart dropped. It wasn't a cupcake-craving patron on the other side of the glass door. Deon was peering into Scandalicious, radiating warmth, love, and a heavy dose of sensuality.

CHAPTER 44

Deon was holding his motorcycle helmet in his hands, wearing a black leather jacket and black leather driving gloves. It was a damn disgrace that one man could possess all the traits that Deon had going on. A hot body, succulent lips, gorgeous face, and he made love like a porn star.

She unlocked and yanked the door open. "Why are you here?" she said coldly.

"We need to talk." He reached for her hand; she snatched it back as if scorched.

"There's nothing to say," she hissed.

"I know how it must have looked…but can I explain?"

"No," she said exasperated. "I'm tired of all your convenient excuses. Go away, Deon. Go be with your wealthy socialite; I don't care anymore." She turned away and headed for the kitchen.

"Baby, baby, baby…" He rushed behind her, following her through the set of swinging kitchen doors. "Hear me out. For one minute! That's all I'm asking."

She kept walking until she reached the sink. Not knowing what else to do, she picked up a sponge, deciding to wipe the metal tables that were already sparkling clean.

With her back turned to Deon, Solay spoke. "I don't... want to hear...any more...of your bullshit," she said, her words separated by gasps, sniffles, and little whimpers.

He came up behind her, gently touched her shoulder, coaxing her to turn around.

It was the tenderness of his touch that caused her to completely lose her composure. She sucked in a huge backdraft of air, filling her lungs and swelling her chest, followed by an anguished wail.

Holding her, caressing her, comforting her as her body caved into his, Deon was wracked by her raw, gut-wrenching, uncontrollable sobs.

Deon murmured in her ear. "Let it out, baby. I'm so sorry. Go ahead, cry. I gotchu. I swear I never meant to hurt you."

Finally, Solay calmed down enough to form coherent speech. "Why did you lie and tell me you had an audition in New York?"

"I did, and I got the part!"

"I don't understand. You said you'd call me if you got the part, but instead, you went out with a client."

"She wasn't a client, Solay. Her name is Quintouria Stevens. She's one of the executive producers of the film. Instead of staying in New York and auditioning for the commercial, my agent wanted me to come back to Philly and go to that charity event with the three producers. It's called schmoozing, babe. That's all I was doing."

Solay let out a long sigh. "I'm really happy for you, Deon. Congratulations."

"Thanks. And what's up with you—showcasing your cupcakes at that event? What was that—top secret? Why'd you keep something like big from me?"

"It wasn't intentional. I was busy trying to make it happen, and I never got around to telling you."

"That makes sense."

"So where do we go from here, Deon? Is this relationship permanently damaged? Do you think there's a future with us?"

"I hope so. But I have to tell you something." There was a sad look in his eyes.

"What?"

"We start shooting soon. I'm leaving for Toronto tomorrow, and I'll be there for the next three months."

"Three months in Toronto!" Her hand pressed against her mouth. Her eyes were wide with startled hurt.

"We have to do the long distance thing. Ninety days—that's not so long," Deon soothed.

Solay nodded, hoping that Deon was right. It was ironic that they were back together but also had to say goodbye. "What time is your flight?"

"Tomorrow at two."

So soon? Anxiety clawed at her. "Do you want to come upstairs?" she asked nervously.

Deon answered with a smile.

Reunited in the bedroom, they tore at each other's clothes. Panting…growling…perspiring. Naked, they fucked like animals. Standing up against the bedroom door, seated in a chair, doggy-style on the floor.

On the bed now, their bodies crashed and collided, almost brutally. Duel emotions fueled their passion…a combination of welcome-back sex and a farewell fuck at the same time.

When Deon finally pulled himself out of Solay's silken clutch, he exhaled. "Damn, that shit was off the chain!"

Breathing hard, still trying to catch her breath, Solay nodded in agreement. When she found her voice and said, "Oh, Deon. I miss you already," he didn't respond. Knocked out cold, Deon was snoring.

Could a long distance romance really survive? Troubled, she stared at his sleeping face, searching for an answer. While Deon slept, Solay studied his image as if she were trying to memorize every beautiful detail. She stared at his body…his hard, broad chest, and the outrageous breadth of his shoulders. With the tip of her finger, she traced the Asian letters of the tattoo that draped the thick, right shoulder. Voyaging downward, her eyes settled on his dick, which was tempting and desirable, even while limp. It was a tremendous effort not to kiss and suck it.

Settling for snuggling, she stretched an arm across his chest, wishing that her arm was a lock that could keep Deon next to her forever. *You're acting clingy and weak*, said a scolding inner voice. But in the throes of separation anxiety, Solay couldn't control her feelings of desperation.

She rubbed the slightly raised letters of Deon's tattoo, comforted by the feeling, until she slipped into an uneasy dream.

Deon's ring tone was loud, awaking Solay early in the wee hours of the morning. He sounded groggy when he answered but he quickly became alert; his voice vibrating in excitement.

Propping himself up, Deon lay on his side with his phone pressed to his ear. "They're changing the script—giving me a bigger part? Yo, man. That's what's up. Good lookin'!" Shaking his head as if in disbelief, Deon chuckled. "Man, you working overtime for that twenty percent!" He erupted in joyful laughter.

Feeling suddenly and completely alone, Solay caressed his back, and eased her hand up to his broad and muscular shoulders.

"It's my agent," he whispered with pride.

The smile she returned was sad and knowing. Something had changed between her and Deon; she'd felt it last night. Their lovemaking was passionate, but something had been missing. The connection last night had been purely physical…their emotional bond had weakened, seemingly beyond repair.

Though Deon was still in bed with her, Solay had a sorrowful feeling that he had already gone.

CHAPTER 45

"Did one of your friends recommend the therapist?" Lincoln asked Chevonne as he cruised along Ivy Hill Road.

"No, I found Dr. Lerner online. She's a certified marriage counselor; licensed in three states. "

"Three states? Wow! I guess she really knows her stuff," Lincoln said sarcastically.

"You promised you'd go into this with an open mind."

"I am. Can't you take a joke? Stop being so sensitive."

Dr. Lerner's office was nestled on a small, quaint street in Chestnut Hill, a prominent section of Philadelphia. Her Colonial-style home doubled as her office.

Lincoln knew immediately, after entering the mosaic-tiled foyer, that the therapist was a little eccentric.

Dr. Lerner met them at the door. She wore her brown hair in spiraled curls that were gray at the roots and blonde on the tips. She was dressed in an oversized, paisley-print smock that was so ill-fitting, it hung off her shoulder, revealing a beige bra strap.

She ushered them to a lime-colored office that was decorated with peaceful floral paintings intermingled with striking Picasso prints. Framed degrees and inspirational quotes were also hung on the wall.

"Have a seat, Mr. and Mrs. Jennings." Dr. Lerner offered, motioning for Lincoln and Chevonne to take a seat on a purple sofa that didn't match anything in the room—not the yellow bean bag chair or the shaggy orange rug.

The woman was obviously colorblind, and a product of the hippie era, but Lincoln didn't want to be judgmental—at least not until he heard what the therapist had to say.

Dr. Lerner dragged a wheeled office chair across the room. She positioned the chair across from Lincoln and Chevonne, and took a seat. She smiled a very pleasant smile, but Lincoln was feeling a bit aggravated. He wondered if Dr. Lerner could sense that he didn't want to be there.

I don't know about this. This woman better know her stuff or I'm out! He cut a glance at Chevonne, trying to convey his sentiments with his eyes, but Chevonne wouldn't meet his gaze.

"Thank you for seeing us at such a short notice, Dr. Lerner," Chevonne said in a nervous tone, breaking the silence.

"No problem. I'm glad you took the first step. Let's not waste any time; let's discuss your issues." She turned on a recording device and grabbed a canary-colored note pad. "Why are you here?"

Why are you here—just like that? Doesn't she need to dig a little deeper; ask more let's-get-acquainted questions before going for the jugular? Lincoln glared at Chevonne for selecting this kook.

Chevonne coughed, putting a cupped hand in front of her mouth. She looked at Dr. Lerner, and then at Lincoln. "We're here because I had an affair. I know it was wrong…I didn't mean for it to happen. Actually, a casual fling turned into something bigger than I ever expected. My infidelity almost destroyed our marriage; I really hope you can help us."

Dr. Lerner turned her attention from Chevonne to Lincoln. "And what role did you play in her affair?"

"What do you mean?" Indignant, Lincoln turned up a corner of his upper lip.

"What did you do that drove your wife to cheat on you?" Dr. Lerner spoke cheerfully as if she were asking a pleasant question.

Lincoln twisted around, frowning at Chevonne and then at Dr. Lerner; resenting being asked such an asinine question.

"Well?" Dr. Lerner asked, pen poised to jot down Lincoln's response.

"I didn't do anything. I love my wife. I've never gone outside of this marriage," he said, looking at Chevonne. Admitting his faithfulness to a stranger heightened his anger. Another man had touched his wife's naked body, had stuck his dick in her mouth and her pussy—places that should have been reserved for Lincoln only. Infuriated, Lincoln sat, bent at the waist with one leg extended, appearing ready to bolt.

"So do you think this is something that can be fixed? Are you both equally committed to resolving your problems?" Dr. Lerner asked.

Chevonne spoke up first. "Yes, Doctor, that's why we're here. We are both committed to our marriage; we want to work this out." She darted a glance at Lincoln. "Right, babe?" she said, grabbing Lincoln's hand.

Though Lincoln felt like punching a wall, he sat upright and reluctantly accepted Chevonne's hand.

"Now that we agree that this marriage can be fixed, let's start at the beginning. What is the real reason you believe the affair began?" Dr. Lerner smiled sweetly.

Lincoln looked over at Chevonne, interested in hearing her answer to Dr. Lerner's question. Despite all her apologies and explanations, Lincoln still didn't get it. He didn't understand why Chevonne would choose a dirty, sweaty, greasy mechanic over him. Why'd she go to that thug for the warmth and love that she could have easily gotten from him?

Chevonne cleared her throat. "Things started changing between us. I didn't feel like my husband cared about me anymore."

"You know that's not true!" Lincoln growled.

"Let her finish," Dr. Lerner intervened in her soft, sweet voice.

"Well, after he started having problems with his career…

um…after the second pay cut, there was no joy in his eyes. He was so angry; it was difficult being around him."

"Uh-huh." Dr. Lerner scribbled on her pad. Lincoln looked over to see what she was writing.

"How did that make you feel, Mr. Jennings? Did you feel like less of a man after your salary was reduced?"

"Yes, I did. But I wasn't pushing my wife away. If anything, I needed her more. I needed her to be there for me—to have my back while I was down. I desperately wanted her attention…her affection. But instead, she pushed me away, and let me suffer, treating me as if I wasn't good enough for her anymore."

Dr. Lerner turned her focus to Chevonne; her blue eyes targeting Chevonne with laser precision. "Did you cheat on your husband because he was making less money?"

Now it was Chevonne's turn to squirm. No longer in the hot seat, Lincoln relaxed and became a spectator.

"No, I didn't cheat over his salary. I love my husband," Chevonne exclaimed while looking over Lincoln. From the look in her eyes, Lincoln could tell that Chevonne was becoming weary of Dr. Lerner's questions. She kept glancing at the door, as if she'd had enough and was ready to leave.

"Was your relationship okay prior to your husband's financial issues?"

Lincoln answered before Chevonne could. "Yes, I think so. We were good."

"Mmm-hmm. You say you and your wife were good.

So…how was your sex life?" Dr. Lerner asked, as if she doubted that his claim was true.

"Great. I didn't have any complaints."

Dr. Lerner laced her fingers together. "What do you think would help you in the process of forgiving your wife?"

Both Chevonne and Dr. Lerner gave Lincoln their undivided attention.

"I'm not sure. Knowing that she had sex with another man…" He shook his head. "No matter how hard I try, I can't get that thought out of my mind. I keep seeing a man's hands on her and them making love. It's killing me to know that during the time that she was denying me—she was out there, giving it away. She was so deceitful, taking time off work to be with her lover…" Lincoln paused to collect himself.

He hadn't expected to be able to open up to Dr. Lerner, but her voice was calming like a teacher on the first day of kindergarten, making him comfortable enough to believe that she would come up with the perfect solution.

"It's okay, Lincoln," Dr. Lerner soothed. "It's very hard to forgive a cheating spouse, but it can be done."

"So what do you suggest, Dr. Lerner?" Chevonne asked, clearly becoming annoyed with being referred to as a cheating spouse. "Do you have any techniques that might help him to stop obsessing about my affair?"

Chevonne then turned her attention back to Lincoln. "I love you. I truly don't want anyone else. It is over,

Lincoln. I ended it. Babe, I'm doing everything in my power to help us heal."

"Well, I've counseled many couples that are dealing with infidelity. Your situation is stastically unusual. Though it happens, it's rarely the wife that has been unfaithful. You may not like what I have to say, Mrs. Jennings…"

Chevonne placed a hand on her chest. "Dr. Lerner, I'm open to practically anything that you think will save my marriage."

With bated breath, Lincoln waited for Dr. Lerner to finish her sentence. He was curious to hear what she had to say.

Dr. Lerner leaned forward. "If you want your husband to forgive you and to move past your indiscretion, you're going to have to allow him the same sexual freedom that you enjoyed."

Chevonne's eyes narrowed. "Excuse me?"

"You need to give your husband a one-night-only pass. A night of complete sexual freedom."

Chevonne gasped; her mouth hung open.

"My methods are unorthodox, but they work. After your husband has explored outside of the marriage, his resentment will dissolve. He needs to feel vindicated. Then and only then, will he be able to forgive you."

"Are you crazy? We came here to get help, and your advice is for me to allow my husband to cheat on me? Please!" Chevonne stood. "We have to get out of here, Lincoln."

Exiting the office, Lincoln was at a loss for words. He couldn't believe that Dr. Lerner would tell him to dip out on his wife, as if more cheating would resolve their problem.

During the drive home, Chevonne would not stop talking. "Have you ever heard anything so absurd? What kind of doctor would suggest that a man cheat on his wife, to make a marriage work? She's a damn quack! I'm so sorry that I chose her. I should report her to the therapy board. That woman should not be allowed to practice!"

"That therapy thing is nothing but a racket. Don't worry, sweetheart. We're going to work this out ourselves." Lincoln reached over and patted Chevonne's hand.

Though Dr. Lerner's advice sounded off-beat and crazy, on second thought, having one night of passion with a stranger might be exactly what Lincoln needed. Maybe she wasn't a quack; maybe she was a genius.

He decided to take Dr. Lerner's advice and secretly use that free pussy card. One of these days. Maybe.

CHAPTER 46

"Guess who the boss is taking to the AIA convention?" Rachel said when Lincoln arrived at work.

"No idea," he said, trying to sound disinterested, but his pulse was thrumming fast. Five years in a row, Lincoln had gone to the American Institute of Architects convention along with Frank, and it would be a sure sign that his job was in trouble if Frank decided to take one of the so-called young, cutting-edge guys.

Rachel leaned forward and whispered conspiratorially. "The boss is looking for some hanky-panky. He's taking Amber." Rachel clicked some keys on the keyboard and turned the computer monitor toward Lincoln.

Dumbfounded, he tried to keep his eyes from physically bulging when he saw the order for two tickets to the convention. One for Frank Clemmons and the other for Amber Ralston.

It almost felt like a sucker punch, but with so many pay cuts, he would have been a fool not to have seen it coming. It was time to make moves. A leap of faith. On the bright side, maybe Frank was doing him a favor by forcing him to free-fall from the ledge.

"I wouldn't be the least bit surprised if those two are getting adjacent hotel rooms. He didn't ask me to book the hotel. Oh, no. Mr. *Family Man* booked the rooms himself." She turned the screen back to its normal position. "I told you those two were up to no good. Do you believe me now?"

"Hmm," Lincoln murmured.

Rachel smirked with self-satisfaction. "Case closed. Mystery solved."

In his office, Lincoln sat staring at nothing. The world was full of surprises. The woman he loved wholeheartedly had proven with her sordid betrayal that nothing is ever the way it appears. Other than to indulge his sexual cravings, there was no reason for Frank to take Amber to that convention. She was only an apprentice drafter—the last person on the totem pole. Lincoln had always considered Frank to be a straight-shooter...the last of the good guys. Amber was ambitious and devious. Perhaps she and Frank deserved each other.

While he was trying to wrap his mind around the Amber and Frank situation, his cell phone rang. A glance at the screen told him that Michelle was calling again. Instead of clicking the IGNORE button, he picked up. The poor woman deserved to have closure.

"Hi, Michelle. How are you holding up?"

"I'm making it," she said solemnly. "You could have at least returned my phone calls; I've been calling you every day."

"Yeah, I'm sorry about that. It gets hectic here at work."

"Well, I was only calling because you told me to let you know if I heard anything about Crowbar."

Lincoln swallowed a lump of fear. "Did he turn up?" He grimaced, his imagination working overtime with the details of Crowbar's fiery demise. Lincoln had never met Crowbar, but he envisioned a charred body discovered in a vacant lot. Burned beyond recognition, it took dental records to identify him. *That man didn't deserve to go out like that*, he thought, bitterly mimicking his brother's words. Lincoln conjured up a newfound hatred for Raheem.

"Crowbar's back home. At least one of those two no-good bums knew how to find his way back to where he belongs. I don't know what Earl's problem is. Why would he do me like this?"

"Crowbar's home? He's all right?"

"Yeah. He never intended to go back to rehab. He took Sharonda's money and went on a long binge."

"Fantastic!" Lincoln blurted.

"What's so fantastic about that? Crowbar went through the rent money, the electric bill money, the money for groceries. He messed Sharonda up."

Despite Crowbar's misdeeds, Lincoln couldn't stop grinning. *Wait until Earl hears this!*

"You need to stop giving me the runaround. You know where your brother's at!"

"You're right, I do," Lincoln said, coming clean. "He

hooked up with another woman, Michelle. I was hoping Earl would tell you himself; I didn't want to be the bearer of that bad news."

Michelle wailed, whooped, and hollered like she was openly grieving at a funeral. Her response was extreme, in Lincoln's opinion. Michelle and Earl had only been together for a short time. But he couldn't judge her. What did he know about a woman's heart?

After she quieted down a little, Lincoln assured her that he'd tell Earl to call her. But Earl wouldn't. In Earl's mind, Michelle was long gone and forgotten, undeserving of even the common courtesy of a phone call. That's how Earl was. He was the younger brother. While Lincoln was taught to stand on his own two feet, their mother—may she rest in peace—made life easy for Earl and did everything for him. When cancer cut her life short, Earl replaced her with a stream of female enablers. Lincoln hoped that Ivella didn't allow him to lapse into a former, trifling behavior.

Earl was at work right now, so Lincoln would give him a call later. A load of guilty weight would be lifted from Earl's shoulders when he found out the good news about his friend, Crowbar.

And Lincoln was somewhat relieved to know that the man that Chevonne had been cheating with, wasn't a cold-blooded killer.

Being nosey, Lincoln checked around the Pennsylvania Department of Corrections Inmate Locator website to find out if Raheem had been sprung from jail. He keyed in Raheem's name and…voilà! More good news; Raheem was still locked up. That dude must have had several open warrants to be locked up for this long over an unregistered gun. It served him right!

Lincoln caught a glimpse of Frank and Amber walking past his office, and was reminded that he had to deal with the current issue of reviving his career. No doubt about it, he had to take the plunge and strike out on his own.

Lincoln arrived at the bank fifteen minutes early. As he took a seat on one of the leather benches, a bank representative approached him. "May I help you?"

"I have an appointment with Mr. Wilkes."

"He's with a client."

"That's okay; I'm early." Lincoln smiled politely. The rep went back to her desk and Lincoln busied himself, scrolling through his digital contact list. There were so many things to do to get a business started. He was confident that he'd qualify for a business loan. His student loans were paid off; he had an expensive house for collateral. And despite his financial suffering—being already deep in debt, he had maintained A-1 credit.

He was fiddling with his mobile device, but something caught his attention. He looked up, and he saw a stunning woman. She looked oddly familiar. She shook hands with a bank rep and then gathered her handbag, and began walking in his direction. She wore a curve-fitting business suit, a strand of pearls, and sexy heels. Her stride was confident as she approached, smiling as if she knew him.

It wasn't until she was directly in front of him, that Lincoln recognized her.

"Fancy meeting you here," the woman said, extending her hand. "Lincoln, right—the honest architect?"

"Ooh, Solay…from the cupcake place!" He shook her hand, looking her over from head to toe with a roving glance. "Wow, you look spectacular. I've only seen you in the shop…in the uniform, and my brain couldn't make the connection."

"I don't know how to take that. Are you saying I look a hot mess at the shop?"

"No, not at all. You look real cute in that apron. But this is different. It's like…Wow! The clothes…even your hair is different."

"Thank you for the compliment. You look extra spiffy yourself," she said, indicating his suit, tie, and briefcase.

He laughed self-consciously. "Yeah, I'm trying to make a good impression."

"I'm impressed." She looked him over, and the gleam in her eyes was somewhat flirtatious.

"How's business?" he inquired, getting serious and trying to ignore his sudden attraction.

"It's going great. But it's time to expand, so I'm taking

the plunge and going into more debt," she said with a sigh and a shrug. "Oh, I have a new cupcake on the menu. I know that you don't like sweet things," she said with a little laugh. "But I have something new and I guarantee that you're going to love it."

"Oh, yeah? What's it called? Oh, wait a minute…let me prepare myself for a scandalous name."

"The new addition is called The Ho Cake," she said, laughing.

Lincoln chuckled in amusement. "Nothing subtle about that."

"You should stop by and try it."

"Maybe I will."

"I'm open until seven."

"I'll be there at six." *Okay, we're definitely flirting. But it's harmless. Just having fun.*

He watched the slight sway of her hips as she walked toward the exit sign. Pretty woman with nice legs and a cute little round ass. Sweet disposition. But being such a go-getter, she probably had a fiery side, too.

"Mr. Jennings?" a male voice broke into Lincoln's thoughts.

Lincoln stood and shook the loan officer's hand.

CHAPTER 47

He arrived at Scandalicious at six o'clock sharp. There was a big after-work crowd, but Solay spotted him the moment he walked through the door. Well, it wasn't hard to miss him; she'd been watching the door.

She waved and pointed to an empty seat in the rear. Lincoln was there by her personal invitation and he didn't have to wait in line for his ho cake.

"Hold down the fort, Vidal. I'm taking a little break."

"You're doing what?" Vidal whipped his head back and forth. "Do you see this long line of pests?"

"You can deal with the after-work rush crowd for a few minutes," she said and pushed open the kitchen doors. She could have given Lincoln a savory cupcake from the bakery case, but she wanted him to taste one that was hot and fresh out of the oven.

She set the red paper plate in front of Lincoln. The Hoecake was large...the size of a muffin. She placed a napkin, plastic knife, and fork beside the plate.

"Looks good; smells good," Lincoln said with admiration.

"And it tastes even better," she said in a slightly seductive voice.

Why am I flirting so hard with this ring-wearing married man? Because I'm lonely, horny, and a married man has responsibilities at home...he won't complicate my life, she responded.

Solay was back where she'd started when she'd first called the Rent-A-Man agency—looking for sex without any emotional entanglements. She hadn't given up on her and Deon, but she refused to live every day of her life, waiting for a phone call or a text. They'd tried Skyping, but that hadn't worked out too well. They'd agree to a time to Skype, and Solay would get dolled up and sexy...only to be staring at her blank computer screen...stood up because the film schedule had run later than Deon had anticipated.

Deon was always distracted whenever they did have a phone conversation. Their long distance romance was dying a slow death, and Solay had no choice but to accept it and move on. Maybe they'd get another chance when Deon finished filming...in the meantime, she had to live her life.

Solay liked Lincoln. He wasn't hot like Deon...no one was, but he had a level of maturity and a chivalrous spirit. It was so sweet, the way he'd gone out of his way to repay the money for those cupcakes that he'd said his coworker had swindled.

"Mmm. This is awesome." Lincoln frowned and shook his head at the scrumptious flavor. He cut into the Hoecake and forked up another big chunk. "Does this have meat in it?"

"Uh-huh. Chunks of slab bacon."

"What else is in it? Damn, this is hitting the spot."

"Cornmeal and bacon are the two main ingredients. But I added extra seasonings and spices, but I can't tell you what they are."

"Why not?"

"Because…they're my sexy little secret."

Lincoln made eye contact with Solay. Her eyes sparkled with desire.

The bell jingled, announcing another stream of customers.

"I have to get back to work."

"Definitely, didn't mean to keep you. Go handle your business."

"I want to extend a more personal invitation…"

"Oh, yeah? An invitation to what?"

"An erotic invitation…a sensual adventure…blissful sex…no emotional complications," Solay said boldly.

Lincoln thought about the fuck-free card he'd gotten from Chevonne at the therapist's urging. "When and where?" he asked without hesitation.

"I have a place upstairs, and if you're interested, I'd like to see you tomorrow night, around eight?" she suggested.

"Sounds good; okay." Lincoln nervously moistened his lips.

"I'm looking forward to it."

On the way home, thoughts of Solay's invitation had his dick as hard as iron, making a tent in his pants that was a hella distraction while he was driving.

He wondered how Chevonne would react when he told her that he was finally going to take the therapist's advice and get some pussy on the side. As appalled as he'd been at the therapist's suggestion, Chevonne would want to know what changed his mind, and he'd be honest. Solay was an attractive woman who'd made him a "sex with no-strings attached" offer.

Tomorrow night was a long time to wait; he needed to do some- thing about this boner as soon as he got home.

He threw his keys in a basket on the kitchen counter, paced across the marble floor, and bounded the stairs. He checked on the kids. Amir was in his room doing homework on his computer. Tori was in her room play-ing with dolls.

And Mommy was where he wanted her to be…in their bedroom. "Hey, baby," Lincoln called as he opened the bedroom door.

"Hi, Lincoln; what took you so long? You know it's gym night." Chevonne's back was to him, and she was wearing workout gear.

"I forgot," he murmured, feeling letdown and horny. There was something else. He wanted to tell her about his plan to start his own firm. But that could wait until later tonight.

He also wanted to have an open and honest discussion

about his sexual attraction toward Solay, and his decision to act on his feelings—get it out of his system.

He sat on the bed, watching Chevonne stuff her gym bag with a towel, a change of clothes, bath gel, and other toiletries.

Rushing, Chevonne zipped up the bag. "Can you make sure that Amir and Tori both take a shower before bed? I think Amir needs to start wearing deodorant. That boy has developed a musky, teenage odor and he's only six." She kissed Lincoln on the forehead, then left the room and disappeared down the hall.

With extra time on his hand, Lincoln checked out office space online. He ran a troubled hand down the side of his face. *Whew!* Renting space in downtown Philadelphia was through the roof. With a disgusted grunt, he shut down the laptop, deciding to focus on more pleasurable thoughts.

His mind wanted to conjure up an image of Solay in that sexy black suit, but thoughts of her would lead to jerking off in the shower. Then he remembered Crowbar!

He called his brother. "You not gon' believe this. Guess who turned up!"

"Crowbar?" Earl said, his voice hushed.

"Alive and well. That dude was out on a long drug-binge."

"Yo, that's whassup!" Earl yelled in delight. "You got a number for him? You know I lost all my numbers when I lost my phone."

"No, but why don't you call Michelle and get that information. She really wants to hear from you. She wants you to tell her why you left her."

"I'm not doing all that. Why can't you call her and get the info?"

"Because…you need to deal with that situation like a grown man. How would you like it if Ivella bounced on you with no explanation?"

"I'd be out there looking for her; she'd have to tell me something!"

"So how do you think Michelle feels? Man, stop tryna dodge shit. Act like a grown man, and call that woman. Be honest with her—tell her why you left her."

"I left her because I thought it was hot in Philly; I had to get out of town."

"Do the right thing, Earl. Call her and let her know that you're sorry that things didn't work out. She deserves some kind of explanation."

"Aye, man. Goddamn. Always preaching. Why you gotta come at me like that? Talking to me like I'm a child," Earl grumbled.

"Then act like a man."

"Yeah, aye. Whatever. Get on my nerves, fuckin' with my high."

Lincoln chuckled as he hung up the phone.

"Tori and Amir! It's bedtime," he shouted in the thundering voice that made his children react more promptly than usual. Five minutes later, he poked his head inside

Amir's room. Amir was slipping his legs into a pair of pajamas.

"Are you allergic to water? Hit the shower, little man."

"I'm tired," Amir complained, dragging his feet toward his private bathroom.

Lincoln went into Tori's bathroom. He turned on the faucets and poured in bubble bath. Unlike her brother, Tori was thrilled about bath time. Carrying an armful of dolls, she jumped in the tub with a big splash.

Lincoln took a moment to count his blessings. Two healthy kids and a beautiful wife who was successful in her field. What had he been thinking when he accepted Solay's invitation? Chevonne and the kids meant the world to him.

Revenge sex wasn't worth upsetting the balance of his happy home.

Close to the time that he expected Chevonne to be back from the gym, Lincoln poured himself a glass of brandy, something he occasionally drank to unwind at the end of the day.

Perhaps it was all the excitement of the day...or maybe it was the brandy that caused Lincoln to doze off while watching TV and bored with the latest cheating politician story that was being covered by every news channel.

Lincoln didn't realize that Chevonne had come home until the sound of her soft laughter lured him out of a dream. She was in the bathroom, talking on her cell phone.

"You should cut out spicy food altogether. I'm sure that's what's been upsetting your stomach." A long pause. "You're too young to have an ulcer." She laughed again. There was something different about her laughter. She sounded happy and girlish—practically giggling.

"So you're going to keep coating your stomach with milk? Who told you to do that? Your grandmother... well, that figures. That old home remedy isn't proper treatment."

Before drifting back to sleep, Lincoln wondered which of her girlfriends Chevonne was talking to.

CHAPTER 48

Mornings were complete chaos inside the Jennings household. Cartoons blared from the TV in the kitchen, Tori and Amir fought at the breakfast table, and complained about the lunches their mother had packed for them. Adding to the bedlam, Chevonne tended to yell out the current time every five minutes. "We're running late; let's get a move-on!"

Lincoln's workday started two hours later than Chevonne's and so he normally stayed away from the pandemonium. Preferring to start his day on a peaceful note, he hardly ever ventured downstairs until he heard Chevonne starting up her car.

Once Chevonne and the kids were gone, Lincoln came down for coffee. He turned those damned cartoons to HLN, creating a much calmer environment.

It wasn't unusual for a lunch bag, backpack, or a sweater to have gotten left behind during the fray. Today, it was Chevonne's cell.

There it was—her city-issued BlackBerry in plain sight on the white marble island. Tempting him. Beckoning him.

The honorable thing to do was to call and leave a

voicemail at her work, letting her know that she'd left the BlackBerry at home, but Lincoln was drawn to the phone as if being pulled by a magnet.

Chevonne's phone felt hot in his hands as he powered it on. He checked recent calls and saw that she'd gotten a call at 10:17 last night.

Next, he checked her texts.

Like someone had pulled a rug out from under him, Lincoln sagged. Annihilated by the words he read, Lincoln was nearly rocked off of his feet. Palms pressed firmly against the kitchen counter, he steadied himself and took a seat.

We on 2nite?

Can't. 2 nights in a row is risky.

I'll make it worth the risk. lls.

I want to, but I really can't. ☹

OK. When?

Next gym night

Ard. But no panties, no thong. Leave dem shits off. Bring my pussy to me raw.

I will.

He leapt to his feet. Kicked a stool over. Muttering obscenities, he paced around the kitchen. The vile… vulgar…disgusting sext messages had taken place a mere half-hour ago, while Chevonne was in the kitchen— supposedly parenting their kids.

That bitch! That dirty…cheating…fuckin' bitch, pulling this same bullshit again! Grim-faced, Lincoln stalked upstairs, grabbed his laptop, and powered it on. Two minutes later, a visit to the inmate information site enflamed Lincoln further.

The gun-toting, pyromaniac mechanic had been released last night at six.

It all came rushing back to him. Chevonne whispering and giggling on the phone last night. She was talking with concern and sweetness in her voice, and now Lincoln realized she'd been talking to that fuckin' Raheem.

Lincoln read the text exchanges so many times, the words were imprinted in his mind. His first thought was to storm into Chevonne's office. Holding the incriminating BlackBerry in his hand, he'd expose her in front of her staff as the dirty, skank hoe that she was. But that idea brought only a small measure of satisfaction.

The only way to feel better was to go upside a disrespectful nigga's head. Remembering that Amir's baseball bat was still in the trunk of his car, Lincoln dressed quickly. Murderously angry, he threw on a pair of jeans, a hoodie, and a jacket—didn't bother to shower or shave.

It took being outside and breathing in the chilly autumn breeze to bring him to his senses.

Calm resolve replaced fury. *Two can play the same game*, he decided.

He went back inside. In the kitchen, he picked up the stool that he'd knocked over, and then returned Chevonne's BlackBerry exactly where he'd found it.

He climbed the stairs purposefully. After showering and shaving, Lincoln dressed for work.

Solay finished mopping the floor and checked the clock. Shit! Vidal had done a shoddy clean-up job and Solay could not turn out the lights out in the kitchen unless it was sparkling clean. Lincoln would be here in five minutes, and she'd never gotten a chance to change out of her work clothes.

She dashed out of the kitchen and went into the dining area. In the rear, she stood before the full-length dressing mirror, examining herself. She looked tired and frumpy. How could she slip into seductress mode, looking like this?

When she'd extended the invitation, she was feeling vibrant and sexy, but tonight she was frazzled and worn.

She was feeling so unattractive and insecure.

Part of the problem was that she hadn't received a text or a phone call from Deon in four days. Finally, she broke down and called him. She usually got his voicemail and was pleasantly surprised to hear his voice. But her joy didn't last long. "Yo, I gotta hit you back. I'm in the middle of something," he'd said brusquely before she could even say a word.

It seemed that her life was on permanent pause…living for Deon's rare phone calls, his occasional texts. It was downright degrading, the way the relationship had declined, yet she continued to hold on to the dim hope that eventually she and Deon would be back together... in love the way they used to be.

If only I'd been more understanding—if I'd had more faith in him, our relationship would have been strong enough to endure the separation.

Soft, tentative knocks announced Lincoln's arrival.

Treading toward the door, Solay smoothed her hair back as she practiced what she would say in her mind. *So sorry, but something's come up. Can I get a rain check?*

Through the glass pane, Lincoln looked like a totally different person, wearing sweat pants, T-shirt, sneakers and a hoodie. Brows knitted together in curiosity, she opened the door.

"Hey," he greeted, but didn't cross the threshold.

"Come on in," she said politely.

He took a few steps, but remained close to the door. "Uh, look... I...uh, just came by to tell you that...well, I have a lot of stuff going on, but I want to be straight with you. That's why I stopped by. Your offer was flattering, but I don't think I'm the right guy."

She flinched. Visibly. Her lips drew into a tight frown of disappointment. *Damn, I'm not even good enough to be a friend with benefits?*

"Hey, don't look like that." He patted her shoulder.

Hurt by the sting of rejection, she squirmed away from his sympathetic touch. "I know I'm not looking my best, but I must be looking a hot mess, any time a man turns down an opportunity for uncommitted sex."

"Nooo. You've got it all wrong. You're beautiful. And smart. You've got a lot going on for yourself. But my life…" His eyes dropped.

She glanced guiltily at his wedding band. "I know… I shouldn't have hit on a married man. That was selfish and wrong."

"It's not that. I'm not at my best self right now."

She shrugged. "You look good to me. You're rocking that 'right off the basketball court' look. Very handsome and extremely sexy."

"Handsome and sexy—really?" Lincoln chuckled, obviously flattered.

The flirtatious words had spilled from Solay's lips without warning. There was something about rejection that was stimulating and challenging.

"Why don't we go upstairs, have a drink, and talk about what's bothering you and see how we can make it all better." She moistened her lips.

Hands shoved into the pockets of his sweats, he came inside, pacing a little awkwardly as he looked around the empty dining area.

Solay hit a switch, turning down the bright illumination. The bakery took on a sultrier and more provocative look with the dimmed lighting.

Solay looked at Lincoln and smiled suggestively. He smiled back, his white teeth grazing his bottom lip. There was a definite attraction between them. Lincoln had a quiet sex appeal—the kind that snuck up on a woman, and took her off-guard.

She led the way upstairs to her apartment. "Welcome to my abode," she said as she opened the door.

"Nice and cozy," Lincoln commented.

"Thanks. Have a seat." She motioned toward the sofa. "Glass of wine?"

"Sure."

She came back carrying two glasses of red wine. "I want to be honest with you, Lincoln," Solay said, sitting next to him. "I'm going through a crisis. My professional life is fine, but on a personal level, I'm an emotional wreck."

"What's going on with you?"

"Well, I'm supposed to be in a long distance relationship. But it's clearly not working. I've been trying to hold on because it's so hard to accept that it's over. My emotions have been all over the place: frustrated, angry, scared, depressed, and lonely." She shook her head. "I think I'm going through a sort of grieving process; at least that's how it feels."

"What went wrong? He had to be a very foolish man to risk losing someone like you."

"I can't blame him; it's not his fault. It's sort of on me. The relationship was already damaged before he went out of town. I had hoped that a little time apart would heal what was wrong. But the distance between us has only made it worse," Solay said bitterly.

"Where's out of town?"

"Toronto," she said sadly. "So, what's your story?" She changed the subject, afraid that she'd start crying if she talked about Deon for too long.

Lincoln held up his hands. "So many changes are happening in my life, I don't know if I'm coming or going. This time a year ago, I couldn't have imagined that my life would turn completely upside down. This is a challenging time for me, but I'll get through it. I have to."

Lincoln had provided only a vague account of his problems, yet Solay could feel his pain.

"I understand," she said, looking deeply into his eyes. She took the glass of wine out of his hand, leaned in and boldly kissed him.

There were no fireworks. It wasn't electrical…or magical. It was a gentle kiss, soft and soothing. She put her arms around his neck, realizing that she didn't need sparks to fly—the only thing she needed was the comfort of a man.

She unclasped her arms, breaking the kiss. "I'm a little sweaty from cleaning up the shop. I'm gonna take a quick shower." Solay stood up. "Turn on the TV." She handed him the remote.

After standing, she bent over slightly and kissed his cheek and then playfully bit his earlobe. "I'll be right back, lover," she said with a wink.

CHAPTER 49

L incoln held the remote. He heard Solay's footsteps as she padded down the hall. Moments
later, he heard the shower curtain being pulled
back, followed by the sound of running water.

He clicked on the TV, and turning the volume low, he
surfed through the channels. Uninterested in watching
any of the programs that flickered past, he settled on a
random sitcom and put the remote down.

Lincoln took another sip of wine. *What am I doing
here?* He felt ridiculous, like a kid in high school, waiting for his girl to come back and join him on the couch
for another session of kissing and groping.

His mind flashed briefly on Chevonne and the children,
and his first thought was to rush home and be with his
family. Then he thought about Dr. Lerner's recommen-
dation—a one-night pass that could potentially heal his
hurt and definitely even the score with Chevonne.

Ironically, he no longer had an interest in getting even.
Revenge was the last thing on his mind. His marriage
was in such bad shape that it would take more than a
one-night stand to repair it. After hearing Chevonne
whispering to her lover late at night in their bathroom,

and after reading those damning texts, it would take a lobotomy for Lincoln to forget the callous way she'd disrespected him and their marriage. For her to have sneakily continued to cheat with Raheem was simply unforgivable.

Solay was in the shower. The idea of her being a few feet away from him, naked and wet, caused his dick to thicken inside his pants. Solay was a beautiful woman. The complete opposite of Chevonne. With her doe-shaped, slanted eyes, silky hair, and cinnamon-colored skin, Chevonne was an exotic beauty, and a complete enigma, always keeping secrets.

Red-bronzed skin and round, expressive eyes, Solay had that wholesome, girl-next-door look. Her open honesty and willingness to show her vulnerability had made her a kindred spirit. She wasn't looking for romance; she needed sex to forget her pain. Lincoln wanted the same thing. They were two hurt people, trying to get a sexual healing. Probably not a good combination, but his throbbing dick had a different opinion.

Unable to resist the temptation of getting close to some naked wet booty, titties, and pussy, Lincoln shed his clothes.

Making a bold move, he entered the steamy bathroom. He hoped he'd read Solay's signals right. It would be embarrassing if she let out a plaintive scream when he pulled the shower curtain back. *Is this what she wanted?* He questioned himself. *Of course, she does. Why else would she kiss me and tell me she was going to take a shower?*

Taking a deep breath, he slowly pulled back the beach-themed shower curtain. Solay's perfectly proportioned body was soapy all over. Her eyes were closed as she rubbed her arm with a bath sponge. When a tiny welcoming smile appeared on her lips, Lincoln stepped inside the shower stall.

He positioned her in front of him. Her butt against his groin. He picked the bath gel from the shower rack and poured a dollop in his palm, and then rubbed both palms together. Going straight for her breasts, he added more soap to the perky mounds. His thumbs toyed with her nipples, rubbing and twisting, forcing them into sharp peaks. Water pelted his back as he soaped her body; his hands began to roam, squeezing her ass cheeks, running over her hips, stroking the mound of her pussy, exploring every area of her feminine landscape.

His hand worked its way to her sleek entry. He stroked and teased her pussy lips, but didn't penetrate. Two fingers rested on either side of her pulsing clit, capturing it in a gentle, undemanding clasp. Lazily, he rubbed the hardened bud, circling it in a leisurely manner.

Heat emanated from Solay's body; she moaned softly—her hips swiveled in a slow rhythm. Lincoln's dick responded by prodding and probing, seeking a warm place. The rigid organ pulsed and probed until Lincoln tucked it inside the warm, moist confines of her lush, soapy thighs.

"Damn, you feel good," Lincoln muttered in her ear. "I wanna fuck you right now."

"Do it. You know what I want," she murmured, clamping her thighs tightly around his dick.

"Not yet."

He slid his dick in and out of the lathered territory between her thighs. His hands became active again, toggling her swollen clit. He slid a finger into her juicy pussy, and Solay let out a loud moan. He pleasured her with a crooked, searching finger, while his thumb worked on her clit.

"I'm ready for some dick," Solay uttered breathlessly. She disengaged, momentarily breaking the passion spell she was under.

She turned around and faced him. He bent his head, and covered her mouth with his. The kiss was not soft and delicate. They kissed with fervor, their mouths open, tongues lashing, hungrily devouring each other. She moaned and writhed; his hot kiss making her yearn for more.

Solay groped and found Lincoln's thick, meaty dick. It felt like a heavy club inside her fist. She stroked it tenderly into her sudsy fist.

"Oh, shit. That feels good. I bet that hot pussy feels even better," Lincoln panted. Roughly, he turned her around, positioning her with her arms outstretched, her hands pressed against the tiled wall, her legs spread widely apart as if he preparing to conduct a strip search.

Feeling highly emotional and sexually charged, Solay looked over her shoulder. "Come on and fuck me; I'm ready."

He entered her slowly from behind, pushing in increment after increment of hot pulsing dick. After embedding every inch of thickness to the hilt, Lincoln became still.

Solay let out a sharp cry. "Oh, Lincoln. I need you." She wriggled and moaned. "I need you so bad."

"I'm here, baby. You got me," Lincoln whispered soothingly. Though his body was still, he could feel his hard dick throbbing against her silken, tight sheath. The feeling was so intense, he was afraid he'd shoot out a hot load with the first dick stroke.

His hands steadied her as her pussy grew more insistent, tightening around his girth, goading him into giving her what she wanted—a long, hard ride.

Don't you punk out on me, muthafucka, he cursed at his pulsing dick, demanding that it exercise some self-control. His strong hands gripped Solay's shoulders as he drove in…delivering long, slow strokes, clenching his teeth to hold back the orgasm that was rocketing through his body.

The way her muscles gripped him, the way she started mumbling words that he couldn't make out, told Lincoln that Solay was close to getting hers. He ignored the hot burn of pleasure that coursed through him; refusing to cum until he was certain that Solay was satisfied.

"Tell me whatchu want," he whispered, while working his dick in and out at a faster pace.

"Pinch my nipples," she said hoarsely.

His hands slid away from her shoulders and traveled

down to her titties. He squeezed the voluptuous, small melons, and then pinched her stony nipples, until her pussy puckered wildly around his shaft. Her body began to buck uncontrollably. Lincoln didn't stop pinching her nipples or pounding her pussy until Solay went completely over the edge of ecstasy, all the while, spewing a litany of sex-induced profanity.

The walls that sheathed his dick were slippery with her juices. There was so much heated moisture inside her pussy tunnel; Lincoln could no longer hold back. He squeezed his eyes shut and let go of every torturous emotion that had plagued him. Inside Solay's tight warmth, he released a rushing sea of passion.

CHAPTER 50

Lincoln came home at two-fifty in the pitch-black gloom of night. There wasn't a star in the sky. He entered his home and was surprised to see Chevonne sitting on the sofa in her bathrobe, obviously waiting up for him. The disgusted look on her face informed that she was none too pleased. At any other time, he would have cared—he would have immediately launched into an explanation, and would have tried to placate her. But tonight, her pissed-off look was almost laughable.

"Do you know what time it is?" Chevonne demanded.

Lincoln looked down at his watch. "It's almost three in the morning," he said dispassionately, striding past Chevonne. "Are you staying down here? 'Cause I'm going to sleep," Lincoln said without breaking his gait, and heading for the stairs.

He listened as Chevonne stomped and huffed up the steps behind him.

Inside their bedroom, Lincoln closed the door and began to undress. Chevonne glowered at him. "Are you seriously going to walk in this house at this time of the morning, and act like it's perfectly normal? Where have you been for all these hours? I've been calling your phone, sending you texts. I though you were in an accident!"

"Sorry about that," he mumbled without emotion.

"That's it…you're sorry. Lincoln, I've been worried sick about you, but you're acting like you don't have a care in the world. Waltzing into this house at three in the morning and acting like it's the middle of the day." She put a hand on her hip. "You better tell me something."

"I don't have to report to you; I'm not telling you shit." Stripped down to his underwear, Lincoln pulled back the covers on his side of the bed.

"Why don't you review what you and ol' boy did last night…and then read some of those sext messages y'all were sending back and forth…" He paused letting his words sink in.

Chevonne's eyes were blinking fast. She opened her mouth to talk, and then seemed to think better of it.

"Now do you really want to question where I've been, or do you wanna take your ass to sleep and leave me the fuck alone," he said with contempt.

"Sex messages?" She scowled as if she found the thought repugnant. "I didn't send any sexually explicit texts."

In bed with the covers pulled over his shoulders, Lincoln pushed himself up and stared at his wife. "Oh, no? Did I read that shit wrong, or did you agree to give up the pussy raw on your next gym night?"

Chevonne grimaced. "What are you talking about?"

"Keep playing dumb; I really don't care. I just wanna get some sleep." He clicked off his bedside light. Lying with his hands clasped behind his head, he observed Chevonne momentarily, and then closed his eyes.

His eyes opened reflexively as she rushed to his side of the bed, and turned the light back on. "Why would you snoop through my phone messages?"

"Do you really have to ask me that? Look, everything you're saying and doing is only irking me, so give it a rest. Go to sleep." He shook his head. "Oh, yeah," he said suddenly. "We may have to start coordinating our after-work schedules. Be sure to let me know when you need me to watch the kids…you know, while you're out there getting it in with your mechanic. I don't want Tori and Amir left home and neglected, whenever Mommy goes out to get a tune-up."

"You cold-blooded bastard; how dare you talk to me like this. I would never neglect my children. Those texts that you read were old, Lincoln. I must have forgotten to delete them," Chevonne said desperately.

"Mmm-hmm. Sure, you're right. You lie so much, you're starting to believe yourself."

Chevonne walked solemnly to her side of the bed. "I'm telling the truth, Lincoln," she said pleadingly.

He glared at her. "You don't know the first thing about truth or decency, so stop embarrassing yourself by continually lying." Lincoln turned the light out again, and curled into a comfortable position.

"You're accusing me of cheating, and I haven't!" She

sounded tearful. "I can't sleep in here with you. There's too much tension." She flung off the covers and sat up.

"Look, either lie the hell down and go to sleep...or take your ass in the basement...the garage...or sleep on the sofa. I don't give a fuck where you go; just shut up and leave me alone."

Snatching her pillow from the bed, Chevonne stormed out of the bedroom.

Having the bed to himself, Lincoln turned over on his stomach, and stretched out his arms and legs. This position would hopefully deter Chevonne from trying to creep back into their marital bed.

"Daddy. Are you awake?"

Lincoln opened his eyes and smiled at his daughter's face. "I am now."

"Mommy slept in my room last night...how come?"

Lincoln searched his mind for a convenient lie, but couldn't find one on such a short notice. "Sweetie..." Lincoln cleared his throat. "Mommy and Daddy are having problems, and we're not going to be able to work them out."

Tori wrinkled her nose in confusion. "Are you getting a divorce?"

"Probably." He nodded his head. "Yes, sweetheart. More than likely."

"When?" she asked, sounding panicked.

Lincoln sat up. He peered intently at his pajama-clad daughter. "I don't know, Tori. Getting a divorce can be a lengthy process. But I don't want you to worry about it. Mommy and Daddy both love you and Amir. That's never going to stop."

"Am I going to have a stepmother?" she asked with horror.

Lincoln chuckled. "Maybe someday—but not any time soon."

Amir entered the bedroom next, with a troubled expression. "Go downstairs and eat breakfast, Tori."

"You can't tell me what to do."

"Get a move-on!" Amir insisted, using his mother's phrase.

"Go eat breakfast, Tori," Lincoln intervened.

"Okay, Daddy." Tori scampered out of the bedroom, apparently relieved that her young world wasn't going to instantly collapse.

"Mommy was crying," Amir said accusingly.

"Your mother and I are having a lot of problems, and she's upset."

"What kind of problems?"

"Serious problems. We're headed for a divorce, son."

Amir flinched. More sensitive than his little sister, tears welled in Amir's eyes.

"We're all going to get through this, somehow. It's going to be all right, man. I promise you."

"But I don't want you to leave us."

"I'm going to have to—eventually. But that won't be for awhile. It's going to be tense around here, until I get my own place. I'm going to do everything in my power to make the transition easy on you and your sister. I love you, son. You know that, right?"

Amir nodded, while tears streamed down his cheeks.

CHAPTER 51

Eighteen Months Later

It was only due to his high spirits that Lincoln didn't groan when he paid the extravagant monthly parking fee. He walked the next block and a half, taking in the sights of the neighborhood.

The past year and a half had been the hardest time of Lincoln's life. Divorced now, he had finally found it in his heart to forgive Chevonne. She was the mother of his children, and he felt great relief that he was finally able to let go of his deep resentment toward her.

She'd cut all ties with that ruthless thug, Raheem. Lincoln had threatened to go after full custody of the kids, if she didn't. Now she had a new man. She went from a thug to a suit; her new love interest was a city official. Lincoln didn't like him very much; he was a smug prick, but at least Chevonne's new man wasn't psychopath—he wouldn't be a bad influence on his children.

Parenting his kids on a part-time basis would take some getting used to. He and Chevonne shared joint custody, and they were all still learning to cope with the changes that had occurred in their lives. Logistically, picking up and dropping off the kids, was a little problematic, but he had no choice but to make it work.

Lincoln put the key in the lock of his newly leased loft-style office. Located in the historic, Old City section of downtown Philadelphia, the place made a great statement to Lincoln's clients. With a smile of satisfaction, he surveyed the high ceilings, hardwood floors, and exposed brick walls.

Wow, I did it! A leap of faith had brought miracles his way. He finally was able to let go of fear and hesitation, and made bold moves—something he should have done years ago.

He'd left Clemmons and Associates at exactly the right time. It turned out that Amber was far more devious than Lincoln had imagined. She sued Frank for sexual harassment and won a huge settlement. Frank's wife filed for a divorce. With mounting legal debt, Frank sold the business.

Lincoln gazed through one of the large windows. Peering down on busy Arch Street, he was so grateful for this new beginning. A year ago, he'd started accepting architectural consulting jobs, many of which came from Solay's business contacts. And amazingly, even his ex-wife had assisted, hooking him up with her city connections.

The realtor had shown him every detail of the ultra-modern space; now Lincoln was delighted to wander around the empty space on his own. He found his way to the full kitchen with an island that separated that room from the office area.

The large space contained an inner office reception area, and huge flex-space that could accommodate multiple workstations. The apprentice that would be working under him would have a lot of room to move around. Once his business grew, he would hire other consultants and expand his business.

Everything in his life was changing for the better. Although he and Solay had both been afraid of getting hurt, somehow they'd made their relationship work. Solay had trust issues and so did he, and so they'd taken only baby steps, never making big demands of each other.

Their strong sexual attraction had blossomed into friendship—and finally—love. For seven months, Lincoln had been staying at Solay's apartment, without officially moving in. Now he wanted to make it more than merely "official." He was prepared to take it to the next level— get married and buy a home. Though he was ready, he would never rush Solay. If she ever wanted to settle down and make it official, she wouldn't have to ask him twice.

This had been a month of big changes: the opening of Solay's second cupcake shop and Lincoln's architectural firm. The deck had been stacked against Lincoln and Solay—two brokenhearted souls. Who would have thought that a rebound relationship could actually work?

After he'd check out the space a few more times, there

wasn't much to do, except wait for Solay. She'd insisted that it would bring good luck if she and Lincoln "christened" the place before the furniture arrived.

He called her cell. "Hey, baby, are you standing me up? Where are you? I can't wait for you to see the space."

"I'm stuck in traffic, but I'll be there as soon as I can." Solay didn't sound very happy; in fact, she sounded distraught.

"This is supposed to be a day of celebration…why do you sound like you've been crying?"

"Because I have."

"Why, sweetheart? What's wrong?"

"Tears of joy, Lincoln. Everything is changing for us. So fast, it's amazing. It's so unreal. I'm ecstatic that I can finally put the past behind me, and move full-speed ahead with you."

"Are you sure about that?"

"I'm positive, Lincoln. I love you, and I'm on my way."

"I love you, too. Drive safe, baby."

It was an action flick…not a tearjerker, yet Solay's purse was filled with tissues, just in case. She spotted a lone seat at the far end of the very last row. She had to squeeze past a row of people, muttering, "Excuse me. Sorry. Beg your pardon," until she reached the prized seat.

Sitting in the back of the movie theater offered a small degree of privacy.

As soon as the opening credits began to roll, Solay braced herself for a big emotional response. She gasped and began weeping when Deon's name appeared on the screen. *Damn, he really did it!* She hadn't believed in him and her doubt had cost her dearly.

Five minutes into the movie—there he was, living out his dream. His scene opened with Deon in swimwear, lounging by a pool, wearing a pair of dark shades.

The female movie-goers began howling and clapping the moment the camera panned in on his ripped stomach and broad chest. Deon removed his shades, and the women in the theater emitted lustful roars when they got an close-up view of his handsome face.

Deon was playing the part of a serial killer, who preyed on rich women that he met while parking their cars at a posh Beverly Hills restaurant, where he worked as a valet.

He was stunning on screen, exuding charm that mesmerized. Deon had once told Solay that he was a natural, and he was so right. He was working his role as if he'd been performing on the big screen his whole life.

The starring role in the film was played by Ian Shelby. He played the tortured detective that was continually taunted and outwitted by the serial killer. Ian Shelby was a Hollywood actor that commanded stop salary. His willingness to lend his name to a small, independent project had given the film credibility.

Deon was costarring with a Hollywood heavyweight, and holding his own. Without a doubt, casting directors would be sending him scripts and big-money offers.

At the end of the film, Deon's character was hit by a barrage of bullets, and Solay boo-hooed as if the real Deon had been murdered. As her tears fell, she realized that she was crying over Deon's untimely departure from her life.

Seeing him on the big screen was actually cathartic. Observing him being murdered, albeit on screen, gave her a morbid kind of closure. Deon had moved on a long time ago, and he'd never looked back. It was time for Solay to release him, and move forward with her life.

Lincoln was waiting for her. And she was ready for him. Solay and Lincoln had a clean slate—no lingering animosity, no infidelities, no resentment. What they shared was respect, faith, and love. Their pressure-free "friends with benefits" relationship had blossomed into something beautiful and real.

Traffic on Walnut Street was bumper to bumper. She groped through her pocketbook when her cell rang. It was Lincoln, asking if she'd stood him up.

"No," she assured him.

While talking to Lincoln, she drove past her newest location, Scandalicious II, on Spruce Street in the Penn campus area. Both Penn and Drexel University students flocked to the cupcake shop, and were spreading the word. During finals and mid-terms, the students hung out at Scandalicious for so many hours, getting their sugar rush and drinking coffee, she had to extend her hours to midnight.

Life was extremely good.

Even Melanee had made big changes in her life. She was doing her own thing. She'd left Scandalicious a few months ago and was now baking sensual delights for private parties. Melanee had been extremely vague when Solay questioned her about her new endeavor. Oh, well. What the heck? That's Melanee for you—always sneaky and secretive. She sounded happy, and that's all that really mattered.

Vidal was running things at Scandalicious II. He was still a smart-mouth pain in the ass, but the college crowd adored him.

Solay arrived at Lincoln's new office space, and found him waiting for her downstairs.

He took one look at her, puckered his lips and whistled. "You're looking good in that skirt, showing off those pretty legs," he said, acknowledging her short paisley-print skirt.

"Thank you, sweetie," Solay said, revealing a generous grin.

Holding hands, they walked the flight of stairs that led to his new office. "This place is huge," she said as they entered. "It's gorgeous! I can see why you fell in love with this spot."

Lincoln excitedly showed her where he was going to

put his desk, and then he waved his hand to the rear of the big, open space. "Until I hire a couple of consultants, my apprentice is going to have all that space in the back."

After Lincoln finished giving Solay the grand tour, he drew her into his arms. "I couldn't have accomplished this without you."

"We're good together." She lifted her mouth to his. Closing her eyes dreamily, she enjoyed the feel of Lincoln's lips and the strong arms that embraced her. She pulled away from the kiss. "Hey, we're supposed to be celebrating—drinking champagne and sexing up this place. Where's the blanket, candles, and the bubbly?"

Lincoln smiled embarrassedly. "As soon as the Realtor handed me the keys, I rushed right over. Baby, I forgot everything. We can't lie on this hard floor."

Solay frowned in disappointment.

"Can I get a rain check?" he asked, with a sneaky smile. "Remember when you gave me that line?" he reminded her.

"Back then, I wasn't being honest with myself. Even though you were married at the time, I saw something in you that was so real, it scared me."

"You don't have to feel that way ever again."

"I know," she said, nodding. "But I don't want a rain check. I wore this skirt just for the occasion. I'm not taking no for an answer; we're gonna celebrate right now."

Lincoln looked around, as if hoping that a blanket had magically appeared.

"We don't need a blanket, baby. Where's your imagination?" Solay motioned toward the kitchen.

"Oh," Lincoln said, catching on to the plan.

In the kitchen, Lincoln lifted Solay onto the island. She pulled up her skirt, and spread her legs, revealing her crotchless thong.

"Baby, whatchu doing to me?" He swiped a finger along the seam of her folds, and brought his finger to his lips. "Mmm," he murmured, licking her taste from his finger.

Her hand wriggled down to his belt buckle, tugged on it, and pulled it loose, and she deftly undid his fly. Lincoln groaned when Solay grabbed his thick, hard shaft, and began stroking it until his dick quivered and throbbed in her hand.

"Hold up; hold up," Lincoln urged as he kicked off his shoes and took off his pants.

Solay sent her skirt and thong floating down; she watched as her garments landed in a soft pile next to Lincoln's pants.

He wasted no time covering Solay with his yearning body.

She groped for his thickness, and guided him to her sweet opening, rubbing it up and down, getting her juices to flow like a river.

Solay let out a sharp gasping moan as she felt his tip nudging and pushing until his length and girth completely filled her.

She cupped his face, and stared into his eyes. "This is real, Lincoln. You're the perfect man for me—the one that I've been waiting for."

"I'm all in," he panted as he delivered gentle thrusts. "I'm talking about the whole nine…church, chapel… whatever, baby. The house in the suburbs. If that's what you want, you can have it."

"I do want all that…and more."

"What else? Name it."

"I want to have your baby."

His pace quickened. "We can work on that right now," he gasped.

Following his words with actions, Lincoln gripped her hips as he drove between her luscious folds.

Solay drew in a sharp breath as she was hit with wave after wave of pleasure. Deeply entrenched inside her, Lincoln shuddered and then released his seed in a titanic burst of passion.

"Solay," he uttered her name, his body quivering.

"Yeah, baby?" Her voice was a satisfied whimper.

"I'm sorry."

"Sorry for what?"

"You said you wanted a baby—I think I messed around and made a set of triplets."

"You're so silly," Solay said, laughing. "And so sweet. That's why I love you."

"And I love you more," Lincoln said, gathering her into his arms.

ABOUT THE AUTHOR

Allison Hobbs is a national bestselling author of twenty-three novels and has been featured in such publications as *Romantic Times* and *The Philadelphia Inquirer*. She lives in Philadelphia, Pennsylvania. Visit the author at www.allisonhobbs.com and Facebook.com/Allison Hobbs.

PUT A RING ON IT

BY ALLISON HOBBS
AVAILABLE FROM STREBOR BOOKS

CHAPTER 1

C all it a woman's intuition. Call it a sixth sense, but instead of driving home after work, Nivea felt an urge to swing by her fiancé's old apartment. When she rolled up in front of the building where Eric used to live, she gave the place a smug look. Eric's former apartment building was a dump. She had no idea why he'd been so resistant to the idea of moving into her upscale townhouse.

But that was water over the bridge. She had introduced Eric to a better lifestyle and she was proud of that fact.

Nivea did a double take when she noticed the Highlander parked at the curb. Her heart rate began to accelerate when she recognized Eric's license plate. *What's he doing here? He's supposed to be working overtime.*

With the motor running, she jumped out of her Mazda and removed a couple of lawn chairs that were holding someone's nicely shoveled parking spot. Brows joined together in bafflement, she parallel parked, cut the engine, and then got out.

Nivea peered up at the second floor apartment that Eric had left six months ago when he'd moved in with her. She could see the twinkling colored lights that adorned a Christmas tree. She frowned at the Christmas tree. It was the first day of December, too soon to put up a tree in Nivea's opinion.

Eric had sublet the place to one of his unmarried friends. *Which one?* She couldn't remember. Feeling a rush of uncomfortable heat, she unbuttoned her wool coat, allowing the frigid evening air to cool her.

There had to be a good explanation for Eric being here. Something really innocent. *He didn't have to work overtime after all, and decided to stop by and visit his buddy,* she told herself.

Even though moving into Nivea's townhouse was a step up for Eric, it had been hard convincing him to give up his crappy bachelor's pad. She was so elated when she'd gotten him to agree to move in, that she hadn't bothered to question him about the details of his rental transaction.

But she was concerned now.

Carefully, Nivea climbed the icy concrete steps that led to the front door. Inside the vestibule area, another door, this one locked, prevented her from forcing her way to Eric's old apartment. She read the name that was centered above the doorbell of apartment number two: D. Alston.

Who the hell is D. Alston? She jabbed the doorbell twice, and then pressed the button without letting up.

She heard a door open on the second floor. "Stay right here. Let me handle this," Eric said gruffly.

Who the hell is Eric talking to?

Eric thumped down the stairs, causing a vibration. At the bottom of the stairs, he looked at Nivea through the large windowpane that separated them. She expected a smile of surprise, but Eric gawked at her, displeasure wrinkling his forehead.

He turned the lock, cracked the door open, and poked his head out. "Whatchu doing here, Niv?"

"I should be asking that question. You're supposed to be at work!"

"Yeah, um…" He scratched his head.

"Who's renting the place now?"

"Uh…"

Refusing to give him time to gather his thoughts, she pushed the door open, and zipped past Eric.

"You can't go up there, Niv."

"Hell if I can't!" Nivea took the stairs two at a time, the heels of her boots stomping against the wooden stairs.

Eric was up to something, and she had to know what the hell was going on.

Eric raced behind her. He roughly grabbed her arm. "You outta pocket."

She yanked her arm away and spun around. "Let me go, Eric!" Eric was a big, stocky man, but she gave him such a violent shove, he fell backward, stumbling down a couple of steps.

Motivated by a suspicious mind, Nivea bolted for Eric's apartment, which was at the top of the stairs. The door was slightly ajar. She pushed it open.

A woman, who appeared to be in her early twenties, stood in the kitchen, clutching a baby. One glance told Nivea that the woman was street tough. Hardcore. She was not cute at all. Light- skinned, reed-thin with a narrow, ferret-like face. The Kool Aid red-colored weave she was rocking looked a hot Halloween mess. Anger flickered across the woman's mean, sharp-featured face.

"Who are you?" Nivea asked, hoping to hear, *I'm Eric's cousin*. Hell, she was willing to accept childhood friend, or even long lost sister. She'd happily go along with any relationship, except jumpoff. She stole a glance at the baby that was buried beneath blankets.

The skinny chick looked at Nivea like she had sprouted a second head. "How you gon' bust in here axin' me who da hell I am?" Her bad grammar and attitude confirmed Nivea's suspicion that the chick was a hood rat.

Nivea scanned the kitchen quickly. The appliances

were as outdated as Nivea remembered, and the cabinetry was still old and chipped, but the room was spotlessly clean and somewhat better furnished than when Eric had lived there. Nivea took in the rather new, but cheap-looking kitchen set that had replaced Eric's old one.

The female tenant had tried to brighten up the dismal kitchen. Matching potholders and dishtowels were on display. The former dusty mini blinds that had once hung at the kitchen window had been replaced with ruffled curtains.

What is Eric doing here with this ghettofied heifer and her child?

As if she'd read Nivea's mind, the thuggish chick turned toward Nivea. Holding the baby upright, she gave Nivea a full view of the infant's face. Nivea felt her heart stop. The little boy, who looked to be around four or five months old, was a miniature replica of Eric.

"Oh, my God!" Nivea squeaked out. She grimaced at the child who was Eric's spitting image.

Okay, I'm imagining things. That child can't possibly be Eric's baby!

CHAPTER 2

Eric barreled into the apartment. Nivea suspected he had been hanging out in the hallway, trying to get his lies together.

"You need to check yourself, Nivea. You know you dead wrong for running up in the crib like this."

Nivea was stunned that Eric, her gentle teddy bear, was growling at her like a vicious grizzly bear.

Nivea stared at the baby and then at Eric. She swiped at the tears that watered her eyes. "What's going on, Eric?"

The skinny chick bit down on her lip, like she was struggling to control her temper. "I'm not with this shit, Eric. You better handle it."

Eric tugged Nivea's coat sleeve. "This ain't the time or the place, Niv."

"Have you lost your mind, Eric? You told me you were at work. I need to know what the hell is going on. Get your coat!" She motioned with her hand. "Talk to me on the way home. We're out of here!" Nivea waited for Eric to go get his coat, but he didn't budge.

The ghetto chick snickered, and then looked down at the baby. "Don't worry, Boo-Boo; Daddy ain't going nowhere."

Daddy! No way! That is not Eric's child, Nivea told herself. With a hand on her hip, she glared at Eric. "Who is this bitch? And why are you here with her?"

"My name is Dyeesha. I ain't gon' be another bitch, *bitch.* I don't know who you is, but you trespassing." The woman with the bad grammar spoke in an annoying scratchy tone, her nostrils flaring as she furiously patted her baby.

"Eric! Tell this girl who I am!" Nivea spoke through clenched teeth.

Looking like a cornered rat, Eric was at loss for words and could only come up with utterances and sputtering sounds.

"How you expect him to remember the name of e'ry hooka he done slept with while I was pregnant with his son," Dyeesha said with a sneer.

The abrasive sound of the girl's voice, her assumption that Nivea was a stripper and a prostitute, and her terrible grammar…it all grated Nivea's nerves. "For the love of God, will you please tell this ignorant-ass, ghettofied, hood chick who I am!" Nivea yelled.

As if his lips were sealed with Super Glue, Eric was mute.